SUSAN MALLERY

FINDING PERFECT

HQN™

Recycling programs
for this product may
not exist in your area.

ISBN-13: 978-0-373-77468-5

FINDING PERFECT

Copyright © 2010 by Susan Macias Redmond

This edition published by arrangement with Harlequin Books S.A.

For questions and comments about the quality of this book
please contact us at Customer_eCare@Harlequin.ca.

www.HQNBooks.com

Printed in U.S.A.

Also available from
Susan Mallery and HQN Books

**And look for more of Susan Mallery's
fantastic stories set in Fool's Gold,
coming in 2011!**

To Jenel—like Pia, you are organized, dedicated and charming. Fool's Gold would be lost without her and I would be lost without you. A thousand thanks for all you do.

CHAPTER ONE

"WHAT DO YOU MEAN she left me the embryos? I'm supposed to get the cat." Pia O'Brian paused long enough to put her hand on her chest. The shock of hearing the details of Crystal's will had been enough to stop the strongest of hearts, and Pia's was still bruised from the loss of her friend.

She was relieved to find her heart still beating, although the speed at which her heart was pumping was disconcerting.

"It's the cat," she repeated, speaking as clearly as possible so the well-dressed attorney sitting across from her would understand. "His name is Jake. I'm not really a pet person, but we've made peace with each other. I think he likes me. It's hard to tell—he keeps to himself. I guess most cats do."

Pia thought about offering to bring in the cat so the lawyer could see for herself, but she wasn't sure that would help.

"Crystal would never leave me her babies," Pia added with a whisper. Mostly because it was true. Pia had never had a maternal or nurturing thought in her life. Taking care of the cat had been a big step for her.

"Ms. O'Brian," the attorney said with a brief smile, "Crystal was very clear in her will. She and I spoke several times as her illness progressed. She wanted you to have her embryos. Only you."

"But I..." Pia swallowed.

Embryos. Somewhere in a lab-like facility were frozen test tubes or other containers and inside of them were the potential babies her friend had so longed for.

"I know this is a shock," the lawyer, a fortysomething elegant woman in a tailored suit, said. "Crystal debated telling you what she'd done. Apparently she decided against letting you know in advance."

"Probably because she knew I'd try to talk her out of it," Pia muttered.

"For now, you don't have to *do* anything. The storage fees are paid for the next three years. There's some paperwork to be filled out, but we can take care of it later."

Pia nodded. "Thank you," she said and rose. A quick glance at her watch told her she was going to have to hurry or she would be late for her ten-thirty appointment back at her office.

"Crystal picked you for a reason," the attorney said as Pia walked toward the door.

Pia gave the older woman a tight smile and headed for the stairs. Seconds later, she was outside, breathing deeply, wondering when the world was going to stop spinning.

This was not happening, she told herself as she started walking. It couldn't be. What had Crystal been thinking? There were dozens of other women she could have left the embryos to. Hundreds, probably. Women who were good with kids, who knew how to bake and comfort and test for a fever with the back of their hands.

Pia couldn't even keep a houseplant alive. She was

a lousy hugger. Her last boyfriend had complained she always let go first. Probably because being held too long made her feel trapped. Not exactly a sterling quality for a potential parent.

Her stomach felt more than a little queasy. What had Crystal been thinking and why? Why her? That's what she couldn't get over. The fact that her friend had made such a crazy decision. And without ever mentioning it.

Fool's Gold was the kind of town where everyone knew everyone else and secrets were hard to keep. Apparently Crystal had managed to break with convention and keep some huge information to herself.

Pia reached her office building. The first floor of the structure held several retail businesses—a card store, a gift shop with the most amazing fudge and Morgan's Books. Her office was upstairs.

She went through the plain wooden door off the side street and climbed to the second story. She could see a tall man standing by her locked office door.

"Hi," she called. "Sorry I'm late."

The man turned.

There was a window behind him, so she couldn't see his face, but she knew her schedule for the morning and the name of the man who was her next appointment. Raoul Moreno was tall, with huge shoulders. Despite the unusually cool September day, he hadn't bothered with a coat. Instead he wore a V-neck sweater over dark jeans.

A man's man, she thought unexpectedly. Which made sense. Raoul Moreno was a former professional football player. He'd been a quarterback with the Dallas Cowboys. After ten years in the game, he'd retired on top and had disappeared from public view. Last year he'd shown up in Fool's Gold for a pro-am charity golf tournament. For reasons she couldn't figure out, he'd stayed.

As she got closer, she took in the large dark eyes, the handsome face. There was a scar on his cheek— probably from protecting an old lady during a mugging. He had a reputation for being nice. Pia made it a rule never to trust nice people.

"Ms. O'Brian," he began. "Thanks for seeing me."

She unlocked her office door and motioned for him to go inside.

"Pia, please. My 'Ms. O'Brian' years are looming, but I'm not ready for them yet."

He was good-looking enough that she should have been distracted. Under other circumstances, she probably would have been. But at the moment, she was too busy wondering if the chemo treatments had scrambled Crystal's brain. Her friend had always seemed so rational. Obviously that had been a facade.

Pia motioned to the visitor chair in front of her desk and hung her coat on the rack by the door.

Her office was small but functional. There was a good-size main room with a custom three-year calendar covering most of one wall. The squares were half dry-erase material and half corkboard.

Posters for various Fool's Gold festivals took up the rest of the wall space. She had a storage room and a half bath in the rear, several cabinets and a filing system that bordered on compulsively organized. As a rule she made it a point to visit rather than have people come to her, but scheduling-wise, having Raoul stop by had made the most sense.

Of course that had been before she'd found out she'd been left three very frozen potential children.

She crossed to the small refrigerator in the corner. "I have diet soda and water." She glanced over her shoulder. "You're not the diet type."

One dark eyebrow rose. "Are you asking or telling?"

She smiled. "Am I wrong?"

"Water's fine."

"I knew it."

She collected a bottle and a can, then returned to her desk. After handing him the bottle, she took a seat and stared at the yellow pad in front of her. There was writing on it, very possibly in English. She could sort of make out individual letters but not words and certainly not sentences.

They were supposed to have a meeting about something. That much was clear. She handled the city festivals in town. There were over a dozen civic events that she ran every year. But her mind didn't go any further than that. When she tried to remember why Raoul was here, she went blank. Her brain was filled with other things.

Babies. Crystal had left her babies. Okay, embryos, but the implication was clear. Crystal wanted her children to be born. Which meant someone was going to have to get them implanted, grow them and later give birth. Although that was terrifying enough, there was also the further horror of raising them.

Children weren't like cats. She knew that much. They would need more than dry food, a bowl of water and a clean litter box. A lot more.

"Oh, God, I can't do this," she whispered.

Raoul frowned. "I don't understand. Do you want to reschedule the meeting?"

Meeting? Oh, right. He was here for something. His camp and he wanted her to...

Her mind went blank, again. Right after the merciful emptiness, there was panic. Deep to the bone, intestine-wrenching panic.

She stood and wrapped her arms around her midsection, breathing hard and fast.

"I can't do this. It's impossible. What was she thinking? She had to know better."

"Pia?"

Her visitor rose. She turned to tell him that rescheduling was probably a good idea when the room began to spin. It turned and turned, darkening on the edges.

The next thing she knew, she was in her chair, bent over at the waist, her head between her knees with something pressing down on the back of her neck.

"This is uncomfortable," she said.

"Keep breathing."

"Easier said than done. Let go."

"A couple more breaths."

The pressure on the back of her neck lessened. Slowly, she straightened and blinked.

Raoul Moreno was crouched next to her, his dark eyes cloudy with concern. She took another breath and realized he smelled really good. Clean, but with a hint of something else.

"You all right?" he asked.

"What happened?"

"You started to faint." Raoul met her gaze as her eyes widened, and, despite the bigger things crowding her thoughts, she couldn't miss the zing of interest.

She blinked, and shook her head. "I don't faint. I never faint. I—" Her memory returned. "Oh, crap." She covered her face with her hands. "I'm so not ready to be a mother."

Raoul moved with a speed that was a credit to his physical conditioning and nearly comical at the same time.

"Man trouble?" he asked cautiously from a safer few inches away.

"What?" She lowered her hands. "No. I'm not pregnant. That would require sex. Or not. Actually it wouldn't, would it? This is so not happening."

"Okay." He sounded nervous. "Should I call a doctor?"

"No, but you can go if you want. I'm fine."

"You don't look fine."

Now it was her turn to raise her eyebrows. "Are you commenting on my appearance?"

He grinned. "I wouldn't dare."

"That sounded almost critical."

"You know what I meant."

She did. "I'm okay. I've had a bit of a shock. A friend of mine died recently. She was married to a guy in the army. Before he was shipped off to Iraq, they decided to do in vitro, just in case something happened to him. So she could have his kids."

"Sad, but it makes sense."

She nodded. "He was killed a couple of years ago. She took it really hard, but after a while, she decided she would have the babies. At least a part of him would live on, right?"

Pia rose and paced the length of the office. Moving seemed to help. She took a couple of cautious breaths, to make sure she was going to stay conscious. Fainting? Impossible. Yet the world really had started to blur.

She forced herself back to the topic at hand.

"She went to the doctor for a routine physical," she continued. "They discovered she had lymphoma. And not the good kind."

"There's a good kind?"

She shrugged. "There's a kind that can usually be cured. She didn't have that one. And then she was gone. I have her cat. I thought I'd be keeping him. We have a relationship. Sort of. It's hard to tell with a cat."

"They keep to themselves."

There was something about the way he spoke. She glared at him. "Are you making fun of me?"

"No."

She saw the corner of his mouth twitch. "Don't mess with me," she told him. "Or I'll talk about my feelings."

"Anything but that."

She returned to her desk and sank into the chair. "She didn't leave me the cat. She left me the embryos. I don't know what to do. I don't know what she was thinking. Babies. God—anyone but me. And I can't ignore it. Them. That's what the attorney hinted at. That I could let it go for a while because the 'fees' are paid for three years." She looked at him. "I guess that's the frozen part. Maybe I should go see them."

"They're embryos. What's there to see?"

"I don't know. Something. Can't they put them under a microscope? Maybe if I saw them, I would understand." She stared at him as if he had the answer. "Why did she think I could raise her children?"

"I'm sorry, Pia. I don't know."

He looked uncomfortable. His gaze lingered on the door. Reality returned and with it, a sense of embarrassment.

"I'm so sorry," she murmured, standing. "We'll reschedule. I'll compose myself and be much better next time. Let me look over my calendar and give you a call."

He reached for the door handle, then paused. "Are you sure you're going to be all right?"

No, she wasn't sure. She wasn't sure of anything. But that wasn't Raoul's problem.

She forced a smile. "I'm great. Seriously, you should go. I'm going to call a couple of girlfriends and let them talk me down."

"Okay." He hesitated. "You have my number?"

"Uh-huh." She wasn't sure if she did, but she was determined to let him escape while she still had a shred of dignity. "The next time you see me, I'll be professionalism personified. I swear."

"Thanks. You take care."

"Bye."

He left.

When the door closed, she sank back into her chair. After lowering her arms to the desk, she rested her head on them and did her best to keep breathing.

Crystal had left her the embryos. There were only two questions that mattered. Why, and what the hell was Pia supposed to do now?

RAOUL ARRIVED AT RONAN Elementary shortly before two. He parked in the lot by the playground. No surprise—his was the only Ferrari in the parking lot. He was a guy who liked his toys, so sue him.

Before he could climb out of the car, his cell phone rang. He checked his watch—he had a few minutes before he was due inside—then the phone number on the screen. As he pushed the talk button, he grinned.

"Hey, Coach."

"Hey, yourself," Hawk, his former high school football coach, said. "Nicole hasn't heard from you in a while and I'm calling to find out why."

Raoul laughed. "I talked to your beautiful wife last week, so I know that's not why you're calling."

"You got me. I'm checking on you. Making sure you're moving on with your life."

That was Hawk, Raoul thought with equal parts frustration and appreciation. Cutting right to the heart of what was wrong.

"You had some bad stuff happen," the older man continued. "Don't wallow."

"I'm not wallowing. I'm busy."

"You're in your head too much. I know you. Find a cause. Get personally involved in your new town. It'll distract you. You can't change what happened."

Raoul's good humor faded. Hawk was right about that. The past couldn't be undone. Those who were gone stayed gone. No amount of bargaining, no sum of money, made it better.

"I can't let it go," he admitted.

"You'll have to. Maybe not today, but soon. Believe in the possibility of healing, Raoul. Open yourself up to other people."

It seemed impossible, but he'd been trusting Hawk for nearly twenty years. "I'll do my best."

"Good. Call Nicole."

"I will."

They hung up.

Raoul sat in his car for a few more seconds, thinking about what Hawk had told him. Get involved. Find a cause. What the other man didn't know was how much Raoul wanted to avoid that. Getting involved is what had caused the problem in the first place. Life was much safer lived at a distance.

He got out of his car and collected the small duffel he'd brought with him. Whenever he visited a school, he brought a few official NFL footballs and player cards. It made the kids happy, and that's why he was here. To entertain and maybe slip in a little motivation when they weren't looking.

He glanced at the main school building. It was older but well-kept. He usually spoke to high-school-aged kids, but the principal and class teacher had both been persistent to the point of stalking. He was new to small-town life and was figuring out the rules as he went. As he planned to settle in Fool's Gold permanently, he'd decided to err on the side of cooperation.

He stepped toward the main walkway, then made his way into the building. Unlike the inner-city schools he usually visited, there weren't any metal detectors or even a guard. The double doors stood open, the halls were wide and well-lit, the walls free of graffiti. Like the rest of Fool's Gold, the school was almost too good to be true.

He followed the signs to the main office and found himself in a big open area with a long counter. There were the usual bulletin boards with flyers for book drives and after-school programs. A dark-haired woman sat at a desk, typing on an ancient-looking computer.

"Morning," he said.

The woman—probably in her midthirties—looked up. Her mouth fell open as she stood and waved her hands. "Oh, God. You're here. You're really here! I can't believe it." She hurried toward him. "Hi. I'm Rachel. My dad is a huge fan. He's going to die when he finds out I met you."

"I hope not," Raoul said easily, pulling a card out of the bag and reaching for a pen.

"What?"

"I hope he doesn't die."

Rachel laughed. "He won't, but he'll be so jealous. I heard you were coming. And here you are. This is just so exciting. Raoul Moreno in our school."

"What's your dad's name?"

"Norm."

He signed the card and passed it to her. "Maybe this will help him deal with his disappointment."

She took the paper reverently and placed a hand on her chest. "Thank you so much. This is wonderful." She glanced at the clock, then sighed. "I suppose I have to take you to Mrs. Miller's class now."

"I should probably get started talking to the kids."

"Right. That's why you're here. It's been wonderful to meet you."

"You, too, Rachel."

She came out from behind the counter, then led him back into the hallway. As they walked, she chatted about the school and the town, all the while glancing at him with a combination of appreciation and flirtatiousness. It came with the territory and he'd learned a long time ago not to take the attention seriously.

Mrs. Miller's class was at the end of the hall. Rachel held the door open for him.

"Good luck," she said.

"Thanks."

He entered the room alone.

There were about twenty young kids, all staring wide-eyed, while their teacher, an attractive woman in her forties, fluttered.

"Oh, Mr. Moreno, I can't thank you enough for speaking with us today. It's such a thrill."

Raoul smiled. "I'm always happy to come talk to kids in school." He glanced at the class. "Morning."

A few of the students greeted him. A few more looked too excited to speak. At least the boys did. Most of the girls didn't seem impressed at all.

"Fourth grade, right?" he asked.

A girl with glasses in the front row nodded. "We're the accelerated group, reading above grade level."

"Uh-oh," he said, taking an exaggerated step back. "The smart kids. You going to ask me a math question?"

Her mouth curved into a smile. "Do you like math?"

"Yeah, I do." He looked up at the class. "Who here really likes school a lot?"

A few kids raised their hands.

"School can change your life," he said, settling one hip on the teacher's desk. "When you grow up, you're going to get jobs and work for a living. Today most of your responsibilities are about doing well in school. Who knows why we need to learn things like reading and math?"

More hands went up.

His usual talk was on staying motivated, finding a mentor, making a better life, but that seemed like a little much for the average nine-year-old. So he was going to talk about how important it was to like school and do your best.

Mrs. Miller hovered. "Do you need anything?" she asked in a whisper. "Can I get you something?"

"I'm good."

He turned his attention back to the students. The girl in the front row seemed more interested in the pretty scenery outside of the window. Oddly enough, she reminded him of Pia. Maybe it was the brown curly hair, or her obvious lack of interest in him as a person. Pia hadn't gushed, either. She'd barely noticed him. Not a real surprise, given how her morning had started. But he'd noticed her. She'd been cute and funny, even without trying.

He returned his attention to the students, drew in a breath and frowned. He inhaled again, smelling something odd.

If this had been a high school, he would have assumed an experiment gone bad in the science lab or a batch of forgotten cookies in home ec. But elementary schools didn't have those facilities.

He turned to Mrs. Miller. "Do you smell that?"

She nodded, her blue eyes concerned. "Maybe something happened in the cafeteria."

"Is there a fire?" one of the boys asked.

"Everyone stay seated," Mrs. Miller said firmly as she walked toward the door.

She placed a hand on it before slowly pulling it open. As she did, the smell of smoke got stronger. Seconds later, the fire alarms went off.

She turned to him. "It's only the second day of school.

We haven't practiced what to do. I think there really is a fire."

The kids were already standing up and looking scared. He knew they weren't very far from panic.

"You know where we're supposed to go?" he asked. "The way out?"

"Of course."

"Good." He turned to the students. "Who's in charge here?" he asked in a voice loud enough to be heard over the bells.

"Mrs. Miller," someone yelled.

"Exactly. Everyone get in line and follow Mrs. Miller as we go into the hall. There are going to be a lot of kids out there. Stay calm. I'll go last and make sure you all get out of the building."

Mrs. Miller motioned for her students to move toward the door.

"Follow me," she said. "We'll go quickly. Everyone hold hands. Don't let go. Everything is fine. Just stay together."

Mrs. Miller went out the door. The children began to follow her. Raoul waited to make sure everyone left. One little boy seemed to hesitate before leaving.

"It's okay," Raoul told him, his voice deliberately calm. He reached for the boy's hand, but the child flinched, as if expecting to be hit. The kid—all red hair and freckles—ducked out before Raoul could say anything.

Raoul went into the hall. The smell of smoke was more intense. Several kids were crying. A few stood in the middle of the hallway, their hands over their ears. The bells rang endlessly as teachers called for their students to follow them outside.

"Come on," he said, scooping the nearest little girl into his arms. "Let's go."

"I'm scared," she said.

"I'm big enough to keep you safe."

Another little boy grabbed hold of his arm. Tears filled the kid's eyes. "It's too loud."

"Then let's go outside, where it's quieter."

He walked quickly, herding kids as he went. Teachers ran back and forth, counting heads, checking to make sure no one was left behind.

When Raoul and his group of kids reached the main doors leading outside, the children took off at a run. He put down the girl he'd been carrying and she raced toward her teacher. He could see smoke pouring into the sky, a white-gray cloud covering the brilliant blue.

Students flowed out around him. Names were called. Teachers sorted the groups by grades, then classes. Raoul turned and went back into the building.

Now he could do more than smell smoke. He could see it. The air was thick and getting darker, making it hard to breathe. He went room by room, pushing open doors, checking under the large teacher desks in front, scanning to make sure no one was left behind.

He found a tiny little girl in a corner of the third room he entered, her face wet with tears. She was coughing and sobbing. He picked her up, turned and almost ran into a firefighter.

"I'll take her," the woman said, looking at him from behind a mask and grabbing the girl. "Get the hell out of here. The building is nearly seventy years old. God knows what cocktail of chemicals is in the air."

"There might be more kids."

"I know, and the longer we stand here talking, the more danger they're in. Now move."

He followed the firefighter out of the building. It wasn't until he was outside that he realized he was coughing and choking. He bent over, trying to catch his breath.

When he could breathe again, he straightened. The scene was controlled chaos. Three fire trucks stood in front of the school. Students huddled together on the lawn, well back from the building. Smoke poured out in all directions.

A few people screamed and pointed. Raoul turned and saw flames licking through the roof at the far end of the school.

He turned to head back in. A firefighter grabbed him by the arm.

"Don't even think about it," the woman told him. "Leave this to the professionals."

He nodded, then started coughing again.

She shook her head. "You went back inside, didn't you? Civilians. Do you think we wear the masks because they're pretty? Medic!" She yelled the last word and pointed at him.

"I'm fine," Raoul managed, his chest tight.

"Let me guess. You're a doctor, too. Cooperate with the nice lady or I'll tell her you need an enema."

CHAPTER TWO

THERE WAS NOTHING LIKE a community disaster to snap a person out of a pity party, Pia thought as she stood on the lawn at the far end of the Ronan Elementary playground and stared at what had once been a beautiful old school. Now flames licked at the roof and caused glass windows to explode. The smell of destruction was everywhere.

She'd heard the fire trucks from her office and had seen the smoke darkening the sky. It had only taken her a second to figure out where the fire was and that it was going to be bad. Now, as she stood on the edge of the playground, she felt her breath catch as one of the walls seemed to shudder before falling in on itself.

She'd always heard people talk about fire as if it were alive. A living creature with cunning and determination and an evil nature. Until now, she'd never believed it. But watching the way the fire systematically destroyed the school, she thought there might be seeds of truth in the theory.

"This is bad," she whispered.

"Worse than bad."

Pia saw Mayor Marsha Tilson had joined her. The sixty-something woman stood with a hand pressed against her throat, her eyes wide.

"I spoke with the fire chief. She assured me they've

gone through every room in the building. No one is left inside. But the building…" Marsha's voice caught. "I went to school here."

Pia put her arm around the other woman. "I know. It's horrible to see this."

Marsha visibly controlled her emotions. "We're going to have to find somewhere to put the children. They can't lose school days over this. But the other schools are full. We could bring in those portable classrooms. There must be someone I can call." She glanced around. "Where's Charity? She might know."

Pia turned and saw her friend standing by the growing crowd of frantic parents. "Over there."

Marsha saw her, then frowned. "She's not getting any smoke, is she?"

Pia understood the concern. Charity was several months pregnant and the mayor's granddaughter. "She's upwind. She'll be okay."

Marsha stared at the destruction. "What could have started this?"

"We'll find out. The important thing is all the kids and staff got out safely. We can fix the school."

Marsha squeezed her hand. "You're rational. Right now I need that. Thank you, Pia."

"We'll get through this together."

"I know. That makes me feel better. I'm going to talk to Charity."

As the mayor moved off, Pia stayed on the grass. Every few seconds, a blast of heat reached her and with it the smell of smoke and annihilation.

Just that morning she'd walked by the school and everything had been fine. How could things change so quickly?

Before she could figure out an answer, she saw more parents arriving on the scene. Mothers and some fathers rushed toward the children huddled together, protected by their teachers. There were cries of relief and of fear. Children were hugged, then searched for injuries, teachers thanked. The school principal stood by the children, a stack of pages on a clipboard.

Probably the master roster, Pia thought. Given the circumstances, parents would probably have to sign out their kids, so everyone was accounted for.

Two more fire trucks pulled up, sirens blaring. The school fire alarms were finally silenced but the noise was still deafening. People shouted, the truck engines rumbled. A voice over a megaphone warned everyone to stay back, then pointed out the location of the emergency medical vehicles.

Pia glanced in that direction and was surprised to see a tall, familiar man speaking with one of the EMT women. Raoul's hair was tousled, his face smudged. He paused to cough and despite it all, the man still looked good.

"Just so typical," she muttered as she crossed the playground and went toward him.

"Let me guess," she said as she approached. "You did something heroic."

"You mean stupid," the medic told her with a roll of her eyes. "It's a gender thing. They can't help it."

Pia chuckled. "Don't I know it." She turned to Raoul. "Tell me you didn't race into a burning building in an attempt to save a child."

He straightened and drew in a deep breath. "Why do you say it like that? It's not a bad thing."

"There are professionals here who know what they're doing."

"That's what I keep getting told. What happened to a little gratitude for risking my life?"

"Odds are, you would have been overcome by smoke, thereby giving the firefighters *more* work to do instead of less," the medic told him. She pulled some kind of measuring device off his finger.

"You're fine," she continued. "If you have any of the symptoms we talked about, go to the E.R." She glanced at Pia. "Is he with you?"

Pia shook her head.

"Smart girl," the medic said, then moved on to the next patient.

"Ouch," Raoul said. "This is a tough town."

"Don't worry," Pia told him. "I'm sure there will be plenty of women who will want to fawn all over you and coo as you retell your tale of bravery."

"But you're not one of them."

"Not today."

"How are you feeling?" he asked.

For a second she didn't understand the question. Then reality returned. That's right—he'd witnessed her breakdown earlier in the day. Talk about an emotion dump.

"I meant to call you," she said, moving beside him as they walked away from the medics. "To apologize. I usually have my meltdowns in private."

"It's okay. I'd say I understand, but you'll probably bite my head off if I do. How about if I tell you I'm sympathetic?"

"I would appreciate that."

She hesitated, wondering if she was supposed to say more. Or if he would ask. Not that she had anything to say. She was still grasping the reality of her friend's bequest and hadn't made a decision about what to do next. Despite the attorney's promise that she had at least three years before she needed to decide anything, Pia felt the pressure weighing on her.

Not that she was going to discuss her dilemma in front of Raoul. He'd already suffered enough.

"What were you doing here?" she asked. "At the school."

He'd come to a stop and was staring back at the school. His gaze moved from one firefighter to another. The chief stood on a garden wall about three feet high, yelling out orders to her team.

"Are you worried about the kids?" Pia asked. "Don't be. I've sat through plenty of preparedness meetings. They're great to attend if you're having trouble sleeping. Anyway, there's a plan for each school, and a master list. Attendance is taken daily and sent by computer to the district office. A list of who is out that day is brought to the disaster site. Trust me. Every student is accounted for."

He looked at her, his dark eyes bright with surprise. "They're all women."

"Most teachers are."

"The firefighters. They're all women."

"Oh, that." She shrugged. "It's Fool's Gold. What did you expect?"

He appeared both confused and lost, which on a tall, good-looking guy was kind of appealing. Assuming she was interested, and she wasn't. If her natural wariness about guys wasn't enough, Raoul was famous-ish, and she didn't need the pain and suffering that came with that type. Not to mention the fact that she might soon be pregnant with another couple's embryos.

A week ago her life had been predictable and boring. Now she was in the running to be a tabloid headline. Boring was better.

"There's a man shortage," Pia said patiently. "Surely you've noticed there aren't a lot of men in town. I thought that was why you'd moved here."

"There are men."

"Okay. Where?"

"The town has children." He pointed to the few students still waiting to be picked up. "They have fathers."

"That's true. We do have a few breeding pairs, for experimental purposes."

He took a step back.

She grinned. "Sorry. I'm kidding. Yes, there are men in town, but statistically, we don't have very many. Certainly not enough. So if you find yourself exceptionally popular, don't let it go to your head."

"I think I liked you better when you were having your breakdown," he muttered.

"You wouldn't be the first man to prefer a woman in a weakened condition. Full strength, we're a threat. Being as big and tough as you are, I'd hoped for something more. Life is nothing if not a disappointment. You didn't answer my question from before. What were you doing here?"

He looked distracted, as if he were having trouble keeping up. "Talking to Mrs. Miller's fourth-grade class. I speak to students. Usually they're in high school, but she wouldn't take no for an answer."

"She probably wanted to spend the hour looking at your butt."

Raoul stared at her.

She shrugged. "I'm just saying."

"You're certainly feeling better."

"It's more a matter of not being on the edge of hysteria," she admitted.

She turned her attention back to the school. It was obviously going to be in ruins when all this was over. "How big is your place?" she asked. "You seem like the mansion type. Could they hold classes in your foyer?"

"I rent a two-bedroom house from Josh Golden."

"Then that would be a no. They're going to have to put the kids somewhere."

"What about the other schools in town?"

"Marsha said they were thinking about bringing in those portable classrooms."

"Marsha?"

"Mayor Marsha Tilson. My boss. You know Josh Golden?"

Raoul nodded.

"He's married to her granddaughter."

"Got it."

He seemed less stunned now, which probably made him feel better. With the smoke smudges on his face, he looked pretty attractive, she thought absently. Not that he hadn't been devastatingly handsome before. He was the kind of man who made a woman do stupid things. Thank goodness she was immune. A lifetime of romantic failures had a way of curing a woman of foolishness.

"We should make another appointment," she said. "I'll call your office and set things up with your secretary."

"There you go, assuming again. I don't have a secretary."

"Huh. Who sets up your calendar and makes you feel important?" she said with a wink.

He studied her for a second. "Are you like this with everyone?"

"Charming?" She laughed. "As a rule. Just ask around."

"Maybe I will."

He was teasing. She knew he was teasing. Yet she felt something. A flicker. Maybe a quiver, down low in her belly.

No way, she reminded herself as she waved and walked toward her car. Especially not with a man like him. Successful, handsome men had expectations. Blonde ambitions. She knew—she read *People* magazine.

Life had taught her many important lessons. The greatest of which was not to depend on anyone to be there for her. She was a strong, independent woman. Men were optional and right now she was going to just say no.

RAOUL SPENT THE NEXT hour at the school. The firefighters got the fire under control. The chief had told him they would have a presence for at least the next twenty-four hours, to control any hot spots. Cleanup would start when the remaining structure had cooled and the investigation was complete.

It was the kind of disaster he'd read about in the paper and seen on the news a dozen times over the years. But even the best reporting hadn't prepared him for the reality of the heat, the destruction and the smell. It would be months, maybe years, before the campus was even close to normal.

The kids had all gone home, as had most of the spectators. Eventually he turned to walk back to his office. His car wasn't in any danger, but it was blocked in by several fire trucks. He would return later and collect it. In the meantime, the center of town was only about twenty minutes away.

Raoul had grown up in Seattle, gone to college in Oklahoma, and then been drafted by the Dallas Cowboys. He was a big-city kind of guy, enjoying the restaurants, the nightlife, the possibilities. At least he had thought he was. Somewhere along the way, going out all the time had gotten old. He'd wanted to settle down.

"Don't go there," he told himself firmly.

Revisiting the past was a waste of time. What was more important was the future. He'd chosen Fool's Gold and so far he enjoyed small-town life. Walking nearly everywhere was one of the advantages. So was the lack of traffic. His friends had joked that he wasn't going to have much of a social life, but since his divorce, he hadn't been that interested, so it was all working out.

He reached his office, a first-floor space on a tree-lined side street. There was a restaurant—the Fox and Hound—around the corner, and a Starbucks nearby. For now, it was enough.

He reached for his keys only to see the lights were already on. He pulled open the door and stepped inside.

The three-thousand-square-foot office was more than he needed, but he had plans to expand. His summer camp was just the beginning. Changing the world would require a staff.

Dakota Hendrix, his lone year-round employee,

looked up from her computer. "Were you at the fire? Didn't you mention you were going to the school?"

"I was there."

"Did everyone get out okay?"

He nodded and briefed her on what had happened—leaving out the part where he went back to check that all the rooms were empty.

Dakota, a pretty woman with shoulder-length blond hair and expressive eyes, listened carefully. She had a PhD in childhood development and he'd been damn lucky to find her, let alone hire her.

One of the reasons Raoul had moved to Fool's Gold had been because of the abandoned camp up in the mountains. He'd been able to get it for practically nothing. He'd updated the facility and this past summer End Zone for Kids had opened its doors.

The camp's mandate was to help inner-city kids be a part of nature—hardly a unique idea, but one that was appreciated by those who lived in the urban center of broken cities. Local kids came as day campers, and the city kids stayed for two weeks at a time.

The initial reports had been favorable. Raoul had an idea to expand the camp into a year-round facility, a challenge Dakota had understood and wanted to take on. In addition to planning and running End Zone, she'd started writing a business plan for the winter months.

"I heard the fire was awful," she said when he was done. "That there was a lot of damage. Marsha called me a few minutes ago." She paused. "Marsha's our mayor."

He remembered Pia mentioning her. "Why would she call you about the fire?"

"Mostly she was calling about the camp." This time

the pause was longer. "The city wants to know if they can use the camp as a temporary school. Marsha, the head of our board of education and the principal would like to see it first, but they think it would work. The only other place big enough is the convention center. But it's pretty much booked and the layout isn't really suitable. The acoustics would be awful—the noise of one class bleeding into another. So they're very interested in the camp." She paused for a third time, drew a breath and looked hopeful.

Raoul pulled out a chair and sat across from her. Hawk's words about getting involved echoed in his head. This was one way to get involved—but from a very safe distance.

"We don't have classrooms," he said, thinking out loud. "But we already have all the beds stored so the bunkrooms could be classrooms. They would be small but workable. With the right kind of dividers, the main building could house a dozen or so classrooms."

"That's what I thought," Dakota said, leaning toward him. "There's the kitchen, so lunch wouldn't be a problem. The main dining hall could double as an assembly area. No one knows how much is salvageable in terms of desks, but they're putting out the word to other districts. We should have some solid numbers in the next couple of days. So they can use the camp? I'll take care of the details and act as liaison."

"If you're willing to take that on." There would be liability issues, but that's why he had lawyers.

"I am."

He and Dakota tossed around potential problems and solutions.

"This will give us a lot of practical information about

having the camp open all year," she told him. "Dealing with the weather. We get a lot of snow in the winter. Can we keep the roads open, that sort of thing."

He chuckled. "Why do I know all those displaced kids will be hoping we can't?"

She smiled. "Snow days are fun. Did you have them in Seattle?"

"Every few years." He leaned back in his chair.

"I'll take care of everything," she told him. "Earn the big salary you've given me."

"You're already earning it."

"I was over the summer. Less so now. Anyway, this is great. The town will be grateful."

"Will they put me on a stamp?"

The smile turned into a grin. "Stamps are actually a federal thing, but I'll see what I can do."

Raoul thought about the kids he'd met that morning. Especially the little redheaded boy who had flinched, as if someone hit him. He didn't know the kid's name, so asking about him would be problematic. But once the school reopened, Raoul could do some checking.

He remembered Pia's teasing comment about moving the school to his house. This was close. It would be moving to his camp.

"Want to drive up to the camp with me?" he asked. "We should go and see what changes have to be made."

"Sure. If there's anything more than basic cleanup and refurbishing, I'll have Ethan meet with us."

Raoul nodded. Ethan was Dakota's brother and the contractor Raoul had used to refurbish the camp.

Dakota stood and collected her handbag. "We can have a couple of work parties, for general cleaning and prepping. Pia has a phone-tree list that would make the CIA jealous. Just tell her what you need and she can get you a hundred volunteers in about an hour."

"Impressive."

They went out, only to pause on the curb.

"My car is at the school," Raoul said.

Dakota laughed. "We'll take my Jeep."

He eyed the battered vehicle. "All right."

"You could sound more enthused."

"It's great."

"Liar." She unlocked the passenger door. "We can't all have Ferraris in our garage."

"How about cars built in the past twenty years?"

"Snob."

"I like my cars young and pretty."

"Just like your women?"

He got in. "Not exactly."

Dakota climbed in next to him. "I haven't seen you date. At least not locally."

"Are you asking for any particular reason?" He didn't think Dakota was interested. They worked well together, but there wasn't any chemistry. Besides, he wasn't looking to get involved, and for some reason he didn't think she was, either.

"Just to have something to share when I sit around with my friends and talk about you."

"A daily occurrence?"

"Practically." She shifted into First and grinned. "You're very hot."

He ignored that. "Pia was saying something about a man shortage. Is that true?"

"Sure. It's not so bad that teenage girls are forced to bring their brothers to prom, but it's noticeable. We're not sure how or when it started. A lot of men left during the Second World War. Not enough came back. Some people attribute it to a rumor that the site of the town is an old Mayan village."

They drove through town. Dakota took the road that headed up the mountain.

"Mayan? Not this far north," he said.

"They're supposed to have migrated. A tribe of women and their children. A very matriarchal society."

"You're making this up."

"Check the facts yourself. In the 1906 San Francisco earthquake, part of the mountain opened up, revealing a huge cave at the base of the mountain. Inside were dozens of solid-gold artifacts—Mayan artifacts. Although there were enough differences between these and the ones found down south to confuse scholars."

"Where's the cave now?" He hadn't seen anything about it in his travels or research.

"It collapsed during the 1989 earthquake, but the artifacts are all over the world. Including at the museum in town."

Something he would have to go see for himself, he thought. "What do matriarchal Mayans have to do with the man shortage in town?"

She glanced at him, then turned her attention back to the road. "There's a curse."

"Did you hit your head this morning?"

She laughed. "Okay, there's a rumor of a curse. I don't know the details."

"That's convenient."

"Something about men and the world ending in 2012."

"Dr. Hendrix, I expected better from you."

"Sorry. That's all I know. You might ask Pia. She mentioned something about doing a Mayan festival in 2012."

"To celebrate the end of the world?"

"Let's hope not."

Talk about a crazy history. A Mayan curse? In the Sierra Nevada mountains? And to think he'd been worried that small-town living would be boring.

PIA CAREFULLY COLLECTED cat food, dishes, cat toys and a bed that Jake had never used. Jo, the cat's new owner, had said she'd bought a new litter box and litter. After making sure she hadn't forgotten anything, Pia got the pet carrier out of the closet and opened it.

She expected to have to chase Jake down and then wrestle him into the plastic-and-metal container, but he surprised her by glancing from it to her, then creeping inside.

"You want to go, don't you," she whispered as she closed and secured the front latch.

The cat stared at her, unblinking.

Crystal had said he was a marmalade cat—sort of a champagne-orange with bits of white on his chin. Sleek and soft, with a long tail and big green eyes.

She stared back at him.

"I wanted you to be happy. I really tried. I hope you know that."

Jake closed his eyes, as if willing her to be done.

She picked up the tote holding his supplies in one hand and the pet carrier in the other. She took the stairs slowly, then put Jake and his things in the backseat of her car.

The drive to Jo's only took a few minutes. She parked

in front of the other woman's house. Before she could get out, Jo had stepped out onto the front porch, then hurried down the steps.

"I'm ready," the other woman called as Pia got out of her car. "It's weird. I haven't had a cat in so long, but I'm really excited."

Jo opened the back door of the car and took out the carrier. "Hi, big guy. Look at you. Who's a handsome kitty?"

The cooing singsong voice was nearly as surprising as the words. For a woman who prided herself on running her neighborhood bar with a combination of strict rules and not-so-subtle intimidation, Jo's sweet baby talk was disconcerting.

Pia collected the tote and followed Jo into her house.

Jo had moved to Fool's Gold about three years ago and bought a failing bar. She'd transformed the business into a haven for women, offering great drinks, big TVs that showed more reality shows and shopping channels than sports, and plenty of guilt-free snacks. Men were welcome, as long as they knew their place.

Jo was tall, pretty, well-muscled and unmarried. Pia would guess she was in her midthirties. So far Jo hadn't been seen with a man, or mentioned one from her past. Rumors ranged from her being a mafia princess to a woman on the run from an abusive boyfriend. All Pia knew for sure was that Jo kept a gun behind the bar and she looked more than capable of using it.

Pia stepped into Jo's and closed the front door. The house was older, built in the 1920s, with plenty of wood and a huge fireplace. All the doors off the living room were closed and a sheet blocked the entrance to the stairs.

"I'm giving him limited access for now," Jo explained as she walked through to the kitchen. "The sheet won't work for long, but it should keep him on this floor for a few hours."

Pia trailed after her.

Jo put the carrier down on the kitchen floor and opened the door. Jake cautiously stepped out, sniffing as he went.

"The house is really big," Jo explained. "That could scare him. Once he gets to know the place, he'll be fine."

"He must have loved my apartment," Pia murmured, thinking of how small it was.

"I'm sure he did. Cats like upstairs windows. They can see the world."

Pia set the tote on the counter. "You know a lot about cats."

"I grew up with them," Jo said wistfully, then leaned down and petted Jake's back.

Pia half expected the cat to take off one of Jo's fingers with his claws. Instead Jake paused to sniff her fingers, then rubbed his head against them.

He'd never done that to her, she thought, trying not to be offended. Apparently being a cat person helped.

Jo set out dry food and water on a place mat in the corner of the kitchen. Jake disappeared into the laundry room. A minute or so later, there was the distinctive scratching sound of litter being moved.

"He found his bathroom," Jo said happily. "He's all set. He'll figure out the rest of it. Come on. Let's go sit in the living room while he explores. I've been working on a new peppermint martini recipe. I'd like it ready for Christmas. You can tell me what you think."

A martini sounded like an excellent plan, Pia thought, trailing after her friend.

They sat on a comfortable sofa, across from the huge fireplace. Jo poured liquid from a pitcher into a shaker, shook it, then tipped the startlingly pink liquid into two martini glasses.

"Be honest. Is it too sweet?"

Pia took a sip. The liquid was icy cold and tasted of peppermint. It was more refreshing than sweet, with a hint of something she couldn't place. Honey? Almond?

"Dangerously good," she admitted. "And I'm driving."

"You can walk home and get your car in the morning," Jo told her. Her gaze sharpened. "Are you okay?"

"I'm fine." Pia took another taste of her drink. "Just feeling kind of strange. Giving up Jake and all."

"I'm sorry," Jo said. "I didn't mean to steal your cat."

"You didn't. He's not my cat. I thought we were getting along great, but you've had more contact with him in the past five minutes than I've had in the last month. I don't think he likes me."

"Cats can be funny."

As if to prove Jo's point, Jake jumped up on the back of the sofa. He stared at Pia for a moment, then turned his back on her. He dropped gracefully to the seat cushion, stepped onto Jo's lap, curled up and closed his eyes. As he lay there, he began to purr.

Pia found herself feeling snubbed, which hurt a whole lot more than she would have guessed.

"He never purred for me."

Jo had begun stroking the cat. Her hand froze. "Did you want to keep him?"

"No. I would say he hates me, but I don't think he put that much energy into it. I just never thought of myself as giving off the anti-cat vibration."

"You weren't raised with pets."

"I guess."

Apparently Crystal had made the right choice in leaving her cat with Jo. The only question was why her friend hadn't given Jo the cat from the start. No, she reminded herself. That wasn't the only question.

She felt a slight burning in her eyes. Before she could figure out what was going on, tears blurred her vision. She set down her drink and looked away.

"Pia?"

"It's nothing."

"You're crying."

Pia fought for control, then sniffed and wiped her cheeks. "Sorry. I don't mean to. I'm feeling all twisted inside."

"You really can have Jake back. I'm sorry to have upset you."

Jo sounded earnest and caring, which Pia appreciated. She gulped in a breath. "It's not the cat. Okay, yes, part of it is he obviously thinks I'm an idiot. It's just…"

The embryos. She knew that's what it was. That if she couldn't get Crystal's cat to like her, what hope did she have with actual children? Every time she thought of giving birth to her friend's babies, she started to freak.

She was totally the wrong person. She had no experience, no support system, no nurturing abilities. She couldn't even bond with a cat.

But she wasn't ready to talk about that. Not until she'd made up her mind about what to do.

"I miss her," she said instead, mostly because it was true. "I miss Crystal."

"Me, too," Jo said, sliding toward her.

They hugged.

Pia gave in to her tears. Jo held on, patting her back, not saying anything—just being a friend. Oddly enough, Jake stayed where he was, as well. His warm body and the vibration of his purring offered their own kind of comfort.

Pia allowed the caring to heal her, just a little. But even as she started to feel better, somewhere deep inside, she heard the call of three yet-to-be-born children.

CHAPTER THREE

PIA STOOD ON THE SIDEWALK, trying to breathe. The sense of panic was becoming familiar, as was the blurring of the world around her. Determined not to faint, she drew in deep, slow breaths, supporting herself by putting a hand on the brick building.

Think about something else, she commanded herself. Cookies. Brownies. Ice cream.

Chocolate-chip brownie ice cream.

After a few seconds, her vision cleared and she no longer had the sense that she was going to collapse—or run screaming into the bright, warm afternoon. Everything was fine, she told herself. And if it wasn't, well, she would fake it until it was.

She straightened, determined to return to her normal professional self. She had a meeting and this time she was going to get through it without doing anything to embarrass herself. No one would know that she'd just—

"You okay?"

She looked up into Raoul's warm, dark eyes. He stood by an open side door she hadn't noticed. His expression was both wary and concerned, despite which he looked plenty handsome. Which was pretty rude of him, if you asked her. The least he could do was be forgettable. Especially when she was feeling vulnerable.

Slowly, she turned toward the glass windows next to her and held in a groan.

"You saw that?" she asked cautiously.

"The part where you clutched your chest, bent over and nearly passed out?"

Oh, God. Heat burned her cheeks. "Um, that would be it."

"Yeah, I saw it."

She wanted to close her eyes and disappear. But that would violate her mature mandate. Instead she squared her shoulders, sucked in a breath and curved her lips into what she hoped was a smile.

"Sorry. I was distracted."

He motioned for her to step into his office. "It seemed like more than that."

"It wasn't," she lied, firmly clutching her oversize handbag. "So, as you can see, I'm here and ready for our meeting. I have several ideas for linking the camp with existing festivals. Either with a booth, or as a sponsor. A nonpaying sponsor. We force our corporate friends to cough up the big bucks to get their names on a banner, but we're more forgiving with the nonprofits."

"Good to know."

His office was large, with plenty of windows. There were four desks and lots of open space. She glanced around at the blank walls, the few boxes pushed next to a copy machine and the lone visitor chair.

"I guess decorating isn't in the budget," she said.

"We're still settling. Currently, it's just Dakota and me. We had more people working in the summer, but they were mostly up at the camp. I wanted room to expand."

"Apparently. It's nice. I would have expected a few football posters on the wall."

"They're not unpacked yet."

"When you do get them out, they'll add plenty of color."

He motioned to a square folding table in the corner.

Once they were seated on the plain chairs, she withdrew a file folder from her bag and set it on the table. She was aware of him sitting close to her but was willing to pretend she wasn't. One crisis at a time, she told herself.

"In case you haven't heard," she began, "Fool's Gold is the festival capital of California. We have a major event every single month. By major I mean we draw in over five thousand people and we fill at least fifty percent of the hotel rooms. The result is a nice influx of cash for our city."

She paused. "Do you want this level of detail?"

"Sure. Information is never bad."

She thought about some of the very tedious city council meetings she'd sat through—especially the budget ones—and knew he was wrong. But she kept that thought to herself.

"Currently tourism is our largest source of income and employment. We're working to change that. In addition to the existing hospital, we'll soon have a new facility that will include a trauma center. We also have the university campus. Those three sectors provide a lot of employment, but in this town, service jobs rule. One of the long-term goals of the city is to bring in more high-paying manufacturing jobs, so we're not constantly exchanging the same tired dollar, week after week. But until that happens, the festivals bring us both jobs and money."

She opened the folder she'd brought. "In addition to the major festivals, we have smaller events that draw a regional crowd. No 'heads in beds,' as the chamber of commerce likes to say. As in no one spends the night. That's less money for the town, but also less work."

Raoul took the list of festivals and scanned them. She'd marked the ones that would get the most family interest.

"If we can come up with a good angle, say a famous football player headlines the right event, we can draw some media attention," she said. "I'm guessing we can get TV here based on your celebrity, but it would be nice if we could find a good tie-in and maybe get on one of the morning shows."

"Bringing money to the town and donations and sponsorship to the camp?" he asked.

"Exactly."

This was good. Focusing on work helped her stay calm. Because if she thought about that morning…

Without warning, the trembling began again. Her chest got tight and she had to consciously deepen her breathing.

Raoul glanced at her over the papers. "You okay?"

She nodded because speaking seemed iffy at best.

He dropped the sheets. "What's going on?"

"Could I have some water?" she managed.

He stood and crossed to a small refrigerator. After collecting a bottle, he returned to the table and handed it to her.

"Thanks."

"What's going on?" he asked again as he settled

across from her. He took her free hand in his and lightly pressed his fingers to the inside of her wrist.

The contact was light, yet warm. She felt something. A little tingly sensation. Right. Because she had time for that now.

"Your pulse is way too fast," he announced. "You're upset about something."

The tingling disappeared. She snatched back her hand and opened the water.

"I'm fine. It's nothing."

He didn't look convinced. "Is it about the embryos?"

She closed her eyes and nodded. "I went to see them this morning."

"How?"

"I drove to the lab and asked if I could see them." She opened her eyes and sighed. "They said no."

"Did that surprise you?"

"A little. I knew they were small but I thought maybe I could peek at them through a microscope or something." She shifted in her seat, trying not to remember the incredulous look the lab guy had given her. As if she were an idiot.

"Apparently that's not possible without thawing them. And if they're thawed without being implanted, they die." She drew in a breath. "When I explained why I wanted to see them, he gave me a bunch of info on IVF."

"You told him about your friend?"

"Uh-huh. Then I read the material." She pressed a hand to her stomach, hoping to ward off another wave of nausea. "Apparently the body has to be prepared." She set the bottle on the table and used her fingers to indicate air quotes. "Which takes a whole lot more than a stern talking-to. An assortment of hormones are sent into my body. After that, there's the implantation procedure." She swallowed. "I won't get into detail."

"I appreciate that."

She managed a slight smile. "Then you wait. Or I wait. In two weeks, I take a pregnancy test. With luck, there are babies."

She felt the panic surging inside of her again. "I don't understand. Why would she trust me with her children? Do you know that Jake can purr? He gets all fluffy and relaxed and purrs."

"Jake's a cat?" Raoul asked cautiously.

"Yes. I've had him over two months. He never purred for me. He barely even looked at me. Then he goes to Jo's and purrs like his life depended on it. Which maybe to him it did."

She shook her head. "I don't get it. Crystal wanted those kids more than anything. After her husband was deployed to Iraq, she talked about getting pregnant when he got home. I went shopping with her and we looked at nursery furniture. She was so excited. After Keith died, she was still determined to be a mother. But that didn't happen. Now I'm supposed to raise her children? And the whole in vitro thing. It's not a hundred percent. Some or all of the embryos might not take. Which is a polite way of saying they'll die. What if that's my fault? What if there's something wrong with me? What if they're the same as Jake and they just plain don't like me enough to hang on?"

She could feel herself slipping past panic and into full-on terror. She glanced at Raoul to see if he'd completely freaked out, only to find him staring at her.

Intense staring, she thought, feeling a little awkward and exposed.

"TMI?" she asked softly. "Too much information?"

"You said Keith and Crystal."

She nodded.

"Keith Westland?"

Now it was her turn to stare. "Yes. How did you know?"

He stood and walked the length of the office, then returned to stand in front of her. He was tall enough that it was uncomfortable to stare up at him. She stood.

"Raoul, what's going on?"

"I know him," he said flatly. "Knew him. Keith is a pretty common name, but he talked about his wife, Crystal. He talked about this town. That's why I came here in the first place. He's the reason I agreed to play in the celebrity golf tournament last year. I wanted to see where he'd grown up."

"Wait a minute. How could you know Keith? Crystal never said anything." Pia was reasonably confident that her friend would have mentioned being friends with someone like Raoul Moreno.

He looked out the window, as if he was remembering a long-ago event. "I was in Iraq. A few players go in the off-season. Just to hang with the troops. Help morale. That kind of thing. We were all assigned a soldier to keep us out of trouble. Keith was mine. We traveled all around the country, to the different bases. We bunked together, got shot at a few times. He saved my ass."

Raoul rubbed his hands over his face. "That last day, we were heading for the airport. It was a big convoy. The players, a few VIPs, some politicians. There was an ambush. IEDs in the road, a couple of snipers in the hills. Keith was shot." He shook his head. "I held him while he died. He couldn't talk, couldn't do anything but gasp for air. And then he was gone."

She sank back into her chair. "I'm sorry," she whispered. "I didn't know." Crystal hadn't known, either.

"Reinforcements came and they helped us get home. When I got the invitation to the golf tournament, I came here. I guess to pay my respects to a place Keith had loved. I liked it, so I stayed."

Pia hadn't thought there would be any more surprises, but she'd been wrong.

He crouched in front of her. "I wanted to talk to Crystal, but I didn't know what to say. I knew her husband all of two weeks and I was there when he died. Would that have comforted her?"

She felt his pain and lightly touched his shoulder. "The man she loved had died. I don't think there was any comfort to be had."

"I wondered if I'd taken the easy way out. I didn't want to intrude or get involved." He smiled faintly. "Now you're responsible for Keith and Crystal's babies."

"Don't remind me."

He returned to his chair and stared at her. "You okay?"

"Trying to recover from the latest bombshell." She winced. "Sorry. Bad word choice. Hearing that you knew Keith, that you were there when he died, feels oddly cosmic. Like the universe wants to make sure I have these babies."

"You're reading too much into it."

"Am I? Don't you think it's just a little strange that we're even having this conversation?"

"No. I moved to town because I met Keith. If he hadn't been assigned to me, I never would have agreed to do the golf tournament and I wouldn't be here, having this conversation with you."

He made sense, but Pia still felt as if she was being pushed into a decision she wasn't ready to make.

There was so much on the line. The three embryos meant she could have triplets. That was three babies. She had a tiny apartment. How could they all fit?

She grasped the water and held on as if the act of squeezing would prevent her from slipping over the edge. But after hearing about Raoul and Keith, even questioning the act of having the children seemed monumentally selfish.

"You don't have to decide today," he reminded her. "Or even this year."

"I suppose. When I start to freak, I tell myself that I'm focusing on the wrong thing. This isn't about me. It's about Crystal and Keith and their children. Who am I to question whether or not I should have their children? Doesn't that make me a bad person? Shouldn't I already be on the hormones, buying cribs and reading that *Expecting* book everyone says is so great? If I was a good person, I wouldn't be hesitating."

Raoul stared into Pia's hazel eyes, amazed by the kaleidoscope of emotions. She was possibly one of the most honest people he'd ever met. Crazy, but honest. Appealing, as well, but thinking she was hot wasn't exactly appropriate.

Slowly, he took the water from her hands and set it on the table. Then he pulled her to her feet and wrapped his arms around her.

"It's okay," he told her.

She stood rigid in his embrace. "No, it's not."

He continued to hold on, moving one hand up and down her spine, enjoying the feel of her body next to his. Not that he was going to do anything about it. "Take a deep breath. In and out. Come on. Breathe."

She did as he requested. A little of the tension eased out of her.

He couldn't begin to imagine what she was going through. He was thrown by the fact that he'd known Crystal's husband. For her, the connection was a thousand times more powerful.

Moving his hands to her shoulders, he stepped back far enough to see her face.

"You're not a bad person," he said firmly. "A bad person would walk away from the embryos without a second thought. As to taking your time to make the decision, why wouldn't you? Having Crystal's babies will change everything about your life. You're allowed to have a plan."

"But she's my friend. I should…"

He shook his head. "No. Crystal didn't give you a head's up. This was dumped on you, Pia. Give yourself a break."

She drew in another breath. "Okay. Maybe."

Her eyes were large and filled with concern. Her mouth trembled. There was something vulnerable about her. Part of him wondered why Crystal *hadn't* warned Pia in advance. Had it been the other woman's advancing illness or something else? Had she not wanted to give Pia a choice?

Instead of finding an answer, he became aware of them standing very close together. He could feel the warmth of her body, the delicate bones under his fingers.

She was tall but still had to look up to meet his gaze. Her curls brushed the backs of his hands. Her lips parted slightly, which made him want to lean in and—

He moved back with the speed that had gotten him signed by the Cowboys, then carefully tucked his hands into his jeans pockets.

Where the hell had that thought come from? Pia wasn't for kissing. No one here was. He planned to live in Fool's Gold for a long time. If he wanted entertainment, he would take it somewhere else. Not here. Besides, since Caro, he *hadn't* been interested. This was not the time for that to change.

Apparently Pia hadn't noticed. Instead of being hurt or annoyed, she gave him a smile.

"Thanks. You've been great. I'm sorry I keep freaking out on you."

"You're dealing with a lot," he said carefully.

"I know, but this is business. For what it's worth, I really am a calm, rational person. Professional even. You probably don't want to take my word for it, but you can ask around."

He forced a chuckle. "Don't worry about it."

"I will, because I believe in worrying early and often. I'd promise to let you speak to my assistant next time, only I don't have one. And with the fire and all, the town can't afford to pay for one."

"I can talk to you, Pia."

"At least I didn't faint this time."

"Improvement."

She sighed. "You're nice, aren't you? I don't trust nice men." She winced, then held up a hand. "Don't take that wrong."

"There's a right way?"

"I'm just saying…" She shook her head, then grabbed her bag. "I'll leave you with the paperwork. We can talk about the festivals and your camp later, if that's okay. I really need to gather the tattered remains of my dignity and move on. Next time we meet, I swear I'll be totally calm and rational. You'll barely recognize me."

He didn't want her to go. For reasons he couldn't explain, he wanted to pull her close again and tell her—

What? What was he going to say? He barely knew her. She had other things to deal with. The meeting didn't matter.

But the problem wasn't the meeting, and Raoul knew that. There was something about Pia. About how she got right to the heart of the problem. She was an intriguing combination of determined, vulnerable and impulsive. If she wasn't careful, life would beat the crap out of her. Only the strong survived, and even they had to take a hit now and again.

Not his problem, he reminded himself. Nor did he want it to be.

"I'll recognize you," he told her. "You're making too much of this."

"So speaks a man who likely has never been hysterical even once in his entire life." She met his eyes. "Thanks for being so…nice."

"Even though it makes you not trust me?"

She winced. "I'm going to regret saying that forever."

"No. I'm sure you'll have other, bigger regrets that fill your mind."

"Ouch. That's not very encouraging."

"We all have regrets. Things we want to change or

undo. Nothing about today is worth a second of your worry."

She hesitated. "I thought you'd be different. Cynical. Self-absorbed. You know—a sports star."

"You should have met me ten years ago."

Her mouth curved into a smile. "Wild and impetuous?"

"A typical college jock. My high school girlfriend dumped me my freshman year. I spent a few months feeling sorry for myself, healed and returned to my sophomore year only to discover I was a god."

"Did you perform miracles?"

"I thought I could."

"I'm glad to know you went through a bad-boy period."

"Mine lasted several years."

Right through his signing with the Cowboys and beyond. He'd been on the team just over a year when Eric Hawkins—otherwise known as Hawk—had burst into his hotel room, waking Raoul and the twins he'd been sleeping with.

Hawk had been his high school football coach and mentor. He'd ushered the girls out of the room, nearly drowned Raoul in coffee, then had taken him to the gym for a workout that had no pity on Raoul's impressive hangover.

But that hadn't been the worst of it. The really bad part had been the disappointment in Hawk's eyes. The silence that said he'd expected better.

"What changed you?" she asked.

"Someone I care about had expectations and I let him down."

"Your dad?"

"Better than my dad. It's impossible to have nothing to lose when someone loves you."

She blinked. "That was profound."

"Don't tell anyone."

"You saw the light and let go of your bad-boy ways?"

"Pretty much."

After the workout, Hawk had taken Raoul to the poor side of Dallas, driving past people living out of shopping carts.

"Get over yourself," was all his former coach had said.

Raoul had gone home feeling like the biggest jerk in the world. The next day he'd moved out of the hotel, bought a house in a normal neighborhood and had started volunteering.

Two years later he'd met Caro at a charity ball, which had proved life wasn't perfect.

"So you believe people can change," she said.

"Don't you?"

"I'm not sure. Does the meanness go away or does it just get covered up?"

"Who was mean to you?"

She sighed. "And here I was supposed to gather up my tattered dignity and just go. You've been great. I'll be in touch, Raoul. Thanks for everything."

She walked out of the office.

Not sure if he should go after her, he hesitated. Then Dakota stepped in from the back and stared at him.

"Did I hear that right?"

Raoul shifted uneasily. "It depends on what you heard."

"You knew Keith Westland?"

He nodded.

She crossed toward him and sank onto the chair Pia had used. "I won't say anything, of course. About you knowing him or the babies. This is a lot to take in. Talk about responsibility. I guess I knew that Crystal would have to leave her embryos to someone, but I never really thought about it. Did Pia know before?"

He remembered his first meeting with her. "I don't think so. She thought she was getting the cat."

"Right. She was taking care of Crystal's cat." Dakota looked stunned. "What's with Crystal not warning her? You can't just leave someone potential children and not even give them a hint. Or maybe she knew Pia would freak and didn't want to be talked out of it." Dakota glanced at him. "Is she okay?"

"She's dealing. She's surprised Crystal picked her."

"Really? I'm not. Pia might not be the obvious choice, but she makes sense. She would do the right thing." Dakota laughed. "After some serious kicking and screaming. Wow—Pia's going to have Crystal's babies."

"She hasn't decided that yet."

Dakota glanced at him. "Do you really think she'll walk away from those babies?"

He shook his head. He couldn't see it, but then he'd been wrong before.

He took the chair behind the desk. "You and Crystal and Pia all grew up in town together?"

"Oh, yeah. Crystal was a few years older, but she was one of those really nice people who wanted to take care of the world. She worked at the library after school. She was always there to help with school projects." Dakota wrinkled her nose. "I can't believe I'm old enough to remember when there wasn't an Internet."

"You're twenty-seven."

"Practically ancient." She laughed. "Pia was a grade ahead of me and my sisters, but we knew her. Or at least of her." Her eyes brightened with humor. "Pia was one of the popular girls. Pretty, great clothes. She had the boyfriends everyone else wanted."

The humor faded. "Then her dad died and her mom went away. Everything changed for her. Back in high school I would have sworn Pia was taking off for New York or L.A. Instead she stayed here."

Which meant something had happened to her.

"I guess it's where she belongs," Dakota murmured.

"You came back, as well," he said. "There must be something about this place."

"You're right." She laughed. "Be careful, Raoul. If you stay too long, you'll never escape."

"I'll keep that in mind."

But the truth was, he wanted a place to call home. Somewhere that felt right.

There had been a time when he'd wanted it all—a wife and a family. Now he was less sure. Back when he'd married her, he would have sworn he knew everything about Caro. That nothing she did would ever surprise him.

He'd been wrong, and in finding out the truth about what she'd done, a part of him had been destroyed. Pia had asked if he thought people could change. He did, because he'd seen it over and over again. But broken trust was different. Even if it was repaired, it was never the same again. There would always be cracks.

CHAPTER FOUR

ONE OF THE PERKS of her job was that although Pia was a part of city government, she didn't have to participate in any of the really boring stuff. Sure, once a year she had to present a budget, and she was accountable for every penny. But that was easily done on a good spreadsheet program. When it came to the city council meetings, she was strictly a visitor, not a regular.

So when the mayor called Pia and asked her to attend an emergency session, she found herself feeling a little nervous as she took her seat at the long conference table.

"What's up?" she asked Charity, the city planner. "Marsha sounded less than calm, which is unusual for her."

"I'm not sure," Charity admitted. "I know she wanted to talk about the school fire."

Which made sense, but why would Pia have to be there for that?

"How are you feeling?" she asked her friend.

Charity was about four months along. "Great. A little puffy, although no one seems to notice but me." She grinned. "Or they're lying. I'm good with either option."

Charity had moved to town in early spring. In a matter of a few weeks, she'd fallen for professional cyclist Josh

Golden, gotten pregnant and discovered she was the mayor's long-lost granddaughter.

Josh and Charity had slipped away for a quiet wedding and were now awaiting the birth of their first child. Marsha was thrilled at the thought of a great-grandchild.

Just another day in Fool's Gold, Pia thought cheerfully. There was always something going on.

Pia glanced around at the other women at the meeting. There were the usual suspects, along with a few surprises including Police Chief Alice Barns. Why would the police chief need to attend a city council meeting? Nancy East sat close to the front. No doubt the superintendent of schools would have information they all needed.

Before Pia could ask Charity, Marsha hurried in and took her seat at the head of the table.

The mayor was as well-dressed as always. She favored tailored suits and wore her white hair pulled back in a tidy bun.

"Sorry I'm late," Marsha said. "I was on the phone. Thank you all for coming on such short notice."

There was a murmur of people saying it was fine.

"We have a preliminary report on the fire," Marsha said, glancing down at the pages she held. "Apparently it began in the furnace. Because of the unusually cool few days we had earlier in the week, it was turned on before it was serviced. The fire spread quickly, as did the smoke."

"I heard that no one was hurt," Gladys said. The older woman had served as the city manager for several years and was currently acting as treasurer.

"That's true. We had a few minor injuries, but

everyone was treated on the scene and released." Marsha looked at them, her blue eyes dark with concern. "We're still assessing the damage, but we're talking millions of dollars. We do have insurance and that will help, but it won't cover everything."

"You mean the deductible?" one of the council members asked.

"There's that, which is sizable enough. But there are other considerations. Books, lesson plans, computers, supplies. As I said, some will be covered, but not everything. The state will offer assistance, but that takes time. Which leads me into the next topic. Where to put all those children? I refuse to let this fire disrupt their education. Nancy?"

Nancy East, a bright, plump woman in her late thirties, opened a notebook in front of her.

"I agree with Marsha—keeping the children in school is our first priority. We considered splitting them up among the other three elementary schools, but there simply isn't enough room. Even with portable classrooms, the infrastructure can't support that many additions. There isn't enough space in the cafeteria or on the playground. There aren't enough bathrooms."

Some of the tension in her face eased. "Fortunately, we have a solution. Raoul Moreno has offered his camp. I toured the facility yesterday, and it's going to work beautifully for us."

Pia leaned back in her chair. The camp was an obvious choice, she thought. It was big and had plenty of buildings. It was closed in the winter, so they wouldn't be displacing anyone.

"There are some logistics for our classes," Nancy continued. "Our maintenance staff is up there right now, figuring out the best configurations. There is a main building where we'll have assemblies and where the cafeteria will be. Calls have gone out to schools all around the state for extra supplies, including desks, blackboards, dry-erase boards, buses. We're making an appeal to the commercial suppliers. As Marsha mentioned, the state will be offering some assistance."

She turned to Pia. "I need your help, Pia."

"Sure. What can I do?"

"I want to mount a supply drive for this Saturday. We'll hold it in the park. We need everything from pencils to toilet paper. Our goal is to have the children back in school by Monday."

Pia remained calm on the outside, but inside there was a very loud shrieky voice. "It's Wednesday."

"I know. That's the challenge. Can you pull something together by Saturday?"

The clear answer was no, but Pia swallowed that. She had a phone tree that rivaled anything created by the government and access to an impressive list of volunteers.

"I can get the word out tonight," she said. "Beg mention in tomorrow's paper, along with Friday's. Do media Friday and get it set up by, say, nine Saturday morning." Even thinking about it was enough to make her woozy. "I need a list of what you need."

Nancy had come prepared. She passed a folder to Pia. "If people would rather give money, we won't say no."

"Who would?"

Pia flipped open the folder and stared at the neatly typed sheets. The list was detailed and, as Nancy had promised, listed every possible need, from chalk to china. Well, not china, exactly, but dishes for the camp.

"I thought the camp already had a working kitchen," she said. "Why would they need plates, glasses and utensils?"

"End Zone for Kids housed less than a hundred campers, even with the day campers," Marsha told her. "We're sending up close to three hundred."

"That's a lot of napkins," Charity murmured. "I'll stay after the meeting and you can tell me what I can do to help."

"Thanks."

It wasn't the size of the project that worried Pia, but the speed. She would need a full-page ad in the local paper. Colleen, her contact at the *Fool's Gold Daily Republic,* wasn't going to be happy.

"I need to make a call," she said, then excused herself.

Once she was in the hall, she pulled out her cell phone and dialed.

"Hi, it's Pia," she said.

Colleen was a woman of a certain age—only no one knew exactly what age that was. She was a hard-drinking, chain-smoking newspaper woman who didn't believe in chitchat and had never met an adjective she didn't want eliminated.

"What do you want?" Colleen snapped.

Pia sucked in a breath. Talking fast was essential. "A full page tomorrow and Friday. Saturday we're going to be collecting donations for the school that burned down. For a new school and supplies."

Damn. Talking to Colleen always made her nervous.

The worst part was the other woman didn't have to say anything to get Pia feeling frantic.

"The kids will be going up to the camp while the burned-out school is repaired. They'll need everything from books to pencils to toilet paper. I have a list. Money donations are fine, too."

"Of course they are. Anything else? How about a kidney? I was told I have two. You want I should cut that out and send it along?"

Pia leaned against the wall. "It's for the children."

"I'm not competing in any beauty pageant. I don't have to give a fig about kids or world peace."

There was a long pause. Pia heard the other woman exhaling smoke.

"Get me the material in fifteen minutes and I'll do it. Otherwise, forget it."

"Thanks, Colleen," Pia said, already running for the fax machine on the second floor.

She made the deadline with eighteen seconds to spare. When the copy and the list of needed supplies had gone through the fax machine, Pia returned to the meeting only to find out they hadn't actually been as busy as she had.

"Charity, is there any chance you've *seen* Raoul's butt?" Gladys asked hopefully. "Could you get a comparison?"

Pia sank into her seat. "Yes, Charity. You should ask Raoul for a private showing, and I'd like to be in the room when you do."

Charity rolled her eyes. "I haven't seen his butt, I'm not going to ask to see it. As far as I'm concerned, Josh is perfection, and that can't be improved upon."

"You're his wife," Gladys grumbled. "You have to say that."

Marsha rose from her chair. "Debating which of our two celebrity athletes is more attractive can be a thrilling way to pass an hour. However, we still have things to discuss. Pia, you got the ad?"

"Yes. Colleen will run the time, the list and all the contact information tomorrow and Friday. I'll get the phone tree up and running tonight. We'll set up tables for those who want to host a bake sale or whatever. The usual stuff."

Marsha passed her a paper. "Here are the local businesses that will be providing drinks and snacks. I told them not to deliver before eight on Saturday." She glanced around the table. "I would be grateful if those of you with a close and personal relationship with God spoke to Him about the weather. Warm and sunny on Saturday would be best."

Gladys looked shocked at the request, but everyone else laughed.

Marsha sat back in her seat. "There's one other item I need to discuss. I was hoping it wouldn't be an issue, but no such luck. I realize that when compared with the unexpected fire that destroyed the school, this will seem small and unimportant. However, it is going to impact our town and we have to be prepared."

Pia glanced at Charity, who shrugged. Apparently Marsha hadn't talked to her granddaughter about the mystery element.

"A few of you may remember Tiffany Hatcher," Marsha said. "She was a graduate student who came to Fool's Gold in the spring. Her field of study is human geography. As in why people settle where they do, why they move, etc."

Pia vaguely remembered a petite, pretty young woman who had been very interested in Josh. As he'd only had eyes for Charity, nothing had come of her flirting.

"I tried to delicately discourage her from writing about the town, but I wasn't successful," Marsha continued. "Her thesis is being published. She called to let me know there is a chapter on Fool's Gold. Specifically about the ongoing shortage of men. She has sent out excerpts of the chapter to many media outlets and there has been, as she so happily put it, interest."

"No," Chief Barns said forcefully. "I'm not going to have a bunch of media types mucking up my town and parking where they're not supposed to. Isn't there enough real news in the world without them paying attention to us?"

Pia's thoughts exactly. But she had a bad feeling that a town with a man shortage would be exactly the right kind of story to capture a lot of attention.

"I don't suppose telling the media we don't want them here will help," Charity said.

"If only," Marsha told her. "I'm afraid in the next few weeks we're going to have to deal with the problem. And not just the media, either."

Pia stared at her boss. The mayor nodded slowly.

"When word gets out, we'll be flooded with men looking for a town full of lonely women."

"That could be fun," Gladys said, looking intrigued. "A few of you need a good marrying."

Pia suspected Gladys meant her, so she was careful to stay quiet. With less than three days to pull together a massive event, getting married or even meeting men was the last thing on her mind. And even if she wasn't so busy, considering the whole embryo issue, getting involved wasn't just unlikely, it was impossible.

SATURDAY MORNING DAWNED perfectly clear. The temperatures were supposed to be in the low seventies. Apparently God had come through, Pia thought as she arrived at the park a little after seven to find work under way.

The city maintenance crew was already setting up the long tables and collection bins. Several signs had been donated by a printer, and ones that had been made by hand were sorted and in place. Pia had drawn up a floor plan of sorts, showing what would be collected where.

Her miracle phone tree had worked perfectly, and she'd heard back from over fifty people with promises of books, supplies and even cash. Liz Sutton, a Fool's Gold native and a successful author who had recently returned to settle in town, had quietly promised five thousand children's books to start the library. When Pia had offered to shout about the donation from every rooftop in town, Liz had insisted on being anonymous.

She wasn't the only one giving big. Local hero Josh Golden had already handed in a check for thirty thousand dollars, again with instructions to keep quiet about him giving it. A cashier's check for ten grand had arrived in her office the previous morning. Just a plain envelope slipped under the door. No return address and drawn on a busy Sacramento bank, so there was no way of tracing it.

Pia had turned the money over to Nancy, along with a list of what else she knew was being donated.

Now as she sipped her coffee, she went over the

events that would happen during the day. The city yard sale would begin at eight. Donations had been delivered the day before, and her volunteers were already sorting through the bounty. To keep things simple, the items would be grouped according to price, at one-, three-, five- and ten-dollar tables.

The bake sale would start at noon, giving the last-minute bakers time to get their goodies finished. The auction was at three, and Pia was still waiting on the list of what would be offered.

Throughout the day, local bands would play, the hospital was offering a mini-clinic for blood pressure checks and the high school senior class was holding a car wash. Pia was less sure about their "Naked for a Cause" theme—even though the class president had sworn that meant bathing suits, not actual nudity, but at this point, she was willing to take every dollar they raised.

By seven-thirty there was a steady stream of volunteers showing up. They checked the master directory Pia had posted and went to their assigned areas. Charity arrived fifteen minutes later, looking pale.

"Sorry I'm late," she said, tucking her hair behind her ears. "I don't get sick in the morning much, but today was one of those days. The good news is the guys did a very nice job installing the floor tile."

Pia winced. "You got a close look at it?"

"For nearly an hour. My knees hurt." She pressed a hand to her midsection. "Not to mention other parts of me." She handed Pia a folder. "The final auction info."

"Thanks for doing this."

"I'm happy to help. There are some great prizes." Charity paused. "Is it a prize if you have to buy it?"

"I'm not sure."

Pia flipped through the list. There were the usual gift cards from local restaurants and shops. She would bundle those into a couple of baskets, so the value was greater. That should up the bidding price. Ethan Hendrix had offered five thousand dollars' worth of remodeling. There were weekends in Tahoe and up at the ski resort, ski lessons, and a weekend in Dallas compliments of Raoul Moreno. His package included airfare, two nights at Rosewood Mansion on Turtle Creek, dinner at the hotel and two tickets to a Dallas Cowboys home game... on the fifty-yard line.

"There's some money in that prize," Pia said, impressed by Raoul's generosity.

"I know. My eyes nearly bugged out," Charity said. "The guy's already donating his camp. That's more than enough."

"He's nice," Pia said absently. "He can't help it."

Charity laughed. "You say that like it's a bad thing."

"It can be." Although Raoul had claimed to have a dark past. Something that should have bothered her but instead made him seem more human.

"He's very good-looking," Charity told her.

Pia looked at her friend. "Don't even go there."

"I'm just saying he's here, he's handsome, successful, rich. I don't think he's dating anyone. He and his ex divorced a couple of years ago."

Pia raised her eyebrows. "You've been checking up on him?"

"Oh, please. I'm with Josh."

As if that explained everything. Which it probably did, Pia thought with only a hint of envy. It wasn't that she'd ever had a thing for Josh, it was more the way he looked at Charity that made Pia feel a little lost and sad. Josh didn't just adore his wife, he worshipped her. It was as if he'd been waiting his whole life to find her and now that he had, he was never letting her go.

Not that Pia would trust that kind of adoration, but it was nice to think about.

"I'm not interested," she said firmly.

"How do you know? Have you spent any time with him?"

Pia wasn't ready to talk about the embryos, but the truth was getting pregnant with them would change everything. Very few men would be interested in raising someone else's kids. Especially triplets. The thought was beyond daunting. And even if there was a guy like that out there, she knew Raoul wasn't him.

"We've spoken," Pia said. "Like I said—he's nice enough. Just not for me."

She eyed her friend's belly. Charity was barely showing, but she knew a whole lot more about being pregnant than Pia. But asking anything, as in finding out what it really felt like, meant answering a lot of questions. Pia wasn't ready for that.

The clock from The Church of the Open Door chimed the hour. Pia glanced at her watch and winced.

"I need to run," she said. "I have fifteen places I need to be."

"Go," Charity told her. "I'll handle the auction. Don't even think about it."

"I won't," Pia told her. "Fool's Gold owes you."

BY ELEVEN IT WAS APPARENT the town had come through to support the school. The items brought in for the yard sale had been snapped up, with most people insisting on paying two or three times the posted price. The donation bins were overflowing, as were the tables, and people just kept on coming.

Pia went from area to area, checking on her volunteers, only to discover she wasn't needed. The event ran so smoothly, she started to get nervous.

Over by the mini food court, she bought a hot dog and a soda, telling the kid manning the cart to keep the change.

"Everyone's doing that," he said with a grin, stuffing the extra bills into a large coffee can nearly overflowing. "We've had to empty this twice already."

"Good news," she said, strolling over to one of the benches and taking a seat.

She was exhausted, but in a good way. Right now, in the middle of a sunny day, surrounded by her fellow citizens, she felt good. As if everything was going to be all right. Sure, the school had nearly burned down, but the town had pulled together and order had been restored. Order had always felt really good to her.

Three boys came running down the path. The one in back, a slight redheaded boy, plopped down next to her and grinned.

"There's free lemonade over there," he said, pointing across the park.

"Let me guess. You've already had a couple of glasses."

"How'd you know?"

"I can see the happy glow of sugar in your eyes. I'm Pia."

"I'm Peter." He wrinkled his nose. "I go to the school that burned down. Everybody's doing all this so we can get back to class."

She held in a smile. "Not your idea of a good time?"

"I like school, I guess."

Peter looked to be about nine or ten, with freckles and big brown eyes. He was skinny but had a wide smile that made her want to grin in return.

"What would you rather do than go to school?" she asked.

A shadow crossed his face then cleared. "I like to play baseball. I used to play T-ball when I was little."

"Are you in Little League now?"

He shook his head. "My foster dad says it's too expensive and takes too much time."

That didn't sound good. "Do you like other sports?"

"I like to watch football. They have those funny things they do with their hands. I try to watch what they're doing, but it's hard to see."

"You know they make those up," she told him. "There's not just one right way."

His eyes widened. "For real?"

"Uh-huh. Come on." She put her soda on the ground and tossed her hot dog foil and napkin in the trash, then she faced Peter. "We'll make one up now. I'll do a step, then you do a step."

She made a fist with her right hand. He did the same. They bumped top and bottom, then fist to fist, followed by an open-palm slap and a back-of-hand bump. He added two finger wiggles, and she ended with a double clap.

"All right!" Peter stood in front of her. "Let's do it really fast."

They went through the sequence twice, without a mistake.

"You're good," Pia told him.

"You, too." He glanced down the path and saw his friends. "I gotta go."

"Okay. Have fun. Don't drink too much more lemonade."

He laughed and took off at a run.

Pia collected her drink and stood. It was time to get back to work. As she grabbed her paperwork, she saw Jo crossing the lawn, headed for the auction postings.

Her first thought was to chase after her friend and ask about Jake. Did he seem to miss her? Was he settling in? Then she remembered how the cat had crawled onto Jo's lap and started purring within ten minutes of arriving at her house. Of course he was doing well.

She turned and ran into someone tall, broad and strong. Jostled soda spilled out of the paper cup and trickled down the front of the man's shirt.

Pia groaned and raised her eyes only to encounter Raoul's amused gaze.

"Small-town initiation?" he asked.

"Sorry." She stepped back and brushed his chest, which proved to be more enjoyable than she would have expected. "It's diet. It won't stain or anything."

"I'm fine." He took her hand in his and stilled the movement but didn't release her fingers. "Are you all right?"

"I'm fine. You're the one who got doused."

His touch was light, barely noticeable, yet she couldn't seem to focus on anything else. His skin was warm.

She could feel individual calluses, the power he kept contained.

The power he kept contained? What was this—a bad movie script? Who thought like that?

Apparently her, she realized as she looked back into his eyes and discovered she didn't want to turn away. Which made her immediately pull free of his hold.

"So, thanks for your donation. It's very impressive. You really did enough with donating the camp."

"It wasn't a big deal," he said easily. "I was happy to help."

"Good. We should all help, especially now. With the whole burned-down-school thing."

His dark eyebrows pulled together. "Are you sure you're okay?"

"Yes, of course. Why wouldn't I be?"

No way she was going to mention that the feel of his skin on hers had thrown her. Not only was it irrational, a declaration like that put her into the scary-stalker category.

She searched around for another explanation.

"I saw Jo," she said quickly. "The friend who took the cat?"

He nodded.

"I wanted to ask if Jake missed me, which is dumb, right? He obviously adores her. I was just a way station in the feline road of life. She's a destination. I just…"

"What?"

"I keep thinking if I can't make a cat happy, what chance do I have with kids?"

His expression sharpened. "You're going to have them?"

"Yes. No. I'm not sure." She sighed. "Maybe. I know

that's what Crystal wanted. And no matter how many times I tell myself they're not my responsibility, I feel they are. I'm female. I'm going to go out on a limb and assume I have all the working equipment."

She could do more than assume, she reminded herself. She knew for sure.

Don't go there, she told herself. Not today. Not now. Wasn't there enough going on without a side trip to Guilt Land?

"You'll have someone else's children and then raise them?" he asked.

"It's not like I'm going to have them and give them away."

"Why not?"

She stared at him. "Excuse me?"

"Why wouldn't you give them away? There are hundreds of couples who are longing for children of their own. Infants are easy to place, aren't they? You could handpick the couple yourself, be sure the babies are going to be well taken care of."

That had never occurred to her. Give Crystal and Keith's babies away? Despite the warm afternoon, a shiver raced through her.

"No," she said firmly. "If that was what she wanted, she would have mentioned it in the will. Crystal took the trouble to pay for three years of storage. She wanted to give me time."

"She didn't warn you about what she was going to do."

"I know and that confuses me, but it doesn't change reality. If I have the babies, I'll keep them. And raise them." No matter how the thought of it made her stomach flip over and over.

He stared into her eyes as if searching for something. "I don't know many women who would be willing to take that on."

"Really? Because I don't know many who would refuse."

"You can't believe that."

She thought about her friends—how they looked out for each other. "I'm fairly sure."

"As sure as Crystal was of you? You're the one she picked."

"Which raises the question why," she said with a laugh that was almost real. "Okay—enough personal stuff for today. I have to compulsively check on things, and you need to stand in the sun so your shirt can dry."

She took off before he could do something really dangerous, like put his arm around her. That would probably get her to babbling like a starstruck fan.

It was the strangest thing. Usually people made her nervous when she first met them. Over time, the feeling went away. With Raoul, it was the complete opposite. She was more tense every time she saw him. At this rate, in a month, just seeing him would send her into catatonic shock. And wouldn't that give Fool's Gold something to talk about?

RAOUL STOOD BY THE main building and watched the kids arrive for their first day of school at his camp. The parking lot was organized chaos as teachers sorted the children into classes.

In less time than he would have thought possible, the camp had been transformed. There were desks and chairs, playground equipment, books, papers and people prepping lunch.

Dakota joined him, a clipboard in hand.

"This is great," she said. "Like the first day of school, only better."

"The kids would have probably enjoyed more time off."

She laughed. "You're right, but education is important." She glanced at him out of the corner of her eye. "Everyone thinks you're amazing for giving the town this place. Such a nice guy."

"There are worse things to be."

She looked surprised. "Most guys don't want to be nice. It keeps them from getting the girl."

He'd never had much trouble getting the girl. "A nice guy changed my life. Being like him would make me a happy man."

Hawk wasn't a pushover. He was a tough guy who did the right thing. Raoul doubted his old friend would have been fooled by Caro. The irony was Raoul had done his best to make sure he *was* choosing the right person. But he'd still managed to screw up.

"I need to check with a couple of teachers," Dakota said and excused herself.

Three more cars pulled up and parked. Pia climbed out of one and waved in his direction.

She wore a dark skirt and boots. Her sweater was the color of her eyes. Not only did he notice, he found himself wanting to walk toward her. Meet her halfway. That image morphed into his mouth on hers, hands everywhere and a whole lot less clothing.

Not a good idea, he reminded himself. Pia was headed in a whole different direction. Besides, he had rules about small towns and the female residents. Pia might tempt him, but making her an exception would be a disaster...for both of them.

"Isn't this the best?" she asked as she approached. "There was actual traffic coming up the mountain. I love it when a plan comes together."

A bus pulled up. When the door opened, kids spilled out. One boy, skinny with bright red hair, ran over to Pia.

Raoul recognized him as the kid who had flinched when he'd tried to help the boy out of the smoky classroom. As he watched, Pia and the kid greeted each other with a complicated handshake.

"You remembered!" the boy crowed. "I knew you would."

"It's our thing," Pia told him with a laugh. "You'd better get to class. Have fun."

"I will."

He turned and ran off.

"You know him?" Raoul asked.

"Peter?" Pia shook her head. "We met Saturday at the park. He was there with his friends. Why?"

He thought about the smoke-filled classroom. Maybe Peter had been scared of the fire instead of him. Maybe he'd imagined the whole thing.

Even as his gut told him he hadn't, he knew he wasn't going to say anything. Not until he had more information.

"I think he was in the class where I was speaking," he said. "When the fire started."

"Oh. Maybe. He's the right age." She shifted her handbag onto her other shoulder. "What's your calendar like over the next couple of days? Technically I still owe you a meeting."

"How about today?"

"What time?"

"Noon. We'll have lunch."

She hesitated. "You don't have to buy me lunch."

He raised an eyebrow. "I was going to let you pay."

She laughed. "Oh, well, in that case, sure. We'll go to the Fox and Hound. They make a mean salad, and you look like a guy who enjoys lettuce."

"I might surprise you."

Something flickered in her eyes. As quickly as it appeared, it faded. She nodded.

"You might at that."

CHAPTER FIVE

Pɪᴀ ʟᴏᴏᴋᴇᴅ ᴀᴛ ᴛʜᴇ ʜᴀɴᴅsᴏᴍᴇ man sitting across from her in the restaurant and told herself to focus on business. She was here in a purely professional capacity—not to enjoy the view. Though Raoul was pretty enough to dazzle anyone.

They'd already placed their orders and their drinks had been delivered. Pia had chosen diet soda, with the passing thought that if she went ahead with the pregnancy, she could kiss her artificial-sweetener habit goodbye, at least for nine months.

"You grew up in Seattle, right?" she asked, thinking a little chitchat was in order. She was allowed to be friendly.

"Until college," he told her.

"I've never been, but I'm guessing it's nothing like Fool's Gold."

"It's a lot bigger and there's a lot more rain. Seattle has mountains, only they're not as close."

"Why didn't you move back there?"

He flashed her a grin that made her pulse do a little cheer. "Too much rain for me. It's gray a lot. I like to see the sun." He picked up his iced tea.

"Is that why you abandoned them during college? You could have gone to the University of Washington."

"The other offers were better and Coach thought I

should get out of the state and see the rest of the country. Except for him and his wife, and my girlfriend, I didn't have all that much I was leaving behind."

"What about your family?"

He shook his head. "I never knew my dad. One of my brothers died when I was a kid. He was shot. My mom—" He shrugged. "I spent a lot of years in foster care."

There was something about the way he said the words. Bad things had happened, and she wasn't sure she wanted to know what. "I spent a year in the system," she admitted. "Here."

"You?"

"My senior year of high school. My dad died and my mom left to live with her sister in Florida. She said it would be better for me to stay here so I could graduate with my friends, but the truth was she didn't want to be bothered." Pia frowned. "I haven't seen her since. She didn't come back for my graduation and she made it clear I wasn't welcome there. So I stayed. Went to community college for a couple of years before transferring to a four-year university. Got a job with the city when I came back."

She forced a smile. "They tried to offer me a football scholarship, but those uniforms don't really suit me."

"This is your home," he said, his dark eyes serious. "Where you belong."

"You're right. Every couple of years I think I should go somewhere else. L.A. or San Francisco. Phoenix, even. But I won't leave. Which probably seems pretty boring to you."

"No. It's what I want, too. I thought I'd settle in Dallas. The fans are great and I enjoyed the city. I came here because of what Keith had said about his home-town. He made it sound like something out of a movie. When I got here for the golf tournament, I found out he'd been right. I liked everything about Fool's Gold. So I came back and then I decided to move here."

She wondered if he was running to something or from something. Not exactly a casual question.

"So this is your first small town," she said. "Then you need to know the rules."

"Didn't I get them in my welcome packet?" The corner of his mouth twitched as he spoke.

She did her best not to smile in return. "No. But they're very important. You mess up even a little and your life will be hell."

He leaned toward her. "What are the rules?"

"There are the expected things—keep the living room and kitchen picked up. You never know when you're going to have company. Don't mess with a mar-ried woman." She paused. "Or man, depending on your preferences."

"Thanks for the news flash."

"Don't favor any one business over another. Spread the wealth. For example, the best places for hair are owned by two sisters. Bella and Julia Gionni. But you can't go to just one. Trust me. Just alternate. When you're at Bella's, she'll trash Julia and vice versa. It's kind of like dinner theater, with highlights."

He looked more wary than amused. "Maybe I should go out of town for my haircuts."

"Coward."

"I know my limitations."

"You're the one who bought the camp here. Now you're stuck."

His face was handsome, in a rugged man's man sort of way. She liked the stubborn set of his jaw and the way his dark hair fell across his forehead.

"Can I get those rules in writing?" he asked.

"I'll see what I can do."

Their server arrived with their meals. Pia had chosen the barbecue chicken salad, while Raoul had picked a burger.

"How did you find the camp?" Pia asked, reaching for her fork. "I've lived here all my life and I barely remember knowing about it."

"I went for a drive," he told her. "I followed some old signs and found it. I'd had this idea about doing something with kids, but I wasn't sure what. When I saw the camp, I knew it was what I'd been looking for."

He held his burger but didn't take a bite. "The summer program is where we're starting, but I'm hoping we can do more. Be year-round. Bring kids in for intensive two- and three-week sessions where we focus on one or two subjects. Mostly science and math. Not enough kids are excited about those subjects."

"You'd have to coordinate with school districts," she said. "To complement their current curriculum."

"That's what Dakota's working on. We're thinking middle-school-aged kids. Get them excited before high school."

He had plenty of passion about the subject, she thought, taking a bite of her salad. What was he like when he was with a woman? Was the same passion there?

An interesting topic, she thought, but not one she would pursue. Even without the potential pregnancy in her future, she knew better than to get involved with a high-powered guy like him. Or any guy. For some reason, men made it a habit of leaving her. If they hadn't wanted to stick around before, what luck would she have getting them to stay when she had three kids?

Three kids? Her head started to swim. She forced herself to think about something less frightening.

"Having the school use the facility is an interesting way to work out any problems," she said. "And here everyone thought you were just being nice."

He chuckled. "It's a win-win for everyone."

"Even if it wasn't, the camp is a great idea. I know a lot of the kids in town appreciated being able to head up there every day this past summer. Or should I say their moms appreciated it. Summer can be a very long three months."

PIA'S HAZEL EYES DANCED with amusement. Raoul found himself watching her rather than eating. He liked her, which was a good start. He wanted to get to know her better, yet even if he ignored the foolishness of getting involved so close to home, there was the issue of the embryos.

"Why did you want to work with kids?" she asked. "Because of the coach who helped you?"

"How'd you know?"

"The way you talk about him."

"Yeah, it was him. He saw something in me I couldn't see in myself. His wife, too, although they weren't married at the time." He smiled at the memory. "My senior year of high school I was one of the football captains."

"Of course you were," she muttered.

"What?"

"Nothing. Go on."

"Each captain was supposed to bring doughnuts to practice. Once we started two-a-days, I had to quit my summer job. I was living in an abandoned building and didn't have any money."

"Time-out. You were homeless?"

"It wasn't so bad." It had been a whole lot better than dealing with his foster father. The man had never met a kid he hadn't wanted to hit. One day Raoul had hit him back. Hard. Then he'd left.

"It can't have been good," she said, sounding worried.

"I'm fine."

"But you weren't."

"I got by. My point is, I tried to steal them."

"The doughnuts? You stole doughnuts?"

"I didn't get away with it. The lady who owned the bakery caught me and she was pissed." She'd also toppled him with a crutch, a fact he still found humiliating.

"I ended up working for her, then eventually I went to live with her. Nicole Keyes. She liked to think she was tough, but she wasn't."

"You loved her," Pia said softly.

"A lot. If I'd been ten years older, I would have given Hawk a run for his money." He chuckled. "Maybe not. I had a girlfriend at the time and she would have objected." He glanced at Pia. "My girlfriend was Hawk's daughter."

"You're making that up."

"It's true." They'd had a lot of plans, he remembered. Marriage. A dozen kids. "We lasted through my first year of college. Then she dumped me. I got over it."

"Are you still friends with Hawk and Nicole?"

"Sure. They got married and are really happy together. I even keep in touch with Brittany."

"Does he know about your crush?"

"Probably."

"Interesting. I can't begin to bond with a story of my own."

"Your best friend left you three embryos. You'd win." He picked up his burger again. "Hawk and Nicole taught me to do the right thing. What's that phrase? They're the voice in my head, telling me what to do next. I don't want to let them down."

"They're your family," Pia said wistfully. "That's nice."

He remembered she didn't have much of a family. A dead father and a mother with the nurturing skills of an insect. If she had the kids, she would belong, he thought. But he would bet she hadn't considered that. Pia would choose to carry the embryos because it was the right thing to do. She didn't need an example—she just knew.

She pushed aside her salad and drew a folder out of her large bag. "Go ahead and eat," she told him. "I'll tell you what I've come up with and you can think of reasons to tell me I'm brilliant while you chew."

"I like a woman with a plan."

PIA GLANCED AT HER WATCH and was stunned to see it was already after two. "Yikes. I have a three o'clock I need to get to," she said, opening her wallet and pulling out a couple of bills.

"You're not buying me lunch," Raoul told her, picking up the check.

"But you said—"

"I was kidding."

"Too macho to let a woman pay for your food?"

"Something like that."

He tossed money onto the bill, then stood. When she rose as well, he moved close and placed his hand on the small of her back as they walked out.

She was aware of every millimeter of contact. Her faux-cashmere sweater only amplified the sensation of heat and pressure.

When they reached the sidewalk, she turned to face him. "I'll get back to you with a schedule of deadlines," she said. "I think coordinating with a few of the festivals will work out well for the camp."

She found herself wanting to babble, even if she avoided looking directly at him. What was wrong with her? This wasn't a date. They weren't at her door and she wasn't debating whether to invite him in. This had been a business meeting.

"Thanks for your help," he said.

She drew in a breath, squared her shoulders and met his gaze. "You're welcome. You know Robert, our former treasurer, was the kind of man everyone thought was nice, and he ended up stealing millions."

"You're saying I'm a thief?" He sounded more amused than insulted.

"Not exactly. But how much do we really know about you? People should ask questions."

"You think too much," he told her.

"I know, but that's because there aren't enough distractions in my life."

"How about this one?" he asked, right before he leaned in and kissed her.

The contact was light enough—barely a brush of lip against lip. Hardly worth mentioning.

Except every cell in her body froze from the shock. The fingers holding her bag tightened into a death grip on the handle. Before she could figure out what she was supposed to do, he straightened.

"Thanks for lunch," he said, then turned and walked away.

Leaving her gasping and alone. And very, very confused.

RAOUL ANGLED AWAY FROM the mirror as he slowly raised and lowered the weight in his hand. He'd been working out long enough that he rarely needed to check his form or speed. The movements were automatic. Unlike some guys, he didn't get a kick out of staring at himself.

Next to him, Josh Golden worked his triceps. Both men were dripping sweat and breathing hard. It had been a hell of a workout.

"In case you were wondering," Josh said as he lowered the weight to the bench in front of him, "I'm the only hero in this town."

Raoul grinned. "Worried, old man? Or should I say, threatened?"

"I've been here a whole lot longer than you. The town adores me. You're some newcomer. The question is, can you last through the long term?"

"I can outlast you."

Josh grinned. "In your dreams." He grabbed a towel and wiped the sweat from his face. "Everyone appreciates that you offered the camp. Without that place, there wouldn't have been a school."

"I'm happy to help."

"Good. That's what we do around here. Those who have more, give more. Life in a small town."

More rules, Raoul thought, remembering the ones Pia had listed. Something about where he was supposed to get his hair cut. Or not. He hadn't really been listening. He enjoyed listening to her speak, watching the emotions chase across her face. Her eyes were expressive. Her mouth…tempting.

"Earth to Raoul." Josh waved his hand. "Who are you thinking about?"

"A friend."

Josh picked up the weight again. Raoul set his down.

"You had lunch with Pia the other day," Josh said flatly.

Raoul raised his left eyebrow. "You're married."

"I'm not interested in keeping her to myself," Josh said firmly. "I've known Pia for years. She's like a sister. I'm watching out for her."

Raoul was glad someone was. From what he could see, Pia was pretty much on her own. "We're working together. Some of the festivals tie in with the work we're doing up at the camp."

Josh bent forward, keeping his upper arm still, moving the weight up and down to work his triceps. "You're getting tied in here. Sure you're ready for what small-town life really is?"

"I'll figure it out as I go. What's your concern?"

"Pia talks tough. She's smart, she's funny, she pretends nothing gets to her. But that's not true. Crystal's death hit her really hard. Before that…" He set down the weight again and straightened. "She's had some tough breaks. Her dad died, her mom left. There were a few bad boyfriends. Nobody wants to see her get hurt. You mess with her, you won't just answer to me. You'll answer to everyone."

Raoul had been a football star since he was sixteen. He was used to being the person everyone wanted to be with. The one who was liked.

"You're saying I'll be run out of town?"

"That'll be the least of it."

"I like Pia," he said at last. "I'm not going to hurt her."

Josh didn't look convinced. "You can't be sure."

"I don't want to hurt her," Raoul amended. "I care about her, too."

"I guess that will have to do for now. But if that changes, you'll answer to me."

"Think you can take me?" Raoul asked, not bothering to hide his amusement.

"Absolutely."

Josh was in good shape and they were about the same height, but Raoul had a good twenty pounds of muscle on him. Not to mention years of playing football. Cycling wasn't exactly a contact sport.

"I'm glad you're looking out for her," he said, because it was true. "Pia needs more people on her side."

Josh studied him. "Nearly everyone would tell you she has the whole town on her side."

Raoul had his doubts. "She's a local girl and they like her. But who does Pia have that she can really depend on? One-on-one? She's all alone in the world."

A reality that was going to complicate her life when she decided to have Crystal's babies. Babies no one else seemed to know about.

He thought about the soldier he'd known—the soldier who had died in his arms. What would Keith think about all this? Raoul had a feeling he would be pleased that his children were being given a chance but suspected he, too, would worry about Pia being on her own.

"You looking to change her situation?" Josh asked.

"I don't do long term."

"You were married. That the reason?"

Raoul shrugged and set the weight back in the rack.

Josh did the same, then hesitated. "I was married before Charity. It didn't go well. Sometimes it's not supposed to."

Raoul nodded because he wasn't going to have the conversation and agreeing moved things along. If he mentioned a bad first marriage, people assumed he'd been cheated on. Or had discovered Caro had married him for his money. Either would have been a whole lot easier than the truth. Hell, he would have preferred if she'd left him for a woman. But the real reason their marriage had ended gnawed at him. It woke him at night and left him wanting to scream at the heavens.

There were things that couldn't be fixed, he reminded himself. Actions that couldn't be undone. Like throwing a rock in a pond. There was nothing to be done but to wait out the ripples and hope no one got hurt.

He and Josh walked to the locker room. After showering and dressing, they agreed to work out together the following week. One of the things Raoul missed most about playing football was working out with his teammates. Josh could be counted on to push him. Sometimes Ethan Hendrix, a friend of Josh's, joined them.

Raoul knew it took time to fit in a place, but he was

willing to take things slow. He liked Fool's Gold, so he was being careful not to make any missteps.

He left the gym, intending to go back to the office, but instead found himself walking home. He couldn't get Pia off his mind. Kissing her had probably been a mistake but was worth it, he thought with a grin. Not only because he'd enjoyed the feel of her mouth against his, but because of the look on her face when he'd done it. *Surprised* didn't come close.

He reached the small two-bedroom he'd rented and went into the study and booted his computer. When it was ready, he sat down and logged on to the Internet, then typed IVF into the search engine.

An hour later he had a clearer understanding of what Pia was going to go through. Two hours later, he knew there was no way he would ever agree to something like that. Not that it was physically possible, but still. Not only was Pia going to have to chemically prepare her body for pregnancy, she would be carrying triplets. Assuming all the embryos took. If they didn't, she would have to deal with the loss and, he assumed, the guilt that went along with it.

Hard enough to be pregnant, but how much worse was it to be pregnant and alone, with no one to depend on? It wasn't like there was a dad she could go after for help or financial support.

Crystal had asked a lot from her friend. He was still convinced Pia would go through with having the babies, even if she hadn't figured that out yet. But he wondered if she really knew what she was getting into.

THE FUNDRAISER FOR THE SCHOOL might have techni- cally lasted only a day, but it had put Pia behind by an entire week. An amount that probably didn't sound like much, she thought as she stared at her scheduling board. But Fool's Gold had a festival every single month. Some were smaller than others, but work was always involved. With success came hours of behind-the-scenes planning.

Summer was the busiest time, but fall was a close second. The city Halloween Party was barely six weeks away, and before that was the Fall Festival. The Thanksgiving Parade was after the Halloween Party but before the Christmas Gift Bazaar. The Saturday Day of Giving led into the Live Nativity outdoor service, which was the Sunday before Christmas. Then there was New Year's and so on.

One project at a time, she reminded herself, making notes on her dry-erase calendar. That's how she got through. It's not as if any of the events were new. The plans pretty much stayed the same. She had master lists that were cross-referenced, decorations stored all over town. If this ever got old, she could probably apply to run the world. There were—

She paused and stared at the calendar square. Instead of noting when she needed to arrange to have chairs and booths pulled out of storage, she'd drawn a string of little hearts. Although sweet, it wasn't exactly helpful. Worse—she knew the cause.

Raoul's kiss.

No matter how many times she told herself he hadn't meant anything by it, she couldn't get her gut, or her heart, to believe it. That one little second of contact had changed everything. Suddenly he wasn't just Raoul, someone she knew, he was a *guy*. And because he was a guy, she had to be careful around him, which she didn't like.

Awareness was everything, she thought grimly. Two days ago, he'd been everyone's definition of tall, dark and handsome, but she hadn't really cared. He'd witnessed her at her hysterical best, had dealt with it winningly and she'd thought of him as a friend.

Now she found herself thinking about that stupid kiss two or three hundred times a day. She'd wondered why he'd done it, wished he would do it again, imagined him doing more than kissing her. It was pathetic, not to mention a waste of time.

She didn't have a type, but if she did, it wasn't him. He was too perfect. In all her "happily ever after" fantasies, the guy in question had been normal. Maybe even boring. Boring was dependable. With boring, a girl had a shot at the guy not leaving. But Raoul? He was heartbreaker material even when he wasn't trying.

"It was just a kiss," she whispered to herself. "Let it go."

Good advice. And someone, somewhere, would probably take it. Just not her. Not when she could feel the light brush of skin on skin, feel the heat of him and wish...

She lightly bumped her head against the wall, hoping to gently pound some sense into herself. Maybe the problem wasn't that Raoul was not her type, maybe the problem was more generic than that. Maybe if she'd had more kissing in her life, she wouldn't feel like she had to read too much into what had happened. Maybe she should date.

Pia rolled her eyes. "Oh, please. Like *that's* going to happen."

If she went ahead with the embryos implantation, her dating days were long over. Besides, she'd never exactly excelled in the man department. They always left, and for the life of her she couldn't figure out what she was doing to drive them away.

The door to her office pushed open. Pia glanced up and was surprised when Raoul strolled in.

He looked good, she thought, telling herself to make sure *she* looked cool and sophisticated. Barring that, she should try to avoid appearing desperate or needy.

"Hi," she said, going for cheerful. "I haven't had an emotional crisis today so we can't possibly have an appointment."

Instead of seeming impressed by her sparkling wit, he stared at her with an intensity that made her wonder if she'd dropped a bit of breakfast on the front of her shirt. As casually as she could, she glanced down. All seemed well.

"Pia," he said, moving toward her. "We have to talk."

Not exactly words one expected to hear from a macho guy. "Okay," she said slowly. "What about?"

Maybe he'd been as rocked by the kiss as she had been. Maybe he wanted to kiss her again and make her his love monkey. A week or two of intense male attention would probably cure her allergies.

"I've been doing research on in vitro fertilization," he said.

She plopped down on her chair and held in a sigh. So much for the love monkey invitation. "That's more than I've done," she admitted. "Is that what we're going to talk about? Because if it's anything gross, I don't want to know. I have a weak stomach."

He moved toward her desk. "It won't be bad. You take some basic tests, then your body is prepared to receive the embryos."

She hadn't liked the sound of that when she'd read the brochures the lab guy had given her, and she didn't like it now. "Prepared, how?" She quickly raised a hand. "Never mind. Are you going to sit?"

He placed his hands on her desk and leaned toward her. Apparently sitting wasn't on the schedule, either.

"Pia," he said, his dark gaze intense. "You can't go through this alone. You need someone to take care of you, and I want to be that person."

CHAPTER SIX

THE WORDS SWIRLED AROUND in Pia's head. This was even crazier than the kiss.

"I haven't decided I'm going to have the babies," she whispered.

"Sure you have. Are you going to walk away from them?"

"No, but…"

If she hadn't been sitting, she would have collapsed. Was Raoul right? Had she already made her choice?

She closed her eyes. There was no way she *couldn't* have them, she thought with some finality. Whether or not she was the best person, she was the one Crystal had picked. It was crazy and scary and life-changing, but it had to be done. Her friend was depending on her.

She opened her eyes. "Oh, God. I'm going to get pregnant." She sprang to her feet, as her chest tightened and her heart rate zoomed into triple digits. "I can't breathe."

He came around the desk, took her hands in his and held on tight. "I'll help."

"This has nothing to do with you."

"I want to help. Be your…" He seemed to be searching for a description of what he was offering. "Pregnancy buddy. I'll drive you to the doctor, go get you pickles, whatever you need."

"I don't need pickles," she told him, ignoring the warm feeling of his skin against hers. This was not the time to indulge in weakness. "I don't really like them. Not enough to binge on them." A pregnancy buddy? "Maybe you took too many hits to the head when you were playing football."

Despite her tugging on her hands, he didn't release them.

"Pia, I'm serious. You don't have any family here. You have friends, but they all have lives. You need someone to depend on for the next nine months. I'm offering to be that guy."

Did kissing come with the offer, she wondered, before pushing the thought away.

She managed to free her hands and take a step back. "You can't know what you're saying. Why would you give up nine months of your life to help me?"

"Why would you offer to have Crystal's babies?"

"That's different. She was my friend."

"Fair enough. I didn't know her, but I did know Keith. These are his kids, too. The man died in my arms, Pia. I was there. I owe him. Helping bring his children into the world seems like the least I can do."

That almost made sense, she thought. Given that everything about their conversation was beyond believable.

"Okay, maybe," she conceded, "but maybe you could just donate something to charity instead. You're a rich, famous guy. You have a life. Probably a girlfriend."

"I don't have a girlfriend. I wouldn't have kissed you if I did."

Which begged the question of why he had, but she

would deal with one weird incident at a time. "Raoul, you're really sweet, but no."

"Why? Don't you trust me?"

She frowned. "What do you mean?"

"I'm not going to offer this, then change my mind. I'm not going to leave."

She did her best not to wince at his words. He knew enough about her past to guess that being left was one of her issues. Slowly, she returned to her chair and sank down. After drawing in a breath, she looked at him, as if she could find the answer in his handsome features.

There was nothing new there—just the same large, dark eyes, high cheekbones, perfect mouth.

He pulled up a chair and sat facing her. "I mean it, Pia. I want to help. For you and for Keith. You should let me try. I'm good at getting stuff done. All that quarterback training. What you're doing is important. Let me help."

She might not be willing to accept a man she barely knew would do this for her, but she could almost get that he would do it for Keith.

"What does being a pregnancy buddy mean?" she asked cautiously.

"Whatever you want it to mean. Like I said, I'll drive you to the doctor, go on craving runs, listen to you talk about how your ankles are puffy."

Something passed through his eyes—a dark, scary emotion that made her wonder about his past. But before she could ask, the emotion was gone.

"I'll be there for you, Pia. In whatever capacity you want. No expectations, no rules. You won't have to go through this alone."

That sounded perfect, she thought wistfully, wondering if it was possible. Could she really depend on him, trust him, know that he would be there for her?

Leaning on other people hadn't been a big part of her life. Not since high school, when both parents had left her—in one way or another. As she and Raoul weren't involved emotionally, the situation was completely different from what it had been with her boyfriends. If he chose to leave, it wouldn't be a big deal. Right?

Which was what it came down to. Depending on someone she wasn't sure would come through for her.

"It's an interesting idea," she began. "And I appreciate it. But why would you do this? What's in it for you?"

"I'll be there," he said firmly, "because I like you. And because you're doing a good thing. Maybe because there are things in my past that didn't work out the way I wanted them to, and this will make me feel better about them."

"How do you know what I'm thinking?"

"I just do, and I'll be there."

A part of her wanted to believe. Being able to depend on someone, especially while she was pregnant and worried about giving birth to three kids and raising them, would be heavenly. But the rest of her knew that leaving was what most people did best.

"Look at it this way," he said. "Use me shamelessly. Then if I do walk away, you get to be right. A win-win."

An interesting point. He sounded really sincere. Not totally sane, but sincere.

"Okay," she said slowly. "Maybe."

"I'll take it." He leaned in and brushed his mouth against hers.

Again, the light kiss had her entire body reacting.

She wanted to haul him against her and have him put some back into it. Instead, she contented herself with remembering to breathe.

He stood. "Let me know when it all starts and I'll be there."

She wasn't clear on the implantation process, but she was pretty sure it was something she didn't want him to see.

"In the waiting room," he amended at her look of squeamishness.

"Okay. That would be fine. I'll let you know."

He left.

She continued to sit on her chair, feeling both stunned and a little relieved. Maybe this would be for the best, she told herself. Having someone else to help. Having someone else looking out for Crystal's babies. And if he got bored or distracted and walked away, so what? She'd been abandoned in ways Raoul couldn't begin to imagine. He couldn't possibly hurt her. So she was safe. And being safe was really what mattered most.

RAOUL TRIED TO BE UP at camp nearly every day. He timed his visits for recess or lunch so he could spend time with the kids on the playground. It was fun to toss a ball around with them. For the most part they were a little small to throw or catch a football, but a baseball worked well and Josh's sporting goods store had donated several balls and mitts.

When he arrived, the kids were still eating lunch. He went to see Dakota.

She was one of those neat people who had trays and color-coded, arranged files. Sort of like Pia's office, but without the huge calendar or the posters proclaiming Founders Day and Kissing Booth—$1 a kiss.

"How's it going?" he asked.

"Great." She motioned for him to enter.

He took the chair next to her desk.

"All the classes are in place and the kids are settled. We're okay on desks, still a little short on blackboards and books. So there's some creative sharing going on. It's probably good for the students to see that life means being flexible."

He chuckled. "Disaster as a teachable moment."

"Sure. Why not?" She pulled out a folder and glanced through it. "We should have an estimate on the cost to repair the school by the end of the week. If you hear a collective groan about ten Friday morning, it's the school-board-and-city-council joint meeting, where they get the actual numbers. I don't think it's going to be pretty."

"Isn't there insurance?"

"Sure, but it's unlikely to make the school whole again. I'm sure there's state money, too, but I see a lot of fundraising in our future."

He remembered the fun Saturday afternoon in the park. "Pia puts on a good party."

"She has a lot of experience."

A group of yelling kids raced past her open office door. "Lunch must be over," he said.

"Apparently."

More kids ran by.

"Does the noise bother you?" he asked. "Do you want an office somewhere else?"

Dakota laughed. "I'm one of six. I'm used to noise."

"Loud, happy childhood?"

"Absolutely. The boys came a couple of years apart, but when we were born, Mom got smacked with three babies at once. I can't imagine how she did it. I know my dad helped and the neighbors pitched in, but triplets? Somehow she managed."

He thought of Pia. She would have the three embryos implanted at the same time. If all of them survived, she would be looking at triplets, as well.

"So you're used to the chaos," he said.

"I don't even notice it. There are complications with a lot of kids, but as far as I'm concerned, the positives far outweigh the negatives."

"Planning a big family?" he asked.

She nodded and laughed. "I should probably get started, huh?"

"Is there a guy in all this?"

"I'd prefer it that way." She wrinkled her nose. "I know—how boring. I want to be traditional. Get married, have kids, a yard, a dog. Not anything a famous football guy would find interesting."

"What makes you think I don't want the same thing?"

"Do you?" she asked, tilting her head as she studied him.

"It would be nice."

"You were married before." She made a statement rather than asked a question.

"It didn't take."

"Is there going to be a next time?"

"I don't know," he admitted. Like Pia, he found it difficult to trust people. In his case, it was specifically women that were his problem.

"It can be different," she said. "Better."

He was less sure. "What about you? Any prospective husbands on the horizon, or are you waiting for the perfect guy?"

"He doesn't have to be perfect. Just a regular guy who wants an ordinary life." She shook her head. "Finding that is harder than you'd think. We have something of a man shortage here in town."

"I've heard that."

"You could ask some of your single football buddies to visit. As a gracious gesture to the lonely women in town."

"Donating the camp was my good deed for the week."

He stood and glanced out the door. A group of boys walked by, including Peter.

Raoul turned back to Dakota. "There's a kid in Mrs. Miller's class. Peter. He got scared during the fire. I went to take his hand, to lead him out. But when I stretched out my arm, he flinched, like he thought I was going to hit him."

She frowned. "I don't like the sound of that." She wrote the name down on a pad of paper. "I'll talk to his teacher and do some quiet investigating."

"Thanks. It's probably nothing."

"It probably is," she agreed. "But we'll find out for sure." She glanced at the clock. "You'd better go. Your fans are waiting."

He shifted uncomfortably. "They're not fans."

"They worship you. You're someone they've seen play football on TV and now you're on their playground, throwing around a baseball. If that's not fan-worthy, what is?"

"I'm just hanging out with the guys. Don't make it more than it is."

"Caring *and* unassuming. Be still my heart."

"I'm not your type."

"How do you know?"

Because from the second they'd met, there'd been no chemistry. Besides, Dakota worked for him. "Am I wrong?"

She sighed theatrically. "No, you're not. Which is why I'm very interested in your football friends."

"I doubt that. You're going to find your own guy."

"Want to tell me when?" she asked with a laugh. "So I can put a star by that day on the calendar?"

"When you least expect it."

PIA SAT ACROSS FROM Montana Hendrix in Pia's small office. She'd known the Hendrix triplets her entire life. The family had always been a prominent one and could trace its lineage back to the founding of the town.

People who assumed that the three sisters acted alike because they looked alike had obviously never met the triplets. Nevada was the quietest, the one who had studied engineering and gone to work with her brother. Dakota was more like a middle child—wanting everyone to get along. Montana was youngest, both in birth order and personality type. She was fun and impulsive, and the one Pia was closest to.

"So everything sold?" Montana asked, folding a letter and putting it into an envelope.

"Yes. The auction was a huge success. Despite the fact that there weren't any minimum bids, we made nearly twice what we'd hoped for."

The letters were going out to the successful bidders at

the school fundraising auction. It provided information on how to pay and when to claim the prize.

"Everyone wanted to help," Montana said.

"Like you today." Pia grinned. "Did I thank you yet?"

"You're buying me lunch."

"Oh, yeah. I forgot."

They talked about what was happening in town and with their friends.

Montana picked up another letter, then put it down. "I've been offered a full-time job at the library."

Pia raised her eyebrows. "That's great. Congratulations."

Montana didn't look very excited. "It's a big deal, right? I've been working there nearly two years part-time. They're giving me a nice raise and I'll have benefits."

"But?"

Montana sucked in a breath. "I just don't want to." She held up a hand. "I know, I know. What am I thinking? This is a great opportunity. They'd want me to go back and get my master's in library science, and they'd even help pay. I love living in Fool's Gold. Now I'd have job security."

"But?" Pia asked again.

"It's not what I want to do," Montana admitted in a small voice. "I don't love working at the library. I mean, I like it. Books are great, and I like helping people and I enjoy working with the kids. But full-time? Every day for eight hours?"

She leaned her arms on the desk and slumped in her seat. "Why can't I be like everyone else? Why can't I know what I want to do with my life?"

"I thought you liked the library. You were really excited to help set up Liz's book signing last summer."

"That was fun. I just…" She motioned to Pia's office. "You knew what you wanted to do."

"No." Pia remembered trying to pick a major in college. "I didn't have a clue. I went with business because it seemed to give me a lot of options. I started in this job as an assistant, then I found out I liked it. I was lucky. This wasn't a plan."

"I need to get lucky," Montana muttered, then grinned. "I was going to say 'not in a boy-girl way,' but that would be fun, too." Her smile faded. "I feel so stupid."

"Why? You're not. You're smart and funny."

Montana lowered her voice. "I think I might be flaky."

Pia did her best not to smile. "You're anything but."

"I can't pick a career. I'm twenty-seven and I don't know what I want to be when I grow up. Shouldn't I already be grown up? Isn't the future *now?*"

"You sound like a poster. This isn't about the future. This is about making yourself happy. There's nothing wrong with trying different careers until you find one you like. You're supporting yourself. It's not like you're living with your mom and watching TV all day. It's okay to explore the possibilities."

"Maybe," Montana said. "I never meant not to know what I wanted to do."

"Better to keep trying until you find something that makes you happy rather than choose something now and hate your job for the next twenty years."

Montana smiled. "You make it sound so easy."

"Fixing someone else's life isn't hard. The one I have trouble with is my own."

Montana raised her eyebrows. "Does any of this trouble have to do with a certain tall, very muscled ex-football player?"

Pia warned herself not to blush. "No. Why do you ask?"

"You had lunch with him."

"It was a business lunch."

"It didn't look like a business lunch," Montana told her.

Small-town life, Pia reminded herself. "How do you know? Did you see it for yourself?"

"I got the play-by-play from three different people." Montana leaned toward her. "One of them claimed there was a kiss, but I can't get confirmation on that."

Pia sighed. "I swear, we need more channels on cable around here. People are starved for entertainment."

"So there's nothing going on with you and Raoul?" Montana asked, looking disappointed.

Pia hesitated.

"There is!" her friend crowed.

"Don't get too excited. It's not what you think. It's not romantic." How could it be? Her soon-to-be pregnancy would scare off any sane man and most of the ones only flirting with sanity.

Pia drew in a breath. "Crystal left me her embryos."

Montana's eyes widened. "I thought you had her cat."

"I did, until I found out about her will. Jo got the cat."

"And you have her babies? That is amazing." Montana

blinked. "Oh my God! You have her babies. You have to decide what to do with them. Did she leave you any instructions?"

"Not specifically. I know that having them is sort of implied in the bequest. It's not like she wants them frozen forever. She left money to help cover some of the medical expenses and to start a college fund."

"You're going to have them?"

Pia nodded slowly. Reality hadn't completely sunk in, and she was okay with that. Accepting that kind of truth *should* take a little time.

Montana jumped up and ran around the table, then bent down and hugged Pia. "I can't believe it. This is so amazing. You're going to have Crystal's babies."

She dropped to a crouch and stared at her friend. "Are you terrified?"

"Mostly. There's a lot of confusion and worry to go with it, as well. Why on earth did she pick me? There are a lot of other people here who have more 'mom' potential."

Montana straightened and returned to her seat. "That's not true. Of course you're the one she wanted to have her babies."

"You say that like this all makes sense."

Montana looked confused. "How doesn't it?"

"I don't know anything about having a baby or raising one. Or possibly three. She didn't talk to me ahead of time, warn me. I was supposed to get the cat. It turns out he never really liked me, so that's probably for the best, but still…" Pia bit her lower lip. "Why did Crystal pick me?"

"Because she loved and trusted you. Because she knew you'd make the right decisions."

"She can't know that. I sure don't know that. What if something bad happens? What if the embryos hate me as much as Jake did?"

"They're not in a position to make a judgment call."

"Okay, not now, but they will be. After they're born."

"Babies are hardwired to bond. That's what they do. They'll bond with you because you're wonderful. But even if you weren't, they'd still bond with you."

"I'd feel better if they liked me for me and not just because of biology."

"That's going to happen, too," Montana assured her. "You'll be a great mom."

"How do you know?" Pia asked, feeling both worried and desperate. "I don't come from a happy gene pool. My boyfriends always leave. Even the cat didn't want to live with me. What do I have to offer to a baby?"

"Your heart," Montana said simply. "Pia, you'll do everything in your power to take care of those kids. You'll sacrifice and worry and be there when they need you. It's who you are."

"The whole single-mom thing scares me," she admitted.

"You might be single, but you won't be alone," Montana reminded her. "This is Fool's Gold. You'll be taken care of by the town. You'll have all the help and advice you need. Speaking of which, if I can do anything, please let me know."

"I will."

Pia knew that Montana was right about the town. If she needed help, she only had to ask. Then there was Raoul's strange "pregnancy buddy" offer. She wasn't sure exactly what he was putting on the table, but it was nice that he was willing to be there.

"I just wish Crystal had talked to me before she died. Explained what she wanted."

"Would you have told her no?" Montana asked.

Pia considered the question. "I probably would have tried to talk her out of it, but in the end, if this was what she really wanted, I would have agreed. But at least I would have had the chance to find out why."

"You really can't figure that out? You're genuinely confused as to why Crystal left you her embryos?"

"Yes. Aren't you?"

Montana smiled at her. "No. Not in the least. I guess that's what you're going to have to come to terms with. And when you do, you'll know why you were exactly the right person for her to pick."

CHAPTER SEVEN

DR. CECILIA GALLOWAY WAS a tall, large-boned, no-nonsense kind of person who had gone to medical school back when women were expected to be homemakers or secretaries. She believed an informed patient was a happy patient, and that until a man experienced mood swings and menstrual cramps, he was in no position to say whether or not they were in a patient's head.

A mother of one of Pia's friends had gently suggested Pia consider visiting a gynecologist before starting college. Pia hadn't imagined ever having sex, but she'd taken the advice and gone in for her first pelvic exam.

Dr. Galloway had made the experience more interesting than scary, explaining the details of Pia's reproductive system in language the teen could understand. She'd also offered blunt advice about fumbling boys and their lack of expertise. She'd told Pia how to find her clitoris and G-spot and suggested she tell the boy in question to spend some quality time with both before having his way with her.

Now, a decade later, Pia sat in Dr. Galloway's office. She had a meager list of questions, which had made her realize she didn't know enough to know what to ask. Rather than hit the Internet and get a lot of half-truths, she'd come to the source of all knowledge.

At a few minutes after ten, Dr. Galloway walked into

her office. She wore a white coat over casual knits. Her steel-gray hair was cut short. She didn't bother with makeup, but her steady blue eyes were warm behind her sensible glasses.

"Pia," the doctor said with a smile as she crossed the spacious room and settled next to Pia, rather than sitting across from her on the other side of the big wood desk. "I was a little surprised when I saw you were coming in today."

When Pia had made the appointment, she'd said she needed to talk to the doctor before being examined and had explained why.

Now, Dr. Galloway put down the folder she held and studied her. "You're young and healthy. Are you sure about this? It's an extreme measure at this time in your life. Wouldn't you rather wait and be in a relationship? Or even if you don't want to be involved with the father, we can look at artificial insemination rather than IVF."

It took Pia a second to realize the problem. "I'm not trying to get pregnant," she said with a shake of her head. "Okay, I *am* trying to get pregnant, but it's not what you think."

Dr. Galloway leaned back in her chair. "What shouldn't I think?"

"Crystal Westland left me her embryos."

The older woman's expression softened. "Did she? I wondered what Crystal would do. Poor child, to have suffered so much. It's a loss for all of us." She drew in a breath. "So you want to have Crystal's babies, do you?"

Want was kind of a strong word, Pia thought. She'd

accepted the shift in her life path and was dealing. Maybe *want* would come later.

"I'm going to have them," Pia said firmly, holding in the need to wince at the words. "What's the next step?"

Dr. Galloway considered her for a moment. "We do an examination to make sure you're healthy. Draw a little blood, that sort of thing."

She got up and walked around to the other side of her desk. After sitting, she pulled out a pad of paper and started making notes. "How many embryos are there?"

"Three."

"You'll have them all implanted at once?"

"I don't know. Should I?"

"It's probably for the best." The doctor raised her head. "The process is very simple. The embryos thaw naturally until they come to room temperature. They're put through several solutions to wash away any lingering cryoprotectant that was used during the freezing. Then they're warmed to body temperature and implanted. I can do that. It's a simple procedure, relatively painless."

She pulled several brochures out of a drawer. "Then you lie on the examination table for a few minutes, giving the embryos time to settle. Two weeks later, we test you to see if you're pregnant."

That didn't sound so bad, Pia thought. "Will I have to take any drugs? The guy at the lab talked about preparing my body."

"It depends. We'll monitor your cycle with a series of ultrasounds. When you're ready, in they go." Dr. Galloway leaned toward her. "It is possible not all the embryos will have survived the freezing process."

Pia hadn't realized that. "We'll know when they're thawed?"

"Yes, they're checked before they're implanted."

The doctor passed her several brochures. "You can read these over. They give more details about what will happen. Implantation is safe and quick. There's no reason to think this will be anything but a normal pregnancy."

Pia opened her mouth, then closed it. She glanced down at her hands, then back at the doctor. "What if I did something bad?"

Dr. Galloway shook her head. "There is nothing immoral in having Crystal's children, Pia. It is an act of love."

"I don't mean that. I mean…" She swallowed. "When I was in college, I had a boyfriend. I got pregnant."

"You had an abortion." Dr. Galloway sighed. "It happens all the time and has no impact on—"

"No," she said quickly. "I didn't. I was so scared, I couldn't believe it was really happening. There was no way the guy I was seeing would marry me, assuming I'd wanted that, which I didn't. I kept wishing the baby would go away. One morning I woke up and I was bleeding. I got my period."

She felt the wave of guilt, the shame that washed through her. "I wished my unborn child would die and it did."

The doctor rose and pulled Pia to her feet, then held her hands tightly.

"No," she said in a firm voice. "You don't have that much power, Pia. None of us do. A significant percentage of pregnancies end spontaneously. It is impossible to predict exactly when it will happen or even know why. Something went wrong inside the embryo. That is why you lost the baby. Not because you wished it so."

Tears filled Pia's eyes. "I prayed so hard."

"God didn't answer your prayer, child. Have you felt bad all this time?"

She nodded, then swallowed. "I don't deserve to have Crystal's babies. I'm a bad person."

"A bad person wouldn't care. You are young and healthy and you will be an amazing mother. Come on. We'll do the exam. We'll rule out any specific physical problems. Then you can decide. As for the child you lost, it's time to let him or her go."

Pia knew in her head that the other woman was right, but in her heart and her gut, the guilt lived on.

AN HOUR LATER, PIA DRESSED. She'd been poked, prodded and gone through her first ultrasound.

"Everything is fine," Dr. Galloway told her when Pia returned to her office. "You are ready. Based on when you last had your period, you're within five or six days of peak thickness in your uterine lining. So within the week if you want to go ahead this month."

"That fast," Pia said, hanging on to the back of the chair.

"You can wait for as long as you want."

Medically, yes, but if she waited, she might chicken out.

"How is your insurance?" Dr. Galloway asked. "You might want to check out how much it will cover."

"I'm with the city plan." The pregnancy itself would be covered. "Crystal left money to cover the implantation." There was also some money in trust for each of the children and a small annuity to help Pia with monthly expenses.

"Then the choice is yours." Dr. Galloway studied her. "Let the past go, child. It's time to think about the future. Whenever you're ready, I'll be here to help."

"Should I do anything special as far as food or vitamins?"

The doctor shook her head. "We've done a blood draw. I'll have the results in a few days. You'll go on prenatal vitamins then, along with any additional supplements you might need. For now, relax." The older woman smiled. "No, I take that back. Go find a good-looking man and have sex."

Pia felt herself flush. "Is that medical advice?"

Dr. Galloway laughed. "Yes. You're going to be pregnant with triplets, Pia. Your body won't be your own for much longer. Enjoy it while you can. Is there anyone special in your life?"

She immediately thought of Raoul—her hunky pregnancy buddy. "Not really. I'm not dating."

"My advice stands. Just make sure you take precautions. Then when you're ready, we'll take the next steps." She rose and walked around her desk. "You're doing an extraordinary thing, Pia. I'm so proud of you."

Pia thanked her and left. Information swirled around in her head. She was pleased that the implantation could happen relatively easily, and she appreciated Dr. Galloway's attempts to reassure her about what had happened in the past. Pia knew logically that she wasn't to blame for the loss of the baby she'd carried before, but she couldn't help feeling that being terrified rather than happy had been wrong. And that she would be punished later.

Which meant what? Did she give in to the fear and not have Crystal's children? That didn't seem right, either. If she went forward with this, she was going to have to take a leap of faith. On her part, she would do everything right. Take the best care of herself, live perfectly. It would be up to the babies to take care of the rest. A reasonable plan, she told herself. A rational response.

But she couldn't help but wonder if Crystal would have left her the embryos if she'd known the truth.

PIA HAD BARELY BEEN BACK in her office five minutes when Marsha called.

"They're here," the mayor said, sounding desperate. "I knew they were coming, but still."

"Who's here?"

"Reporters. They're everywhere. I need you to come to City Hall and dazzle them."

"Is this where I tell you I don't feel especially dazzling?"

"No, it isn't. We're desperate. Charity is going to take questions, as well. I need young, confident and sexy. Anything that doesn't scream pitiful spinster."

Despite everything that had happened that morning, Pia burst out laughing. "I don't think we use the 'S' word in this century, Marsha."

"They're going to use it. Count on it. You'll come?"

"I'll be there. Give me fifteen minutes."

"Make it twelve."

PIA MADE IT TO CITY HALL in ten minutes, only to find that the mayor wasn't kidding. There were several news vans parked along the street, with reporters setting up for outdoor shots. It was a perfect fall day—crisp without being too cold, blue sky, the changing leaves adding bursts of red and yellow.

She could see Charity talking to two reporters at once, and a crowd of residents starting to gather. Sucking in a deep breath and reminding herself to speak in coherent sound bites, she stepped toward the cluster of reporters.

"Hello," she said as she approached. "I'm Pia O'Brian. I work for the city. Mayor Tilson asked me to come by and see if you have any questions."

Immediately three cameras focused on her. Bright, blinding lights clicked on. Pia did her best not to blink like a mole in the sun.

"What's your name?" one guy asked. "Can you spell it?"

She didn't think Pia was a tough one, but she did as he requested.

"What's with the man shortage?" a young male reporter asked. "How are you driving them away?"

"Is it a sex thing?" another man asked. "The women in town not putting out?"

The assumption being they *must* be doing something wrong, Pia thought, but she did her best not to let her irritation show.

"Demographically, we're not as balanced as other communities," she said calmly. "There are fewer males born per one hundred births than in other places. As the father determines the gender of the child, you'll have to speak to the men in town to get your question answered."

The youngest of the three reporters around her blinked, as if he couldn't remember what he'd asked. All the better for her, she thought.

"Fool's Gold is a family community," she continued. "We have an excellent school system, a low crime rate and are a popular tourist destination. Businesses thrive here. We've recently signed a contract that brings a second hospital to the area. This one will include a trauma center, something this part of the state needs."

"Are the women in town excited about the man invasion?" the second reporter asked. "Maybe some of you will get lucky."

"Oh, joy," Pia murmured, knowing slapping someone when on camera was never a good idea. "Tourists are always welcome."

"We've heard there are busloads of men coming this way. From all over the country."

That couldn't be good. Busloads? What were they supposed to do with them? The kind of men who could drop everything, hop on a bus and travel to a place they'd never seen with the hopes of finding women didn't sound especially stable. Or community oriented. If this was true, it was a nightmare in the making.

"Lucky us," she said. "Fool's Gold is always ready to make visitors feel at home. Families especially."

"But you're short on men," the older of the three said. "So you'll be personally interested in the guys coming. You can't get a date, right?"

Pia raised her eyebrows, fighting a sudden flash of temper. "Do I look like I can't get a date? Is that what you're implying? That we should be *grateful* for anyone who comes here and gives us the slightest hint of affection? Do you really think we're desperate and—"

"There you are," a smooth male voice said, as a hand slid against the small of her back.

She turned and saw Raoul had joined her.

He gave her a warning glance, which was totally unnecessary. Obviously it was dumb to try to best a reporter while on camera. They had the last word in the editing room. But the assumption that she or any of the women in town were dying for a busload of guys from who knows where to show up was beyond insulting. Sure, many of the women in town wanted to meet someone special and get married, but that was a far cry from being desperate for any man who happened to glance their way.

Raoul extended his right hand to the reporters. "Raoul Moreno. Nice to meet you."

Pia had the satisfaction of watching two of the three guys' mouths drop open.

"The football player?" the youngest guy asked. "You played for Dallas. Jesus, you live here?"

"Fool's Gold is a great town. Family friendly, supportive of businesses. I've opened a camp for kids up in the mountains. There's a new hospital being built and a cycling school run by Josh Golden."

The oldest reporter frowned. "That's right. Josh Golden *does* live here. Hey, I thought there was supposed to be a man shortage."

Pia felt smug but was determined not to let it show. "We might have some demographic challenges, but we're still a thriving, happy community. If single men want to be a part of that, great. If they're thinking they've just entered the land of desperate women, they're sadly mistaken."

As she spoke, she was aware of Raoul's hand still pressing against her back. His touch was sure and warm and very, very nice. She found herself wanting to lean in, maybe rest her head against his chest, but that wouldn't be her smartest move. They weren't involved. Although there was a teeny-tiny chance she was thinking about asking him for sex.

How far did the pregnancy-buddy offer extend?

"There's a lot of regional industry that might interest you," Raoul told them. "We have a local contractor who builds wind turbines. He and his staff are designing some cutting-edge blades using special materials."

The reporters exchanged glances, as if wind turbines didn't exactly get their hearts beating faster. But Pia saw what Raoul was doing. Focusing on all the businesses owned by men, trying to get the reporters confused enough that they wouldn't have a story.

"If you're looking for local color," Pia said in her most helpful voice, "there's Morgan's Books. He's been around for years. When I was little, he always made sure the next Nancy Drew book was in stock for me."

Raoul pulled a business card out of his shirt pocket. "If any of you want to contact me about an interview, I'm available."

"Great," the youngest reporter said. "I'll call you. We can do a feature. Life after football, that sort of thing."

"Sure."

The three men drifted away. Pia watched anxiously, then had to hold in a cheer as the bright lights were extinguished and the cameras turned off.

She spun toward Raoul and grinned. "You did it. You saved the town."

He guided her away from the crowd. "Don't get too excited. They've been fooled, but it won't last long. This problem isn't going away."

She didn't want to think about that. "How'd you know to come here?"

"The mayor called and asked me to help. She's worried about the kind of men who will show up based on a news story."

Pia grinned. "She begged, didn't she?"

He shrugged. "It was uncomfortable. Besides, I'm not looking for bad press, either. This is my home, too." He glanced at the milling reporters. "We've bought ourselves some time. But if there really are busloads of men heading in this direction, the reporters will be back."

Not exactly a happy thought. "I guess we'd all better figure out what we're going to say when they return. Not to mention the logistics of herds of single men. What are we going to do with them? Do you think they're here to settle down or just hoping to get lucky?"

His gaze met hers. "That was rhetorical, right? You weren't actually looking for an answer."

She laughed. "You've saved us for the moment and that's enough. But if you get any brilliant ideas…"

"You'll be the first to know."

They stared at each other. He really *was* good-looking, she thought. Talk about an excellent gene pool. And those hands. They seemed…large.

Dr. Galloway's teasing words filled her brain. On a practical level, Pia knew that once she had Crystal's babies, her dating days were long over. Not that she'd been going out all that much before, but still. There had always been the promise of a great guy. Instead she would be the single mother of triplets.

"What?" Raoul asked. "You're thinking something."

It would be asking too much. On some level, it was probably wrong. Still, he was tempting.

"Would you like to come over for dinner?" she asked before she could stop herself. "So we can talk about the pregnancy some more? I saw my doctor today and she gave me a lot of good information."

"Sure. Want me to bring something?"

"Wine would be nice. If I'm going to get pregnant, then there won't be any in my future for nine long months."

They settled on a time and she gave him her address. As he walked off, she stared after him. Between now and dinner, she had several hours to decide if she really was going to ask Raoul for one last fling before she started down the pregnancy road.

The thought of being with him made her feel all squishy inside. Based on what she knew about his past, he had plenty of practice when it came to the wild thing. It would probably be the night of a lifetime. Which was about how long the memories would have to last her.

PIA HAD NEVER BEEN MUCH of a cook. Yet another skill she would need to be a successful mother, she thought as she climbed the two flights of stairs to her apartment. She'd bought a rotisserie chicken from the grocery store, along with a couple of different salads. She would steam broccoli and serve berries over ice cream for dessert. Assuming they got that far in the meal.

The more she thought about asking Raoul for a

single night of wildness, the more she liked the idea. Of course that same thought was accompanied by stomach-clenching panic, but that was a problem for another time.

She put the groceries in the refrigerator, showered quickly, then smoothed on jasmine-scented lotion. She kept her makeup light, then chose a simple green dress that buttoned up the front. The scooped neck wasn't so low as to be obvious, but it hinted at curves.

She'd changed her sheets the previous day, so that was good. She checked the box of condoms she kept around, mostly because she felt she should rather than because of actual need. There were still three inside, and according to the box she had a whole month until they expired. Lucky her.

Now it was just a matter of waiting until Raoul showed up then deciding if she should proposition him. The downside was if he said no, it would be awkward between them and she could kiss the whole pregnancy-buddy offer goodbye. Not that she was counting on it, really.

She had no idea what he thought of her. He probably liked her, but liking and wanting were two very different things. The last thing she wanted was mercy sex. Being pitiful was about the worst outcome possible.

There was also his past to consider. All those groupies throwing themselves at him. They'd probably been a lot more perfect than she could ever hope to be. On her best day, she was pretty, but most of the time she was firmly average.

She spent the next ten minutes making herself crazy by deciding she wasn't going to ask, then changing her mind. The back-and-forth reasoning was making her dizzy, and she was grateful when she heard a firm knock on the door.

She pulled it open. "Right on time."

That was as much as she got out. Raoul stepped into her small apartment and seemed to fill the space. He was tall and broad and suddenly there wasn't enough air in the room.

"Hi," he said, handing her a bottle of white wine, then leaning in and kissing her cheek. "You look great."

There were probably words she was supposed to say, but speaking was impossible.

He'd changed for their evening. Maybe even showered. His knit shirt was casually tucked into khakis, but the fabric seemed to cling to every muscle. He smelled clean and sexy and looked so tempting he was probably flirting with breaking the law. Her mouth watered.

"Thank you," she managed. She thrust the wine back at him. "You want to open this?"

"Sure."

He glanced around, found the kitchen and made his way there. She followed, then fished the wine opener out of a drawer and handed it to him. She collected glasses and set them on the counter.

"I saw my doctor today," she said. "We talked about the next steps and I got my physical."

He turned to face her. "What did she say?"

"That there's no reason why I can't deliver Crystal's babies to term. Apparently getting them implanted isn't too bad."

Saying the words made it all seem a little too real, she thought, feeling a bit light-headed. "Two weeks later, I take a pregnancy test."

His dark gaze never wavered. "You'd have all three done at the same time?"

"She thinks that would be best. Apparently there's a chance some of them might not survive the thawing process. But even if they all do, three is considered okay."

He handed her a glass of wine. "You ready for this?"

"No, but it's not like I'm suddenly going to get ready. I think plunging ahead is the best plan. I don't want to talk myself out of this."

"You don't have to do it. You don't have to have Crystal's babies."

She clutched her wine in both hands. "Yeah, I do. It's what she wanted and she's my friend. I would have done anything to save her. Bone marrow, a kidney, whatever. None of that would have helped, so I'm going to have her children and raise them as my own."

Emotions moved through his eyes, but she couldn't tell what he was thinking. "You're a helluva woman, Pia O'Brian."

"Not really, but thanks for thinking I am."

She led the way into the living room. She curled up in one corner of the sofa, and Raoul sat at the opposite end. He faced her.

"Nervous?" he asked.

She was, but not for the reasons he thought. "Yes, but I'm dealing."

He looked around at her bright apartment. "How many bedrooms do you have here?"

She blinked at him. "One." Reality hit her. "I'm going to have to move, aren't I? I'll need more bedrooms." She thought of the two flights of stairs she went up and down several times a day. There was no way she could deal with them and a stroller…or three.

He reached his arm across the back of the red sofa and patted her shoulder, then left his fingers lightly resting against her. "You don't have to move today. Don't worry about it. When the time comes, I'll help."

"I've lived here six years," she murmured, aware of the heat of his touch. "I don't want to move."

What other changes would there be? How many things hadn't she thought of?

"Can we please change the subject?" she asked. "I'm starting to freak."

"Don't freak. You're not even pregnant yet."

"Yet" being the key word.

She forced herself to breathe slowly, then she took a sip of her wine. "I can do this," she said, more to herself than him. "I'm strong. The town will help."

"Don't forget me," he added. "Your pregnancy buddy."

She still thought there was something odd about that, but why spoil his fun?

"Have you been a pregnancy buddy before?"

His expression tightened, then he relaxed. "No, but my girlfriend in high school thought she was pregnant."

"What did you do?"

"Offered to marry her."

"Of course you did."

"What does that mean?"

"It's the nice-guy thing." She sighed. "I'm sure everyone adored you in high school."

"I wouldn't say adored."

"Sure they did." She sipped her wine. "I was a cheerleader."

He raised an eyebrow. "Still have the uniform?"

She laughed. "Yes, but that's not the point. A lot of people don't like cheerleaders. It's the whole popular-girl thing."

"Were you popular?"

"Sort of." At least until her life had crashed in around her. "I wasn't exactly humble and caring," she admitted. "The phrase 'mean girl' has been tossed around."

"You're not mean."

"I was. I made fun of people, flaunted what I had. I know now it was an uncomfortable combination of immaturity and insecurity, but it's not as if that information will make any of my victims feel better."

"You had victims?"

"I had people I picked on." They were having the last laugh now, she thought sadly. Most of them had wonderful lives, while she lived in a one-bedroom apartment and couldn't even get a cat to like her.

"You're pretty hard on yourself," he said.

"Maybe I deserve it."

"Maybe everyone gets to screw up every now and then."

"I'd like it to be that simple."

"Why does it have to be complicated?" he asked.

An interesting question, she thought, allowing herself to get lost in his eyes.

Raoul was one of the good guys. Around him a girl could let herself feel safe. Not to mention a lot of other things that were a lot more yummy than safe.

A flash of courage swept through her. She set down her wine, braced herself for flat-out rejection and said, "Do you want to have sex?"

CHAPTER EIGHT

RAOUL FELT LIKE A CARTOON character. He wanted to shake his head to make sure he was hearing right. Assuming he was, he was pretty sure his eyes were about to bug out.

"Excuse me?" he asked, standing and staring down at her.

Pia sighed. "Do you want to have sex? With me. The doctor mentioned it. Not that it was important for the implantation procedure, because it isn't. Her point was I'm about to be pregnant and then I'll have babies and little kids and it's probably going to be a long time before a guy finds me the least bit desirable, assuming that even ever happens again. So having sex now, sort of a last fling, makes sense."

She'd said most of that without drawing in a breath. She did so now, then stared at him, her hazel eyes wide and wary. "You don't have to if you don't want to. I have no idea what you think of me. I'm not hideous or anything, but it's not like I have a plaque proving I'm really great in bed. I thought maybe it would fall under the pregnancy-buddy umbrella, but maybe not."

She tilted her head. "Fall under the umbrella. Is that a mixed metaphor?"

She was asking him if he wanted to have sex with her and then had switched the conversation to grammar?

She stared at him with wide eyes. Hope fluttered there, along with a hint of apprehension. He would guess she was braced for rejection.

Sex with Pia? He definitely found her sexy and attractive, but he'd never planned to go further than looking. There were plenty of reasons *not* to do this—the biggest of which was they would be living in a very small town together. There wasn't much room for awkward.

She bit her lower lip. The vulnerable movement hit him like a fist to the gut. Pia was pretty. The proud set of her shoulders, the faint glow on her cheeks. The way her brown curls tumbled to her shoulders.

He'd always been the kind of guy who tried to look past external appeal to the person inside. The fact that Pia was going to have someone else's children, simply because she'd been asked, made her one of the best people he'd ever known. And he'd really liked the kisses they'd shared.

The idea of sex—no, making love—appealed more and more with every passing second. He knew this was a one-time deal. That after she had the babies, she would have other things on her mind. But something inside him told him a single night with Pia would be a night worth remembering.

He took a step toward her. "I did offer to be your pregnancy buddy," he said quietly. "To do anything you asked, to take care of *all* your needs."

"This isn't exactly the same as running out for ice cream in the rain."

He pulled her to her feet, then put his hands on her shoulders and stared into her eyes. "It's a whole lot more fun than that."

She swallowed. "You really don't have to do this. I

shouldn't have asked. I don't want you to feel pressured or like it's—"

He leaned in and pressed his mouth against hers. The act cut off her words, which wasn't a bad thing. Sometimes silence was better.

Her lips were soft and yielding. Tempting. Her arms wrapped around him. She was warm and slight, but tall enough that he didn't have to bend too far to kiss her again. A good thing, because he found he liked kissing her and wanted it to go on for a good long time.

Pia had expected something of a discussion, or at the very least, ground rules on the whole pregnancy-buddy-sex thing.

Apparently not, she thought as Raoul's warm mouth claimed hers. The kiss was both hungry and tender, his lips making her want to melt into his tall, strong body.

He held her against him, her body pressing against his. He was all broad shoulders and hard planes. He smelled as good as he looked—masculine, but clean. There was a slight rasp of stubble on his cheeks, but not so much that she minded.

It had been a long time since a man had swept her away, she thought as she wrapped her arms around his neck and gave herself over to his kiss. She slid her fingers through his dark hair. The short, layered strands felt like cool silk. He moved his hands down her body to her hips. One had slipped to her rear.

When he cupped the curve, squeezing gently, her stomach clenched. She surged closer, bringing her belly up against him. She was immediately aware of the hard thickness—proof that he wasn't doing this out of pity. Thank God!

He touched his tongue to her bottom lip. She parted

for him, then rested her fingers on his broad shoulders. He slid into her mouth, moving with slow, languid strokes designed to make her beg for more.

She held in the whimper and gave herself over to the kiss. Everything about this moment felt right. Hunger filled her, burning hard and hot, making her want to get closer, to touch him and be touched.

She moved her tongue against his, going faster than he had, urging him on. The hands holding her hips tightened, then began the slow journey up her sides. She held her breath until he cupped her breasts in his hands, then she exhaled slowly. He moved from underneath, squeezing her breasts gently, then rubbed his thumbs against her already hard nipples.

At the first brush, she felt a jolt all the way down to her toes. At the second, she had to hold back the need to cry out for more. She reminded herself not to beg—men found it very unattractive. But it was difficult to stay rational and focused when every whisper of contact against her sensitized breasts made her want to scream.

He lowered his head to her jaw and kissed his way to her ear. Then he dipped lower, nibbling along her neck to her collarbone. He paused there to taste her skin, an openmouthed kiss that was surprisingly arousing. Or maybe it was the way he continued to tease her breasts, or the feel of his body so close to hers.

Before she could decide, he'd cupped her face in his hands and was kissing her again. Deep, soul-stirring kisses that made her ache with longing and need. Without realizing what she was doing, she found herself unbuttoning the front of her dress. Suddenly the fabric gapped open to her waist.

Before she could figure out how to stop or what to do next, he'd straightened and pulled her arms free, leaving the dress to pool at her hips. He ran his fingers from wrists to shoulders, then down over her breasts and behind her. With an expert flick of his fingers, her bra came undone and fell away.

In less than a heartbeat, he'd replaced the silky lace with his bare hands. Skin on skin, she thought, her eyes sinking closed. He touched her gently, exploring her curves.

She focused on every stroke, each brush of finger and palm. He moved closer and closer to her nipples but didn't touch them. The contact heightened her arousal, making her knees weak and her body hungry. Then, when she was about to grab his hands in hers and place them where she wanted, he bent down and took her left nipple in his mouth.

The hot, wet, openmouth kiss made her breath catch. He sucked deeply, making her arch against him. A ribbon of erotic connection tugged deep in her belly. Between her thighs she felt herself swelling, wanting.

He shifted to the other breast. She touched his head, then his shoulders, feeling his strength. Wanting poured through her, making her feel delicious and alive.

He straightened. "We should move the party," he whispered, unbuttoning his shirt, then shrugging out of it.

She nodded, even as her gaze was caught by the sight of his broad chest. She wanted to touch and taste, to explore, but he was already moving away. As she followed, she undid the rest of the buttons on her dress and stepped out of both it and her shoes as she walked.

By the time they met up again in the bedroom, he was

naked. She'd never gotten the concept of male beauty before seeing him, but she did now. His chest was a series of defined muscles, his waist narrow, his legs strong. He was hard and ready, his expression intense and focused. Just looking at him made her tremble. As she moved toward him, he grabbed her around the waist and they both tumbled onto the bed.

"You have condoms, right?" he asked, right before he kissed her.

She nodded.

"Good. We don't want my sperm swimming around with Crystal's embryos. It would get crowded down there."

He grinned as he spoke, his eyes alive with humor and desire. It was an irresistible combination. Then he was kissing her again. She let herself get lost in the feel of his mouth on hers.

Their tongues tangled in an erotic dance. Then he moved to her neck, as he had before. The man had skills, she thought dreamily, feeling every part of her heat and melt. When he took her earlobe into his mouth and sucked, she had to bite her lower lip to keep from crying out. When she felt the weight of him as he stretched out next to her, it was all she could do to keep her legs from falling open in a shameless invitation. She wanted him…all of him…on top, inside, pleasuring them both into madness.

He moved to her breasts, and it was just as good as it had been before. With each tug of his mouth on her nipples, she felt an answering shiver between her legs. She could feel herself swelling for him.

His mouth moved lower. He paused long enough to pull off her panties in one smooth, easy move. She waited for the feel of his kiss on her belly, but there was nothing. Her heart beat once, twice, a third time. Then she felt the warmth of his lips on the inside of her ankle.

"What are you doing?" she asked.

She felt as well as heard him chuckle. "And here I thought you were pretty *and* smart."

He kissed his way up to her knee, then moved between her legs and nibbled higher. Up and up until he pressed an openmouthed kiss on the very inside of her thigh.

She opened her legs even wider, knowing it was either that or plead. Then his mouth was on the most sensitive part of her. She exhaled as warm, soul-stirring pleasure flooded her.

He moved slowly, as if discovering all of her. The touch was perfect—quick enough to excite, gentle enough that everything he did was magic. He paused to tell her how good it felt to do this to her, which was nearly as arousing as the finger he slipped inside her.

As he stroked her, he settled his mouth on that one tight and swollen spot. He brushed it with his tongue, which made her squirm. He moved in tandem, his tongue keeping time with his finger. Back and forth, in and out. She couldn't remember the last time a man had done this to her. The last time she'd felt that liquid heat flowing through her body, the promise of release only seconds away.

She tried to hold back, wanting to savor the moment for as long as possible. Although the end would be great, there was something to be said for anticipation. But it was like swimming upstream. Exhausting and ultimately impossible. Every flick of his tongue pushed her closer. When he closed his lips around her very center and sucked, she lost herself to the explosion.

Muscles clenched and released. Every cell in her body quivered as the pleasure crashed into her, through her. She surrendered to the sensations, arching back her head and gasping as she came again and again.

When she could think again, she managed to open her eyes and saw Raoul smiling at her, his expression self-satisfied.

"You're not all that," she told him breathlessly.

"Sure I am."

He leaned in and licked her nipple. She shuddered and had to resist the need to draw him closer so they could do it all again. Instead she pulled open the nightstand drawer and removed the box of condoms.

Raoul frowned. "Is this it?"

"What do you mean? Are they the wrong kind?"

One corner of his mouth turned up. "There are only three."

Her mind went blank. "Only?"

"This is supposed to be your last fling. Shouldn't it be memorable?"

"I figured once was enough."

He pulled out a condom and tossed the package on the nightstand. "Then I'm going to have to show you otherwise."

PIA LAY ON THE BED, doing her best to catch her breath. Her mind was still fuzzy, her body unable to obey even the slightest command. Apparently the body had involuntary systems for a reason. Something had to keep her heart beating. Otherwise, a session with a guy like Raoul could be deadly.

Had she been able, she would have turned her head to look at him. But that would have required more energy than she could muster. Blinking was about all she could manage. As he'd predicted, they'd used all three condoms. She'd come in ways she hadn't known were possible, in positions that were at the very least questionable. In the last five hours, she'd had more orgasms than she'd probably had in her entire life. If doing him was wrong, she didn't want to be right.

He rolled toward her. His handsome face came into view, along with a bit of bare shoulder. His skin had a golden cast and looked as good as it tasted. Talk about temptation. She was exhausted and still shuddering through her recovery, but the thought of being with him again was enough to cause her nerve endings to cheer.

"You okay?" he asked.

She managed a smile. "Fishing for compliments?"

"Maybe."

"The earth didn't just move—it did a two-and-a-half somersault with a twist."

"Good." He brushed the hair off her face, then lightly kissed her. "Can I stay?"

She swore softly. Of course he would ask to stay. Because he was perfect. Funny, smart, good-looking, great in bed and sensitive. Oh, and rich. The man had money. So why wasn't he involved with someone? Why wasn't he married? She knew there was a divorce in his past, but why hadn't some enterprising woman snapped him up?

Not that she cared, she reminded herself. She had embryos to worry about.

"Earth to Pia," he said, still gazing down at her.

"You can stay," she whispered.

Under normal circumstances she would have forced him out in the name of self-preservation. Having him around could be dangerous to her heart. But that wasn't going to be an issue. In a few days, she would return to her doctor's office and possibly be implanted with Crystal's embryos. Then she would be pregnant. Falling in love wasn't going to happen to her—at least not in the romantic sense. No guy would be interested in a woman with three kids who weren't even hers, and she couldn't imagine having even an extra ounce of energy left over for anything close to dating.

So it was perfectly safe to roll on her side and have him slide in next to her. She snuggled against his warm body, feeling his strong arms circle her waist and pull her close. She closed her eyes and allowed herself to believe it was all real. At least for tonight. No matter what, she could count on reality to return in the morning.

FOOL'S GOLD HIGH SCHOOL sat above town on the road that led up to the ski resort. The campus was only about five years old, with a state-of-the-art science building, a large stadium and an auditorium that held five hundred.

Raoul stood onstage, facing the students filling every seat. He'd pushed aside the podium, preferring to walk back and forth.

"I didn't start out rich and famous," he told the kids. "When I was your age, I was in foster care, fighting the system responsible for feeding and clothing me. I knew no one cared about me. Not as a person. I was a case number to the social worker and steady income for my foster family."

He paused and met the gaze of several of the younger guys in the audience.

"Some families really do care about the kids they take in, and I applaud them. I've heard the stories, but I didn't see it much in action. The social workers I knew were overworked. They tried their best, but they weren't given the tools or the resources. So I got involved in some things that I should have avoided."

He walked to the edge of the stage and stared out at the students. "Gangs can look pretty good from afar. They give you a place to belong. You get status from being with the right crowd. You're around people who accept you. If they're crazy enough, you never know what's going to happen next and that can be fun, too."

He shrugged. "It can also leave you worse off than you ever thought. Pregnant. In jail. Or dead." He let the words hang there for a long time.

"When you're sixteen, the future seems a long way away, but I'm here to tell you the value of thinking long term. Of knowing what you want and going after it, regardless of how many people tell you it's not possible. I spent the first few months of my senior year homeless, living in an abandoned building. I had friends who helped out, but what made the biggest difference was I found someone who could believe in me. And he taught me to believe in myself. That's what you have to do. Believe you can make it."

He crossed to the other side of the stage and looked out at those kids. "The dictionary tells us a mentor is a trusted coach or a guide. Be what you want to see in someone else. Find a younger kid and get involved. It's like throwing a rock in a lake. The ripples stretch out forever."

He talked a little more about the importance of doing the right thing, then said he would answer questions.

There were the usual ones about playing for the Cowboys and what it had been like to take his college team through two undefeated seasons.

"I didn't do it," he told them honestly. "I was one member of an excellent team. Everyone did his part and that's why we won. Football isn't golf. It's not just you and the ball. It's everyone around you. Any team is only as strong as its weakest player."

A small girl in the third row raised her hand.

He pointed to her. "Yes?"

"Have you ever been a Big Brother? My uncle has a boy he's been helping for a couple of years now."

"Good for him," Raoul said. "As for being a Big Brother, it's hard for a guy like me to help someone one-on-one. The media finds out and it gets messy. So I give back this way—talking to schools, sharing ideas, working with teachers."

He rattled on for a couple more minutes and was relieved that the students seemed to buy it and the teachers in the room were nodding.

He wanted them to stand up and yell at him. On what planet would a former football player be so damned famous that he couldn't take a kid bowling? Guys way better known than him had private lives.

The truth was less pretty. He didn't want to get personally involved. He didn't want to care. The price was too high. Better to keep things superficial. That way no one got burned, including him.

A philosophy Pia wouldn't agree with, he thought as he finished the speech. She was the kind who would leap in first and ask questions later. That's what she was doing with the embryos. Talk about a woman with conviction and courage.

And a way about her, he thought as he finished up and smiled as they applauded. Three nights ago, he'd stayed with her. Ever since his bed had been a little colder, a little more empty.

But he knew the value of going it alone and the danger of making something more than it was. He knew how a heart could be ripped apart and left for dead. No way he was going through that again.

PIA WAITED NERVOUSLY on the padded table.

"It's okay," the tech told her. "Ultrasounds don't hurt."

Pia eyed the wand. "There has to be a downside."

"Sorry, no. We even heat the goopy gel we use on your tummy. This is one of the easiest medical tests."

"It beats a barium enema."

The other woman, Jenny her name tag said, laughed. "Have you ever had a barium enema?"

"I've heard rumors. They can't be fun."

"No, they can't, but this is easy."

Jenny pulled up Pia's paper gown and squirted warm gel onto her lower stomach. Then she lowered the wand and rubbed it along Pia's skin.

There was no pain at all. Just a sensation of something warm and flat moving across her. Okay, she thought. Note to self—ultrasounds aren't bad.

A few minutes later Jenny covered her then excused herself. Pia lay there in the dimly lit room, doing her best to breathe. Soon she would find out if she was ready for implantation. If she was, then it was crunch time. Was she really going to go through with this? Have

Crystal's babies? Once they were thawed, there was no backing out.

Before she could scramble from the table and run screaming through the building, Dr. Galloway appeared.

"I heard you're ready," the doctor said with a smile. "Let's see."

She squeezed on fresh gel and studied the monitor.

"Very nice," she murmured. "Yes, Pia. I would say we could implant tomorrow, if you want." The doctor touched her arm. "We can also wait a month, if you need more time."

Ready, as in ready? As in now?

Pia opened her mouth, then closed it. Her chest got tight, as if something heavy pressed down. She felt nauseous and light-headed. Ready.

"The e-eggs can be ready by tomorrow?" she asked, her voice faint.

"Yes. We'd schedule you back for right after lunch." Her doctor put down the wand and wiped Pia's belly. "You don't have to decide today. You'll be just as ready next month."

True, but a month was a long time to wait. Pia was afraid she would freak out even more, or at the very least, try to talk herself out of moving forward.

She sucked in a breath and braced herself. "What time tomorrow?"

APPARENTLY DR. GALLOWAY'S definition of painless and Pia's weren't exactly the same. Having a catheter inserted was a borderline creepy experience, but Pia did her best to relax and keep breathing.

"All done," her doctor told her seconds later. She

stood and drew the gown down over Pia's legs, then put a blanket on her. "Lie here for about twenty minutes to let things settle. Then you're free to go."

"And I don't have to act any different?" Pia asked. "Avoid strenuous activities, that sort of thing?"

"I'd stay quiet for the next few hours. You have the vitamins I gave you?"

Dr. Galloway had given her samples the previous day, along with a prescription she'd already filled. She'd taken the first prenatal vitamin that morning, downing the pill with a disgustingly healthy breakfast.

"Yes."

"Then that's all you need for now."

The doctor dimmed the lights and left the room. Pia tried to get comfortable on the padded table. She closed her eyes and placed her hands on her lower stomach.

"Hi," she whispered. "I'm Pia. I knew your mom. She was amazing and wonderful and you would have really loved her."

Thinking about her friend made her eyes burn. She blinked away tears and drew another deep breath.

"She, ah, died a few months ago. Over the summer. It was sad and we all miss her. Your dad is gone, too, which might make you think you're getting off to a rough start. But you're not. You see, both your parents wanted to have children. Your mom especially. She wanted to have all three of you. But she couldn't, what with being dead and all."

She groaned. Talk about screwing up the conversation. "Sorry," she murmured. "I should have planned this better. What I'm saying is she really wanted this. She wanted you to be born. I know I'm not her, but I'm going to do my best, I swear. I'm going to read books and talk to women who are good moms. I'll be there for you."

She thought about her own mother abandoning her to move to Florida. "I'll never leave you," she vowed. "No matter what, I'll be there for you. I won't run off and forget about you." She pressed lightly on her stomach. "Can you feel that? It's me. I'm right here."

Fear lurked in the background. The possibility of cosmic punishment for wishing away her pregnancy in college. But the truth was, she couldn't change the past. She could only pray that the souls of the innocents were protected. That if anyone was to be punished, it would only be her.

"I'm sorry about that, too," she whispered. "I was wrong." Despite Dr. Galloway's promise that it hadn't been her fault, she couldn't help wondering if it was.

She heard a light knock on the door.

"Come in."

Raoul entered, looking impossibly tall and male. "Hey. The doc said it's done."

Pia tried to smile. "That's what they tell me. I don't feel any different."

"Not hearing voices?" he asked with a grin.

"I don't think hearing voices is ever a good sign."

He pulled up the stool and sat, taking her hand in his. "Scared?"

"Beyond terrified. I was telling them to hold on tight and that I'd be here for them."

He gazed into her eyes. "I'm going to tell you the same thing, Pia. Keep holding on."

Once again she was fighting tears. "For Keith?"

"And for you. I need to do this."

She managed a quivering smile. "So it's all about you? Typical male."

"That's me." He leaned in and kissed her forehead. "What happens next?" he asked.

She tried not to focus on the warmth of his skin and the way he made her feel safe. Even if Raoul lasted through the pregnancy, there was no way he was sticking around for anything else. Getting used to having him around wasn't an option.

"I stay here until the nurse kicks me out. In theory I can go back to work, but I'm heading home. I'm going to spend the afternoon on my sofa. It's the whole gravity thing. I want to give these little guys a real shot."

"Okay. What are you in the mood for?"

For a second she thought he meant sex. The part of her that had been dazzled and satiated wanted to beg for a repeat performance. But there was no way they could do it. Not right after the implantation.

"Italian?" he asked. "Mexican? I'll get takeout."

Oh, sure. Food. "Either. I'm not that hungry."

"You will be in a few hours, and you have to eat."

"For the babies," she said, keeping her free hand on her belly. "Do you think I should sing to them?"

He chuckled. "Do you want to?"

"I'm not very good."

"You could give them a cheer. Do you remember any from high school?"

She laughed. "I appreciate the thought, but it's even too weird for me."

He stroked her cheek. "Look at you. Having babies. What would your friends say?"

"My current friends will be completely supportive. The ones who know aren't even surprised. But my friends from before…" She sighed. "As I told you before, I wasn't exactly the nicest girl in high school. Too much attitude and money. Not enough compassion."

He looked interested rather than judgmental. "When did that change?"

"Early in my senior year of high school."

The door opened and the nurse looked in. "You're free to go, Pia. When you're dressed, stop by the desk. We've made an appointment for two weeks from now."

"Thanks."

She sat up. Raoul brushed her mouth with his.

"I'll wait outside for you," he said.

"Okay."

She watched him leave, then carefully slid to her feet and started to dress. As she pulled on her jeans, she realized she trusted Raoul to be there for her. At least for now. After all this time, it was nice to have someone to depend on.

CHAPTER NINE

PIA SAT AT A TABLE IN front of the high school stage. "You're kidding, right?" she asked the mayor.

Marsha rested her elbows on the table and dropped her head to her hands. "I wish I was. I went to the bathroom. I swear I was gone all of two minutes. By the time I got back, they'd voted to have a talent show featuring the single women in town. I guess they want the busloads of men to get a good look at what's available."

When Pia had been asked to attend an audition, she'd had no idea what she was getting into. At least fifty women were here, which she found stunning, and not in a happy way. They were dressed in everything from tutus to shepherdess costumes. A few wanted to start by listing everything they could cook and/or bake. One woman even smiled broadly, saying she had all her own teeth and not a single cavity.

"Like that makes her good breeding material?" Pia asked, eyeing the crowd. "Tell me this isn't happening."

"I wish I could."

"When did we get desperate? I've always known there was something of a man shortage, but so what? We're happy—things get done. There are more women doing traditionally male jobs in town than probably anywhere else in the country. Isn't that a good thing?"

Marsha raised her head and sighed. "I've been told that there are women who want to settle down—get married and have a family. That's more difficult here. The choice is to pick from the limited stock on hand or move."

"Stock on hand?" And women complained that men objectify them. "I don't understand this."

"Me, either, but it's too late for us to stop the flood. Men are arriving daily."

A young woman in her twenties got up onstage. She wore a pale pink leotard and a short, wrapped skirt. She nodded and music poured out of the hidden speakers. Within seconds, the contestant was singing and dancing to a popular Broadway musical.

"She's good," Pia murmured. "What am I supposed to do? Make notes on who I like best? Are we really going to have a talent show?"

"I don't see any way around it. I'm just so humiliated."

"Um, no. That honor goes to the woman who juggled pies she'd baked." Pia had always loved Fool's Gold. The town had traditions and polite residents. People cared about each other. Had a single chapter in a thesis and a busload or two of men really changed everything?

Maybe there was something in the air, she thought. Something promoting change. Look at her. Just two days ago, she'd had embryos implanted. She'd been there for the procedure and had spent the rest of the afternoon lying on her sofa, and she still couldn't seem to wrap her mind around the concept. Being pregnant was just a word. More concept than reality. How could she possibly be pregnant?

Yet Dr. Galloway had put the embryos in her. Were

they hanging on as she'd asked them to? Were they growing, getting bigger and stronger?

She touched her hand to her belly, as if she could feel them inside of her.

Scattered applause brought her back to the auditions. She clapped as well, then turned to find Marsha staring at her.

"Where did you go?" the mayor asked. "She was pretty good, so it can't have been the singing and dancing."

"Sorry. I'll pay attention." Pia picked up her pen and pulled the notepad closer. "Who's next?"

Marsha continued to study her. "Is everything all right?"

"I'm fine."

The mayor didn't look convinced.

Pia drew in a breath. "Crystal left me her embryos."

Marsha's face relaxed into a smile. "Did she? I knew someone would get them. You must be very touched, and equally terrified. That's a lot of responsibility."

"Tell me about it. It's not about owning the embryos. Crystal expects me to have her babies."

Marsha nodded. "That's a lot to ask of a friend. Are you going to agree?"

"I…" Pia drew in a breath. "I had them implanted two days ago. There were three embryos. They all survived the thawing, which I guess doesn't always happen. We'll know in two weeks if they were able to embed or implant or whatever it's called."

Marsha looked stunned for a moment, then hugged her. "Good for you. What an amazing thing to do. I'm so proud."

The words made Pia feel good. "I'm mostly in shock," she admitted. "Nothing about this is real to me."

"That will take time."

"I have nine months." A number that she couldn't relate to. Knowing the facts about a pregnancy was very different than it actually happening to her. "I guess even now my body could be changing, but I don't feel any different."

"You will. Especially if you have triplets."

Pia winced. "Don't say that. I can't comprehend one baby, let alone three. I'm going to have these babies by myself."

Marsha squeezed her hand. "We'll all be there for you, Pia. You know that, don't you?"

She nodded. "Everything is surreal. I keep going back to the same question. Why would Crystal pick me?"

"Because she loved you and trusted you."

"I guess."

The mayor smiled. "I have a personal request."

"Sure."

"Can you please have boys?"

Pia laughed. "That part is already determined. Sorry. You should have had the talk with Crystal."

"I hate being late to anything." She turned back to the stage where a couple of guys were dragging on two-dimensional cardboard trees. "Dear God, what now?"

RAOUL WALKED THROUGH the main building of the camp. Less than a month ago, the last of the summer campers had headed home, and the cleaning crew had begun the process of winterizing the structures. Now, several hundred kids filled the various rooms, pinning flyers to walls and driving away the silence with their laughter.

He still had ideas for a year-round camp, but until he could make that happen, using the facility for the temporary elementary school was the right thing to do.

The preliminary meeting on repairing and rebuilding the burned school had been grim at best. The damage was extensive, the funds limited. Realistically, the new elementary school wouldn't be ready for occupancy for nearly two years. Which put his plans on hold for at least that long. His biggest concern was keeping Dakota Hendrix working for him. She was smart and capable. He had a feeling headhunters called her regularly. All he had to offer her was a good salary, work close to her family, running the summer camp and the promise that when they got the camp back she would be in charge of the new program.

The school had contracted her services for a few hours a week. She provided counseling and acted as the liaison between the school and the camp. So far there hadn't been any problems, and while Raoul didn't anticipate trouble, he'd learned it was always best to be prepared.

He glanced at the big clock on the wall. It was a few minutes before noon. Now the hallway was relatively quiet, but in about two minutes the bell would ring and children would explode out of their classrooms and head for the cafeteria.

He knew because he was here most school days. Somehow he'd gotten roped into playing ball with a group of kids during the lunch hour. He didn't mind too much and he was careful not to spend more time with any one kid. In a group they were great, but he didn't want any of them getting too attached.

He was willing to get involved—to a point. But some distance was a good thing.

When the bell rang, releasing the kids for lunch, doors opened and slammed into the wall. High-pitched voices broke the silence. In a matter of seconds, he found himself surrounded by a dozen or so boys, all clamoring for him to have lunch with them.

He was about to refuse them all—with the promise that he would meet them on the playground after—when he spotted that skinny redheaded kid. Peter, Pia had said his name was.

"You know my friend Pia," he told the boy.

Peter grinned. "Yeah. We met in the park. She's really cool, you know, for a girl."

"I'll pass along the compliment."

"You gonna have lunch with us?" Drew, Peter's friend, asked. "We'll save you a seat and everything."

Raoul hesitated, then nodded. "Sure. I can do that." Maybe he would get a chance to talk to Peter and find out if there was any kind of a problem at home.

They headed for the cafeteria and got in line. Raoul grabbed a tray with the rest of the kids, then smiled at the older woman scooping out mac and cheese.

"I won't take any if there's not enough," he said.

"Oh, we always make extra. Most of the teachers eat here, too," she said and dumped a portion of the pasta onto a plate.

Green beans followed, along with fruit. He passed on very green pudding, grabbed two cartons of milk in one hand, then had to hold in a grin as the boys with him tried to do the same.

Their hands were too small to pick up both cartons at once, so they settled for one and followed him to a low table by the window.

He stared for a second, not sure he would fit on the bench, then realized all the tables were scaled down. Kid-size, he thought humorously, wondering if he was heavy enough to tip one. He lowered himself carefully, centering his weight on the bench. Things seemed steady enough.

The kids gathered around him, pushing to sit closer, until he was crammed in on the bench seat. He picked up the first carton of milk, opened it, then drained it in three long swallows. When he set the carton back down, every boy at the table was staring.

He wiped his mouth self-consciously. "So, ah, how are you guys liking the new school?"

"It's great," one boy said. "When it snows, my mom says we're going to have trouble getting up the mountain. Maybe we'll have snow days."

"Sweet!" another boy crowed.

"Tell us what it was like when you played football," a third boy pleaded. "My dad says you were the best ever."

"Tell your dad thanks," Raoul said with a grin. "I was good, but I'm not sure about being the best. I always tried to do better. That's what defines success."

"I'd like to play football," Peter said. "But I'm small."

"You're not short," his friend told him. "Just skinny."

"Don't worry about being small," Raoul told him. "You'll grow. Now's the time to work on basics. Running, coordination. You can get that from any sport. You can also start learning about the game."

"I want to play football, too."

"Me, too!"

Raoul made a note to talk to the principal about starting a spring football program. Nothing too physical—just some practice with kids split into teams. To give them a taste of the possibilities.

"My sister says she wants to play football," the dark-haired boy sitting next to Raoul said. "I keep tellin' her, girls don't play football. But she's bigger than me and when she gets mad, she hits me."

A couple of the guys laughed. "Then maybe you should stop saying it," Raoul suggested.

"I guess. But you could tell her. She'd have to listen to you."

He held up both hands. "No, thanks. Your sister can do anything she sets her mind to."

The boy sighed heavily. "That's what Mom says, too, and Dad just keeps quiet."

A smart man, Raoul thought.

"My parents are divorced," the boy on Peter's right announced. "I live with them on different weeks. They have houses right across the street from each other."

"How's that working?" Raoul asked.

"I dunno. It's kind of stupid. If they can live that close, why can't they live together?"

"Marriage can be tough," Raoul told him. "The important thing is that your parents love you. Do you have anyone to talk to, like an older brother or an aunt or uncle?"

"My uncle Carl is really nice. He listens."

"Then keep talking to him. Don't let stuff build up inside. That's never good."

"My parents are divorced, too," another boy said.

"I have five sisters," the kid on the end said. Most of the boys at the table groaned.

"That's a lot of girls," Raoul told him. "Are you the youngest?"

"No. I'm in the middle. They're everywhere. My dad built me a tree house so I'd have my own man cave."

"Good for you."

During the conversation, Raoul had been watching Peter. The boy finished his lunch without saying much. Just when Raoul was about to suggest they head to the playground, Peter spoke.

"My parents are dead," he said, staring at his plate. "They died in a car crash two years ago."

"I'm sorry," Raoul told him.

Peter shrugged. "It was bad, but stuff like that happens."

Peter's friend Drew leaned toward Raoul. "He was in the car when it happened. He was there when they died."

Raoul swore silently. What a nightmare for the kid. He had no idea what to say.

Peter looked at him. "You really think I'll get big enough to play football in high school?"

"I really do. In fact, let's go practice some drills right now."

Peter's sad face slowly transformed into a smile. "Yeah?"

"Come on. It'll be fun."

The boys all stood and grabbed their trays. After dumping them on the counter by the kitchen, they ran for the door leading outside. Peter walked more slowly than the rest.

Raoul caught up with him. "I'm sorry about your folks," he said. "I never knew my dad. I lost my mom when I was a little older than you. It's hard."

Peter nodded without speaking.

Raoul wanted to give him a hug, but he knew there was a firm "no touching" policy at the school. Not knowing what else to do, he vowed to pay attention to the kid whenever he was around, then asked, "Want to learn how to throw farther than everyone else?"

"You can teach me that?" Peter asked eagerly.

"You bet."

"All right!" The boy laughed and ran toward his friends.

Maybe, for today, it was enough.

"YOU SHOULD HAVE BEEN more clear about the food," Pia said as she scooped kung pao chicken onto her plate, then licked her finger where a little sauce had dribbled.

Raoul sat across from her at the small table in his kitchen. "Because then you would have jumped right on the pregnancy-buddy wagon?"

"Absolutely. I know it's not sophisticated or elegant, but offer me a snack and I'm practically your slave."

"Good to know."

Humor danced in his dark eyes. Humor that made her want to smile. Of course looking at his face, or any other part of him, made her want to do other things, too. Like ask him to get naked. Or let her get naked. Or touch her. Although she really appreciated the theory of "one last fling," making love with Raoul had left her hungry for more.

Even if he hadn't been very explicit on the temporary nature of their relationship, she couldn't have asked for a replay. Not with the embryos hanging on by a thread…or whatever it was they hung on by. Maybe in a few weeks, when the doctor said everything was normal, she could consider doing the wild thing. But until then, she was only thinking pure and maternal thoughts.

"This may be my last Chinese for the duration," she said, scooping up a mouthful of fried rice on her fork. "I've been reading one of those pregnancy books and I have to watch my salt intake. I also have to give up alcohol, caffeine, over-the-counter medicines and in six or seven months, my ankles. Babies are really demanding."

He grinned. "Don't they also say it's worth it?"

"Sure, but that's a whole lot easier to write than live. And that's for later. Right now I'm living in month one of being pregnant. Assuming I am."

"Any symptoms?"

"Just the voices."

He grinned.

She picked up an egg roll. "Nothing, really. They say some women can tell the second they conceive, but I guess I'm not that sensitive. Probably a good thing. I have a feeling I'm going to make myself crazy worrying as it is."

She glanced around at the modest house. The kitchen had been updated with new appliances and counter-tops, but nothing about the space especially screamed "famous sport celebrity abode."

"What was your place like in Dallas?" she asked.

"Big."

"Two bedrooms? Five?"

"Three stories and some rooms I never saw." He shrugged. "It was more an investment property."

She tried to remember what else she'd read about him. "Did you move to Los Angeles a while ago?"

He nodded. "About a year after I got married. When we split up, I moved back to Dallas but never settled. Then I retired and here I am."

She wondered about the ex-Mrs. Moreno but wasn't sure she was comfortable asking questions. From what she could see, Raoul was annoyingly close to perfect. Why would any woman let him go?

Maybe it hadn't been her choice. Maybe he'd dumped her.

"Are you going to buy a house in town?" she asked.

"I've been looking around," he admitted. "There's no hurry. This place works fine."

"You're renting from Josh, right?"

Raoul grinned. "He seems to own a lot of the town."

"He's into real estate. He had to do something with all his winnings." She tilted her head. "Is it tough for the two of you to share the spotlight? I mean with your large egos and all."

He raised an eyebrow. "You've seen my ego—you tell me."

"Very funny. I guess if anyone would have the problem, it would be Josh. He's been the favorite son for years. But I don't think he's the type to care if you get more of the attention."

"You like Josh." Raoul didn't seem to be asking a question.

"Sure. I've known him most of my life. He was a few years ahead of me in high school. Very crush-worthy."

"Did the two of you ever…"

She looked at him, pretending confusion. "Did we ever?"

"Get involved. Date."

"Oh," she said with mock understanding. "Did I ever see his ego?"

Raoul stared at her without speaking. She wanted to believe his interest was an important clue into how he felt about her. That even as they sat there, he was realizing he was wildly infatuated with her and seconds away from falling in love.

Or maybe not. Did she really need a guy in her life right now? Weren't three potential children enough?

"We never dated," she said. "I've never seen his ego." She grinned. "Although his butt *is* on a screensaver, so I've seen that." She lowered her voice. "Yours is better."

"It's not a competition," he grumbled.

But he had been asking, she thought, amused. Raoul was such a guy.

She sipped her water, studying him. His dark hair fell across his forehead.

"You need a haircut," she told him.

"No, thanks. It sounds too complicated, what with the warring hairdressers and all."

"I'll take you. Show you off."

"Thanks." He leaned toward her. "Have you told anyone about the embryos?"

"Marsha knows. She may or may not have told

Charity. I'm waiting. I guess until it's sure. I just didn't want a lot of people speculating until there was something to speculate about. It seems wrong. This is Crystal's moment, not mine."

"You're the one who's going to be pregnant."

"I'll be peeing on a stick in a few days," she said. "I'm thinking that will be a wake-up call."

"I want to be there."

"Okay, although that's lovely, we're really not that close."

He shook his head. "In the house, not in the room."

She wasn't sure about peeing on command, especially with someone waiting to know the results, but she supposed she could run water or make him hum loudly.

"Okay."

"Good."

He handed her the last egg roll. The overhead light caught the thin scar on his cheek.

"What happened?" she asked, pointing to the scar. "Let me guess. You were helping an old lady across the street."

"Would you feel better if I told you I got it in a bar fight?"

"Yes, but I'd think you were lying."

"How about if I ran into a fence during practice."

And impaled his cheek? She shuddered at the thought. "Maybe the bar fight makes a better story."

"Whatever makes you happy."

After dinner, he insisted on walking her home.

It was already dark and the night was cool. Pia pulled her sweater around her and crossed her arms over her chest. "We'll have snow by November," she said.

"Do you like winter?"

"Most of the time. We don't get a ton of snow, which is nice. The resort is only a few miles up the mountain, but even a couple thousand feet can make a big difference. They usually get several feet. At least I don't have to worry about shoveling a driveway. I can walk everywhere."

He put his arm around her and drew her against him. "If you have any shoveling needs, just let me know."

"More pregnancy-buddy duties?"

"Absolutely."

"You should put out a brochure, so I can know what to expect."

"I'll do that."

He felt warm, she thought as she leaned into him. Safe. All the things a pregnant woman could want in a man. Or a nonpregnant woman.

Once again she thought about the woman he'd been married to before and wanted to ask what had happened. But she wouldn't. For reasons she couldn't explain, Raoul wanted to take care of her for a little while. For someone who had been on her own since she was seventeen, having someone to lean on felt good. Especially now, she thought, pressing her hand to her belly.

They reached her apartment building. He held open the front door, then followed her up the stairs. When they reached her door, he turned and faced her.

"You going to be okay by yourself?" he asked.

"I've been living here for years. I can handle it."

"If you need anything, call me."

"I don't want to interrupt your hot date."

He adjusted the front of her sweater. "You're my hot date."

Words to make her heart beat faster, she thought,

knowing giving in to emotional temptation would be a really bad thing.

"Raoul…"

Before she could say anything else, he pressed his mouth to hers.

The kiss was soft and tender, more caring than passionate. He didn't try to deepen it or even touch her anywhere else. Yet the feel of his lips against hers was devastating. Not from wanting in a sexual way, but because the gentleness ignited a longing she rarely allowed herself to experience. The kiss made her dream about what it would be like to fall in love, to risk her heart, to believe she could have someone to care about. Someone who wouldn't leave.

Unexpected tears burned in her eyes. She pulled back, dug her keys out of her pocket and opened the door.

"Thanks for dinner," she said, doing her best to keep her tone light. "Especially for the last egg roll."

"All part of the full-service plan. You'll let me know when you're going to pee on the stick?"

Despite the emptiness inside of her, she laughed. "No one's ever asked me that before, so I have to say yes."

"Good. Night, Pia."

"Good night."

She waited until he started down the stairs, then she closed the door, locked it and leaned back against the sturdy surface.

"Don't go there," she whispered into the quiet room. "Don't believe in him. You know what will happen if you do."

What always happened. He would leave. She had

a feeling that telling herself she was used to being on her own wouldn't make dealing without him any easier to take.

CHAPTER TEN

"IT WAS THE WEIRDEST THING," Pia said as she and Montana sat in Pia's office, going over details for the bachelor auction. Technically now an auction/talent show.

"I don't understand," Montana said, frowning slightly. "Isn't the auction enough?"

"Apparently not. Nearly thirty women will be getting up onstage and performing in one way or another. They have a three-minute limit." Pia told her about the woman who bragged about a lack of cavities. "I grew up here. When did the women in town get so distressed about the lack of men?"

"Some women want to be in a relationship."

"I agree, but not like this." Pia looked at her friend. "Have you noticed all the extra men in town?"

Montana nodded. "Three guys in a car whistled at me yesterday. It was strange. But kind of nice."

Pia winced. "Tell me you're not going to be there, meeting the bus."

Montana laughed. "I can barely hold down a job, let alone find and keep a man."

"Tell me about it," Pia grumbled. "I've never had a guy stay. And I can't figure out why. Is it me? Do I give off the leave-me vibe? Is there something fundamentally wrong with me?"

"No. You're great. Smart, funny."

"Well, so are you."

Montana wrinkled her nose. "No, I'm scattered. I feel like it's been harder for me to grow up than for everyone else. Maybe that's why I haven't found the one."

"I don't have an excuse," Pia told her. Not that it would matter now, what with the implantation and all.

Without meaning to, she found herself thinking about Raoul. She appreciated the pregnancy-buddy support, but she was going to have a serious talk with him about the kissing. They couldn't keep doing it. She was finding it confusing. Not the kissing itself—that was easy. But the wanting that followed. She was fine wanting sex. But wanting more...that was the real danger.

"I want to find where I belong," Montana said, then sighed. "Don't laugh, but I have an interview for a job."

"Why would I laugh at that?"

"Okay—not laugh exactly. I'm really excited, but just, I'm nervous."

Pia patted Montana's arm. "As long as it's not starring in porn, I'm good with it."

Montana's mouth twisted. "Well, crap."

Pia stared at her. "Oh, God. You're seriously going to be in a porn movie?"

Montana laughed. "I'm kidding."

"Very funny. What is it?"

"There's this guy named Max. He lives outside of town and he trains therapy dogs. They're the ones who go into hospitals and nursing homes. Being around them makes people feel better. He also trains dogs for a reading program. They've done studies and kids who have trouble reading do a lot better reading to a dog rather than a person. I guess they feel they're not being judged. Anyway, he's looking for someone to help him run the kennel and help with the training and take the dogs to their various programs."

Montana drew in a breath. "There's a lot to learn. When I spoke to Max, he said I would have to take a couple of classes online and get certified as a dog trainer. While I was doing that, I would work in the kennel and get to know the dogs. He's giving me a four-month trial period. If that goes well, he'll start me actually working with the therapy dogs. I have an interview in a couple of days."

Pia was still reeling from the porn joke. "You sound excited."

"I am. I like the idea of working with the dogs and helping people. I want to make a difference, but I still don't know if this job is the right one. Dakota and Nevada both just knew what they wanted to do with their lives. I'm an identical triplet. Shouldn't I be like them?"

"You have to follow your own path and figure out what's right for you. It sounds like you might have found it."

"I hope so. I'm tired of messing up."

"Montana, don't beat yourself up. When have you messed up?"

Her friend shrugged. "I just turned down a full-time job with benefits. Who does that?"

"Someone who's thinking long term."

"I want to be good at something. Look at you. You're great at your job."

"I organize festivals. That's hardly saving the world."

"You're an integral part of the community. What you do marks the passage of time and makes memories. Parents look forward to bringing their kids to their first Fall Festival or the Saturday of Giving. People plan their travel schedules to come here for their favorites. What you do changes the way people live."

Pia stared at her. "Wow. I should ask for a raise."

Montana laughed. "I'm serious."

"So am I." She'd always loved her work, but it had never seemed all that important. Montana's words made her rethink that concept. "I'd always focused on the fact that I bring tourists to town, which means more money for all the local businesses."

"It's not just about money."

"You're right. Which is why you shouldn't feel bad about turning down the full-time library job. You have to think about what's really important to you."

"I want to make a difference," Montana said firmly. "I've watched some videos about the service dogs. They're wonderful. I could be a part of that."

"Then I hope you get the job."

"Me, too. It would be nice to find where I belong. I want to be more than my family name."

"Don't discount being a Hendrix," Pia told her. "You're already part of something wonderful."

"I know, but they're just family."

Pia thought about her relatively solitary life. How she'd been on her own for so long, with no one to depend on. Now she was going to be responsible for three new lives. At least that was the hope.

"Family can be the most important thing of all," she said, thinking it was sad that Keith and Crystal had only had each other, and now the babies would only have her.

Montana rolled her eyes. "Now you sound like my mother."

"Denise is wonderful, so thanks for the compliment."

"You're welcome."

"I DON'T NEED MY HAIR CUT," Raoul told Pia as they walked down the street.

"You sound whiny," she told him. "I expect a fairly high level of maturity from my pregnancy buddy. Don't let me down."

"When did you get bossy?"

"I always have been," she said with a laugh. "I thought you would have noticed."

The day was cool. Pia had pulled on a bright red coat over her jeans and sweater. Her boots made her a little taller, which meant she was the perfect height for kissing, he thought absently.

He liked kissing Pia. He'd liked doing more, but under the circumstances, that wasn't on the table. She might be pregnant, and neither of them would do anything to hurt the babies. Not that she'd shown any interest in getting back in his bed. Although given what had happened the last time they'd been together, he doubted either of them would say no.

Still, he had a higher purpose here: taking care of Pia as she took care of Crystal's embryos.

"It's a simple rule," Pia told him. "You alternate between the sisters. Today we're seeing Bella. Next time you'll go to Julia's shop."

"I still think getting my hair cut out of town solves the problem."

"Coward."

"Football taught me when to drop back and let my guys cover me."

She paused by the glass door of the salon. "It doesn't matter if you go out of town, Raoul. They'll still be mad at you. Haven't you figured it out? There's no way to win this fight, so why not get a front-row seat and enjoy the show?"

"There's a show?"

She smiled. "Actually, you're the show."

She walked inside. He hesitated for a second, then followed her into the salon.

It was midday, midweek and still nearly every station was full. As he entered the well-lit, modern space, every single person—aka woman—turned to stare at him.

A middle-aged woman with dark hair and beautiful brown eyes studied him appraisingly. "Pia, what have you brought me?"

Pia linked her arm through Raoul's. "Bella, you can borrow him, but you can't keep him. This is Raoul Moreno. Raoul, please meet Bella Gionni."

Bella moved toward him, her hand extended. "My pleasure," she purred. "So strong, so handsome. Josh is my favorite. After all, I've known him since he was a boy, but you... You come very close."

Raoul shifted uncomfortably, then shook hands with the woman. "Ah, thanks."

"You're welcome. I'm ready for you."

He leaned toward Pia. "You're not leaving, are you?"

"No. I'm here to protect you."

"Good."

He was aware of every woman in the place watching him. He was used to attention, but it usually wasn't so blatant.

Bella seated him in a chair and wrapped a plastic cape around him. Then she stood behind him, her hands on his shoulders, and met his gaze in the mirror.

"What would you like?"

"Just a trim," Pia said, her eyes sparkling with amusement. "This is his first haircut in town."

Bella smiled. "And you came to me."

"Where else would we go?" Pia asked.

"Exactly." Bella reached for a spray bottle and dampened his hair, then combed through it. "Are the two of you together?"

"No," Pia said quickly.

"Yes," Raoul insisted just as fast.

Bella raised her eyebrows. "You should probably get that part figured out."

Pia looked at him. "We're not dating."

"We're together."

"Okay, but not in that way. Just because we've…" She stopped and glanced around, as if aware of everyone listening.

He'd been talking about him being her pregnancy buddy, but he realized she'd been thinking about their night together.

"Men," she muttered, as she stalked off and started talking to one of the other hairdressers.

Bella combed and cut efficiently, her hands moving confidently. "So you like our Pia, do you?"

"Very much."

Bella's expression sharpened. "As a friend or more?"

"We're friends."

"Then you're a fool."

He held in a grin. He'd always enjoyed women who spoke their minds. "Why?"

"Pia is worth ten of whatever women you've been dating. She's a good girl. Smart, caring, beautiful."

He turned his head so he could see Pia in the mirror. She'd shrugged out of her coat and he could see the way her sweater clung to her curves. She laughed at something he couldn't hear, but the sound of her amusement made him smile.

She was all Bella said and more. She had heart and character. No one knew about the embryos. She could have walked away from them, had them donated to science or simply thrown away. But none of the options had occurred to her. There weren't a lot of people he admired, but she was one of them.

"What happened to her was sad," Bella continued. "Losing her father that way, then having her mother run to Florida. There was Pia, in her senior year of high school, and she lost everything. She had to go into foster care."

"I'd heard," he murmured, wondering what kind of mother simply abandoned her kid without a second thought. The grief and loss could have drawn them closer together. Instead Pia had had to deal with all the crap on her own.

He found himself wanting to fix the problem—even though it had happened over a decade ago. Still, the need was there, to do something. To act.

"She's had boyfriends, you know," Bella announced.

"I'm sure she has."

"They never stay. Poor girl. I don't know what goes wrong, but they leave."

Not a conversation he wanted to be having with Bella, he thought. His gaze once again returned to Pia. She'd had a difficult road and her life was about to get three times more complicated. Who was going to take care of her? Who would be there when she needed help?

He knew she had friends and they would help. The town would pull through. Fool's Gold seemed like that kind of place. But on a day-to-day basis, Pia would be on her own.

He wondered if she'd thought that part through. If she knew what she was getting into. She turned and met his gaze in the mirror, then smiled. He winked at her and she returned her attention to her conversation.

He'd been in love twice in his life. He and his first girlfriend had grown apart, and Caro had betrayed every part of their marriage vows. He wasn't looking to feel that way ever again. Not getting involved was safer. But there was still the reality of wanting a family—needing that connection. He couldn't have one without the other. Or so he'd always believed.

"I CAN HEAR YOU," Pia yelled through the closed bathroom door.

"I'm just sitting. There's nothing to hear."

Even so, she was sure there were noises. Or maybe the problem was there weren't. Talk about pressure, she thought as she stood and pulled up her bikini panties and jeans. Is this what it was like to be a guy? Pure performance anxiety?

She opened the bathroom door.

"I can't do this with you in the room," she said, then held up a hand. "Don't bother saying you're not in the room. It's practically the same thing."

Raoul shook his head as he got to his feet and turned to face her. Laughter brightened his dark eyes. "Can't stand the heat, huh?" he teased.

"The heat isn't the problem."

"Have you tried turning on the faucet? The sound of running water might help."

"I'm not going to stand here having a conversation with you about my inability to pee."

"You already are."

She rolled her eyes, then pointed at the front door. "Go stand in the hall until I'm done."

"I've had my tongue in your mouth."

"So not the point."

"We can have sex, but I can't be in the next room while you go to the bathroom?"

"Exactly."

"Fine." He crossed the room and let himself out. Then he stuck his head back in. "What should I tell the neighbors if they ask why I'm loitering?"

"Don't make me kill you."

He laughed and shut the door behind him.

"Men," she muttered, then returned to the bathroom and pulled down her pants.

After sitting on the toilet, she turned on the faucet and reached for the plastic stick from the pregnancy test. Everything was fine, she told herself. She peed several times a day. It didn't require a lot of thought or effort. It was natural. Easy.

But at that moment, it felt far from easy. It felt impossible. She turned off the water, tried humming, shifting, breathing more slowly. Her bladder stubbornly refused to empty.

Never again, she told herself. Pregnancy was too hard. When she finally managed to pee on the stick, she was going to get ice cream. The fact that it was chilly outside didn't matter. She wanted a hot fudge sundae with whipped...

"Oh, no!"

When she'd finally stopped paying attention, her body had responded. She did her thing with the stick, set it on a tissue, then got up, flushed and pulled up her pants. After washing her hands, she walked out to get Raoul.

"Finally," he said when she opened the door. "Success?"

"I have peed."

"I'm so proud."

"Be nice or I'll make you touch it."

She went back into the bathroom and carefully carried out the stick on the tissue and set it on a paper towel on the kitchen counter.

"How long?"

"Just a few minutes."

They stared at the little screen, which showed an hourglass. She could hear the faint ticking of a clock and feel the rapid thudding of her heart. According to the test, the result would announce her condition. Pregnant or not pregnant. As simple as that.

She didn't allow herself to speculate. Part of her was afraid that she'd lost Crystal's babies—that they hadn't been able to hang on. But another part of her was terrified they had.

Raoul put his arm around her. She leaned into him and hung on.

The screen changed and she saw a single word.

Pregnant.

There was no misunderstanding that.

Her body went cold, then seemed to heat from the inside. Her stomach flopped over, making her wonder if she was going to throw up. Reality loomed, like a really big storm, but she couldn't take it all in. Pregnant. She was pregnant.

"You did it!" Raoul crowed, then grabbed her around the waist and spun her in the center of the room. "You're going to be a mom."

He sounded delighted. She felt like she was going to pass out, although that could have been from the world blurring around her.

A mom? Her? "I can't," she whispered.

He set her down. "Sure you can. This is great, Pia. The embryos implanted. This is great news."

Intellectually, she could agree. This is what Crystal wanted. But in her gut, she was deathly afraid of screwing up.

"I have to sit down," she said, making her way over to a kitchen chair and dropping onto it. She closed her eyes and focused on breathing.

Pregnant. Right now there were babies growing inside of her. Babies who would be born and become actual children, then real people. Babies who would depend on her and expect her to take care of them.

Raoul pulled up a chair and sat across from her. He took her hand in his. "What's wrong?"

"I don't think I can do this. I can't have children. I don't know how."

"Don't they do all the hard work themselves?"

"The forming and growing, maybe, but then what? They're going to have expectations. I'm not prepared for this."

He leaned toward her. "You have eight and a half months and I'll help."

"You're going to be my pregnancy buddy." She pulled her hand free and stood. "Don't get me wrong—I appreciate the support. But I'm less concerned about being pregnant than what comes after. I'm going to have to buy stuff. I haven't got a clue what. There must be a list somewhere, right? On the Internet?"

He rose. "I'm sure there is."

"And I'll need to move. This place is too small. I'll need a house." She made okay money, but it wasn't a fortune. Could she afford a house? "And there's college. I should start saving, but I don't know what to invest in. I don't understand the stock market."

He moved close and put his hands on her shoulders. "One thing at a time," he told her. "Relax. Breathe. I can help with all this. We'll find you a great place, and I can get you the best investment advice available. It's going to be okay, Pia. I promise."

She nodded, because that was the expected thing to do. And sure, he would help and she would appreciate it. But when the babies were born, his work was done. He would walk away and she would be left on her own. With triplets.

"THIS IS FUN," JENNY SAID as she ran the wand over Pia's belly. "I don't usually do ultrasounds this early." She kept her gaze on the monitor. "You know we won't be able to see anything specific. Just whether the embryos have implanted."

"I know," Pia whispered, hanging on to Raoul's hand with all her strength. Under normal circumstances she would worry about hurting him, but he was a tough football player. She was sure he could take it.

Besides, he'd offered to come with her to the doctor's office. If any part of this freaked him out, he would have to deal with it himself.

She'd had less than forty-eight hours to get used to the idea of being pregnant. So far the information hadn't become any more real. She alternated between shock and panic. Neither was especially comfortable.

She'd tried a little reading from the pregnancy books she'd bought, but that only made things worse. Knowing the statistical odds of getting hemorrhoids by the end of term wasn't exactly the sort of information she was looking for.

"Okay," Jenny said cheerfully. "Let me get the doctor."

Pia waited until the tech left, then turned to Raoul. "Did we know she was going to do that? Is it okay she's getting Dr. Galloway?"

He bent over her, smoothing her hair back with his free hand. "It's fine. She said she would be getting the doctor before she started. This is all routine, Pia. You're doing great."

Did all mothers-to-be feel such a numbing sense of responsibility? Because whatever happened wasn't just about her—it was also about Crystal and Keith.

"I want them to be all right. The babies. I hate being scared all the time."

"You need to relax. Keep breathing."

She did her best. Fortunately, Dr. Galloway returned quickly and stood by the monitor as Jenny moved the wand.

"There they are," the doctor said, pointing at the screen. "We have three implantations." The older woman smiled. "Good for you, Pia. They're all in place."

Pia stared at the screen, trying to see what they were pointing at. It all looked blurry to her, but she didn't care. It was enough to know that for now, everything was going the way it was supposed to.

Although, honestly, the thought of triplets was enough to send anyone over the edge. Two months ago, she'd had a cat who didn't like her. Now she was carrying triplets.

Dr. Galloway wiped off her stomach. "Go ahead and get dressed, Pia. We'll meet in my office and discuss what happens next."

Pia nodded.

Raoul helped her to sit up, then waited as she got to her feet.

"I'm right here," he told her.

She nodded because speaking seemed impossible.

After dressing, she went out into the hall. Raoul was waiting. He took her hand in his and led the way to the doctor's office.

She went in first, trying to smile at Dr. Galloway.

"You've begun the journey," the other woman told her. "I'm so proud of you, Pia. Not many people would do what you're doing."

Probably because they were sane, she thought as she took a seat. Raoul settled next to her.

"What's next?" he asked.

"Many things," Dr. Galloway said, pulling out papers and brochures. "A multiple birth brings much joy but also a few challenges. We know early and can make the preparations. Pia, you need to focus on good food and good sleep. You're healthy and I don't foresee any problems, but we will take a few precautions."

She passed over the papers. "I want to see you in a month. I'll be monitoring you more closely than if you were carrying only one baby. Between now and then, do the reading I've highlighted. You can call the office with any questions. Everything will be fine."

Pia thought about pointing out there was no way the doctor could actually know that, but why state the obvious? She and Raoul said their goodbyes and somehow made it to the parking lot. She knew, because suddenly they were standing by his sleek, red car. She stared at him across the low roof and saw he looked as stunned as she felt.

"So it's not just me," she said. "That makes me feel better."

"I was faking it," he admitted, then swore. "Triplets. Did you see them on the screen?"

"No, but I wasn't looking too hard. I'm already weirded out by the whole thing."

"They're real," he said slowly. "The babies were just an idea before, but they're going to be born. You're having triplets."

She nodded, wishing people would stop saying that. She didn't need the pressure. Then she looked more closely at him. There was something odd in his eyes. A tightness.

He was going to tell her he couldn't do it, she thought sadly. That this was more than he'd signed on for. Not that she blamed him. She was living in stunned disbelief, as well. But for her, there was no going back. The babies were in her body, doing their thing.

Even though a part of her wanted to beg him not to abandon her, she knew that wasn't fair. He'd already been more than generous. The right thing, the honorable thing, was to release him. Sort of a "Go with God" moment.

"It's okay," she told him. "I understand. I'm going into a place that makes me uncomfortable. I can't begin to imagine what you're feeling. You've been great and I thank you for everything. Please don't feel obligated to do anything more."

He frowned. "What are you talking about?"

"I'm giving you an out. You don't have to be my pregnancy buddy anymore."

"Why would you do that?"

"You look like you want to bolt. I get that."

He walked around the car and stood in front of her. Despite her heels, the man still loomed over her. He was close enough that she had to tilt her head to meet his gaze.

"I'm not running," he said. "But you're right about one thing. I don't want to be your pregnancy buddy anymore."

She hoped her disappointment didn't show. She refused to think about going through the pregnancy by herself. Once she got home, she would have a big hissy fit, followed by a breakdown. But for now, she would stay in control. "I understand."

He took her hand again. He seemed to do that a lot. The problem was she liked it—too much. And now she was going to lose the hand-holding and pretty much everything else when it came to him.

"No," he said. "You don't. Pia, I want more. I want to marry you."

CHAPTER ELEVEN

RAOUL HADN'T PLANNED TO PROPOSE, but he wasn't completely surprised by what he'd said. He'd been thinking about her a lot lately, about the babies she carried and their future. He admired her and respected her. Despite her fear and worry, she'd plowed ahead, taking each next logical step. His desire to help was something he'd learned from Hawk—to step in and make a difference.

He also hadn't been able to get Keith out of his mind. The man had died fighting for his country. He would have assumed that Crystal would go ahead and have their children. He would have believed his family would go on. Thanks to Pia—it would. But it wasn't right that she do all this alone.

Pia stared at him, her eyes wide, her mouth open. She tried to speak, swallowed, then said, "Excuse me? What?"

"I want to marry you."

She shook her head slightly, as if not sure of her hearing. She looked stunned and a little dizzy. He wondered if he should get her into the car so she could sit. She solved the problem by opening the door herself and slumping into the seat.

He went around to the other side and got in, then he angled toward her.

"I mean it, Pia. Marry me."

"Why?"

A reasonable question, he thought. "I admire what you're doing. Most people would have run in the opposite direction, but you didn't. And don't say you had doubts and questions. If you didn't you wouldn't be competent to have the children."

He leaned toward her. "I've seen a lot of different kind of people in my life. Those who give and those who take. Those who think about others and those who think about themselves. I've told you about my coach and how he changed everything for me. Nicole opened her home and her heart to me. They taught me what's important. I want to do what they did—make a difference to someone."

Her expression of shock changed to something that looked a lot like annoyance. "Thanks, but I'm not interested in being your charity case of the week."

"No, that's not what I mean."

"It's what you're saying."

He reached for her hands, but she snatched them back. "Don't."

She was pissed. Damn. He'd screwed up. "Pia, I'm saying this wrong. I want to take care of you. That's all. I want to be there for you and the babies. I want to be a part of your lives."

"If you're so hell-bent on being a husband and father, go marry someone else and have your own kids."

"I tried that," he admitted. "And failed."

"One divorce," she muttered. "Big deal. It happens to more than half of marriages. So what? Try again."

"That's what I want to do. With you."

They were words Pia had never thought she would

hear. A proposal of marriage. Only everything about the situation was wrong. Okay—not the man. He was pretty amazing, but she didn't want him proposing like this. Out of some weird sense of obligation to a former mentor. She wasn't interested in being anyone's merit-badge project.

"You can't fix whatever's wrong with you by marrying me," she told him. "Go get therapy."

She'd thought the words would annoy him, but he simply smiled at her.

"Do you really think that's what I'm doing?"

"Yes. You don't love me. We haven't even dated." There'd been that single, amazing night, but that wasn't enough to build a relationship on.

She supposed on some level she should be flattered he was offering to help, but instead she felt cheated. Even though she'd never had a relationship get to the "I love you, please marry me" stage, she'd always dreamed one day it would happen. That the man of her dreams would propose.

But it was supposed to be a romantic event—a magical time. Not a mercy offer made in a medical parking lot.

"Pia, I like you a lot," he said, sounding annoyingly earnest. "I respect and admire you. You're smart, funny, charming and you lead with your heart. You've given up your life to have your friend's children. How many people would do that?"

The switch in subject startled her. "Crystal left me her embryos. What was I supposed to do? Ignore them?"

"That's my point. You couldn't. You had to take care of your friend, even after she was gone. I might not have known Crystal, but I did know her husband. I can't explain it, but I know that I owe him. These are his kids, too. I want to take care of you. Of them."

The Keith part made sense, she thought. But marriage? "You barely know me." Although she had to admit his assessment of her character had been very flattering.

"I know enough. Is it that you don't know me? Ask me anything. What do you want to know?"

She felt as if she'd stepped into an alternate universe. "I don't know enough to figure out what to ask."

"Then I'll tell you." This time when he reached for her hand, she let him. "You know about parts of my past. I told you I had a serious girlfriend in high school. I was crazy about her. I never even looked at another girl while I was with her. I never cheated. Once we broke up, I had my wild times, but after Hawk got me on the right track, I calmed down. I dated a lot of women, but one at a time. When Caro and I started dating, that was it. I was all in."

He shifted in his seat, as if trying to get closer to her. As if his words weren't enough to convince her and that he would use the magnetism of his presence to tip the scale in his favor.

"When I commit, I give a hundred percent. It doesn't matter if it's football or marriage or my business. I'll be there for you."

She felt overwhelmed. Everything was happening too fast. Worse—she was tempted. Hearing that a guy was "all in" was a leap-without-bothering-to-look-first moment if there ever was one.

It wasn't love. She understood that. Raoul wanted a family without the trauma of giving his heart. He wanted to help her and Keith, and in return he got all the trappings of family without a whole lot of risk.

"I have my flaws," he continued. "I can be impatient. I'm not a morning person and can push back to try to get my way. But I can be reasoned with." He touched her cheek with his free hand. "I'd never hurt you."

She had a feeling he meant what he said. But no one could promise not to hurt another. It didn't work that way.

"Raoul, you're being really nice, but this isn't going to happen."

"Why not?"

"Marriage? It's a huge step and we barely know each other."

"I want you."

As much as she wanted to bask in the words, she couldn't. "No, you want a cause."

"So you get to be someone who loves your friend, but I'm just a guy doing a good deed? You're not the biological mother to these babies, but you're giving up your life to take care of them. Why can't I want to do the same? That's what I'm offering. You need support and a partner. I want a wife and kids. I want to be their dad. Permanently. Yes, getting married is a practical solution for both of us, but that doesn't make it any less real."

She stared into his eyes, wishing she could see down to his heart. Did he mean it?

"Define real," she said softly.

"The whole thing. A ring, a judge, a piece of paper. We'll live together, raise the kids together. I'd like it if you'd take my name, but I'll pretend it's okay if you don't. We'll be listed as the parents on the birth certificates. We'll buy a house, make love, argue, make up, raise kids, get a dog and grow old together. I'm not talking temporary, Pia. I'm offering you everything I have. I'll be a husband to you and a full-time father to those kids. And if you decide to leave me, you can take me to the cleaners in court."

He was saying all the right things, but more than that, he seemed to believe them. Which made her want to believe him.

She would admit to being tempted. On a practical level, having someone to depend on while raising triplets would be amazing. Raoul had already shown he was responsible and supportive. On a personal level, she *did* like him—probably more than she should. The thought of sharing a bed with him for the next fifty years was kind of exciting.

He wasn't offering her love. At least he was honest about it. She'd always expected to fall madly in love at some point, but it hadn't happened yet. And once she had kids, what were the odds? Was a practical marriage based on mutual need such a bad thing?

"What about kids of your own?" she asked.

"I'm hoping you'll agree in a couple of years. Wouldn't you like a baby of your own, too?"

She nodded slowly. That, too, had been part of her fantasy. And Raoul offered an enticing gene pool.

"I meant what I said," he told her. "I'm all in, Pia. I'll be there for you, no matter what. I'll be your husband and partner in every way possible. I give you my word. You'll be able to count on me until the day I die."

She knew enough to recognize he was the kind of man whose word meant something. He was offering her all he had—except his heart. She believed he would take care of her and after all she'd been through, that was nearly impossible to resist. Compared with security, love came in a very distant second.

But this wasn't just about her. "It's one thing to marry me without being in love," she said. "But the babies are different. You can't be any different with them because they're not biologically yours."

"I know. They have my word, too. Marry me, Pia. Say yes."

She looked into his dark eyes and knew that he would be with her every step of the way. That for reasons she couldn't explain, this man wanted to take on her and three unborn children that were no relation to him.

The thought of not having to do everything herself, of knowing there was someone else who would have her back, was tempting. The fact that the guy in question was Raoul made it irresistible.

"Yes," she whispered.

He stared at her. "Yes? You're accepting?"

She nodded, once again feeling slightly faint. Maybe it wasn't the pregnancy, she thought as he pulled her into his arms. Maybe it was him.

Then his mouth claimed hers and she couldn't think at all. She could only feel the warmth and affection and even a slight hint of passion.

"You won't regret this," he told her. "I'm going to buy you the biggest house, the biggest diamond ring. I'll take care of everything."

She drew back slightly and eyed him. "You're not going to become some freakish, controlling guy, are you?"

He grinned. "No. Are you objecting to the diamond or the house?"

"It was the 'I'll take care of everything' part that threw me."

"How about I'll take care of everything after running it by you?"

"That works."

"Good."

He kissed her again, then straightened in his seat and grabbed his seat belt. She did the same. He started the car and they drove out of the parking lot.

Pia stared at the familiar road and told herself it was okay. That the fluttering sensation in her stomach was anticipation, not frenzied dread. Marrying Raoul was a good thing. It's not as if she would ever get tired of looking at him, and despite the fame and fortune, he was a nice guy. In marriage, nice mattered.

This would work, she told herself. In fact, she was downright lucky. It was the right thing to do for the babies. As for her dream of falling in love and being swept away by a handsome prince…given everything going on in her life, this was as close to the fantasy as she was going to get.

AFTER DROPPING PIA OFF at her office, Raoul returned to his house. He walked through the two-bedroom place and knew there was no way it was going to work for a family of five. He'd been thinking about buying something permanent for some time now, but there hadn't been a rush. That had all changed. Now he had a family to provide for.

The thought would have brought some guys to their knees, but Raoul was excited by the prospect. He was ready to be married again, ready to be a father. If things had gone the way they were supposed to with Caro, he would already have at least one kid.

Sure, his arrangement with Pia wasn't traditional, but little about his life had been. He was a street kid who'd been blessed with the ability to think on his feet and throw a football a hundred yards. Now he was getting lucky again. Besides, Hawk and Nicole would be thrilled to be honorary grandparents to the triplets. Hawk would be proud of Raoul for doing the right thing.

He left his rental and headed downtown. On the way, he passed a jewelry store. Jenel's Gems was located in a small square of exclusive shops. He'd probably passed it a dozen times and hadn't noticed. Now he changed direction and went inside.

The interior was all glass and light. Sleek and so-phisticated, it was the kind of place that made you feel as if everything you bought was special.

A tall, pretty blonde walked over to him. "Hi. Can I help you?"

The last time he'd gotten engaged, he'd designed the ring himself. He'd had very specific ideas and had spent two days picking out the diamond. He'd had this idea that the ring had to represent who he was and what he wanted his marriage to Caro to be. The ring was to have been a statement.

Talk about a crash-and-burn, he thought to himself.

"Are you good at keeping secrets?" he asked.

The woman smiled. "I sell engagement rings. I have to be."

"Good. Do you know Pia O'Brian?"

Surprise and pleasure flickered in the woman's blue eyes. "Yes, of course. I like her very much."

"Me, too. I want a ring for her. Something that suits her taste. Something she'll love."

"I see. And may I ask what this ring is for?"

"She's agreed to marry me."

The woman tilted her head and smiled. "Then you're a very lucky man."

"I think so."

"I have a ring," she began. "The design is unique but classic. Let me go get it."

She disappeared into the back for a few minutes, then returned with three rings on a lavender velvet display tray.

"This is the engagement ring," she said, holding out a diamond ring. "The center stone is two carats. It's surrounded by a bead-set diamond border." She turned it upright. "See how the stone is set up to catch the light, but the border not only protects it, it makes it less likely to catch on anything. Like a sweater."

Or hurt a baby, he thought.

The woman turned the diamond ring again, to show the profile. "These are channel-set square diamonds on the side. As you can see, I have two matching bands of the square diamonds. They would slide in on either side, completing the look."

"They're the wedding bands?"

She nodded. "They can be worn alone, if Pia prefers."

He picked up the ring. It glittered in the overhead lights. There was something right about it. Something that told him Pia would like it.

"Let me show you a few other things," the woman said. "For comparison."

They went through the cases. He asked to see a couple

of things, then shook his head. "The first one," he told her. "That's it."

"I think so, too. Are you going to faint when I tell you the price?"

"No."

"It's a high-quality diamond and a custom setting."

"That's okay."

Fifteen minutes later, he had all three rings in boxes tucked into his jacket pocket. He'd refused the shopping bag, not wanting anyone in town to see him carrying it. He was starting to get a handle on Fool's Gold. He knew how word would spread.

Now that he had a ring, it was time to go see a man about a house.

PIA STOOD IN FRONT OF her dry-erase and corkboard calendar, checking the events against her master list. Some of the festivals only required minimal prep work, but others took weeks of planning. If decorations were required, they had to be pulled out of storage and installed. The city maintenance workers appreciated plenty of lead time, and she knew better than to annoy the muscle portion of her operation.

With Halloween coming soon she would need to get the decorative flags changed and put out the scarecrows and hay bales, which reminded her that she needed to order fresh hay. The stuff they'd used last year had looked a little ragged.

She crossed to her desk and had started to pick up her phone when her office door burst open and Liz Sutton and Montana surged into the room.

"I can't believe it!" Montana shrieked. "We sat right here talking about my boring life when you had news like that? How could you keep it to yourself? I may never forgive you."

Pia might have been worried except she had no idea what her friend was talking about, and the fact that Montana and Liz were both grinning like fools meant that it wasn't bad news.

Liz reached her first and hugged her. "Congratulations. He seems really sweet. And hunky, which is always a nice plus. I know I get a little shiver every time I see Ethan. Especially when he's naked."

Montana winced. "Hello, that's my brother we're talking about. Don't share details."

"Sorry," Liz said with a laugh, then turned back to Pia. "Well?"

"Well, what?"

Montana and Liz grabbed each other's arms and actually jumped up and down. It was a little bit scary, Pia thought, taking a step back.

"You're marrying Raoul!" they shrieked together.

"I'm going to forgive you for not telling me if you promise to spill all the details," Montana said. "Start at the beginning and talk slow. You said hi and he said?"

Oh, no. Pia sank into her chair and groaned. This wasn't good at all. It had been a matter of—she checked her watch—four hours. How could word already be spreading?

The truth was she'd barely accepted that he'd proposed to her, let alone the fact that she'd accepted. The impossible situation had left her too confused to do much more than pretend it hadn't happened. It had been the only way to get work done.

"Pia?" Liz asked, her smile fading. "Are you all right?"

"I'm fine. Just confused. How did you hear?"

Montana and Liz exchanged glances.

"Raoul went to see Josh," Liz said. "Ethan was there and heard the whole thing. Raoul said he wanted to buy a bigger house. One with a lot of bedrooms. Josh wanted to know why and Raoul said the two of you were getting married but not to tell anyone. Josh and Ethan swore they wouldn't, then Ethan called me."

Pia winced. It wasn't his fault—he probably thought the information was safe with his close friends. He wasn't a small-town guy and would have no idea how this sort of news fed on itself. In a matter of hours, it would be everywhere.

"I ran into Montana on my way over here and told her," Liz continued. "But you don't look very happy. What's wrong?"

They each pulled up a chair and sat close, looking concerned. Pia wanted to bolt, but these women were her friends. If she couldn't explain the situation to them, how could she possibly go through with it? Not that she was having second thoughts—she wasn't. It was just that everything was complicated.

She drew in a breath. "Crystal left me her embryos," she began, then explained how she'd made the decision to have the babies.

"At first Raoul offered to be my pregnancy buddy," she continued. "He said he would help out while I carried the babies."

"That's so sweet," Montana said with a sigh.

But Liz was more like Pia—less of an overt romantic. Her gaze narrowed. "Why?"

"That was my question." She hesitated. "It turns out he knew Keith. Raoul went over to Iraq with some football guys and Keith was part of their escort team. They became friends. Keith told him about Fool's Gold and Crystal. Raoul was there when he died."

"I didn't know any of this," Montana said, her eyes wide. "Is that why he came here?"

Pia nodded. "Normally he wouldn't have paid extra attention to our invitation to the pro-am golf tournament, but he recognized the name of the town and wanted to check it out. He liked what he saw and decided to move here."

"Did he talk to Crystal?" Liz asked.

"No. He didn't know what to say. So he didn't know she was dying or about the embryos until I found out she'd left them to me and had a bit of a breakdown in front of him. Everything sort of spiraled from there."

"And now he wants to marry you," Montana said with a sigh. "It's so romantic."

It was more practical than romantic, but why state the obvious?

Pia shrugged. "He really wants to be a part of things. And I sort of liked the idea of not being so alone."

"You're not alone," Montana told her. "You have us."

"I know and that's great." She hesitated.

Liz got it right away. "But having friends with lives isn't the same as having someone who is always there for you. When I was pregnant with Tyler, I was scared and confused. You're having triplets."

Pia nodded. "I try not to think about the actual number. Anyway, Raoul's been with me as I made every decision. He's been a rock. Today, after the ultrasound confirmed all three embryos have implanted, he asked me to marry him."

"You're having Crystal's babies," Liz said, her eyes filling with tears. "That's such a blessing for both of you. She would be thrilled."

Pia was still in the confused camp, but she smiled anyway. "I'm committed now."

"Babies," Montana said. "And a proposal. Was it wonderful? Did he get down on one knee?"

Pia hesitated. "Montana, we're not in love. Raoul wants to marry me and be a part of the babies' lives. He wants to be their father. When I asked him why, he pointed out that I'm not their biological mother and no one is questioning my commitment. I'm willing to have them for a friend, because it's the right thing to do. He wants to be their father, and me to be his wife, because of Keith and because it's the right thing to do."

Just saying the words was tough. Believing them would take some time.

"I wasn't sure whether to say yes at first," she admitted. "But he can be really convincing. We like and respect each other. He's a good man and I trust him. I haven't been able to say that about a guy before."

Liz hugged her. "I have a good feeling about this," she said. "Arranged marriages have worked for generations."

"But you're not in love," Montana said, looking crushed. "Don't you want to be in love?"

"Sometimes you have to be practical," Liz told her. "Love can grow."

Pia hadn't thought of that. She wasn't sure if she could make herself that vulnerable—especially with so much at stake. It would hurt too much if he didn't return her feelings and, worse, it could make their arrangement awkward.

"Maybe he'll fall madly in love with you," Montana told her.

"I don't think so," Pia said firmly. "To date, all the men in my life have resisted the process…and me. Men who claim to want to be with me tend to leave. I'd rather have the truth up front. Raoul's been honest and I appreciate that."

"I guess." Montana didn't sound convinced. "It's just not romantic, you know?"

"Romance can be painful," Pia reminded her.

Liz sat back down. "So there's no love allowed?"

"We haven't discussed the rules," Pia admitted. "But it's understood."

"Hmm. You'll need to be careful, then. The heart is a tricky beast."

"Trust me. I have big plans to stay emotionally whole." She hesitated. "Could you two please not say anything about why we're getting married? It's okay to tell Charity, but no one else."

"Of course we won't talk," Liz promised. "You don't need that kind of speculation right now. But brace yourself. Everybody is going to find out about you and Raoul, not to mention the pregnancy. You're going to be a star."

"I can handle it." Pia had been the center of attention in town once before and it had been awful. Now the reasons were different and she was sure everything would be fine.

Raoul had given his word and she chose to believe him. He would stay with her and the babies. Maybe they weren't crazy in love, but that was okay. There were a lot of different ways to make a happy family and they would find theirs.

CHAPTER TWELVE

PIA AVOIDED GOING TO THE grocery store as long as she could. If there was one place in Fool's Gold where she was likely to run into people wanting to talk about her upcoming marriage, it was somewhere between produce and the frozen-food aisle. But she'd used up the last of her milk that morning and there was absolutely nothing in her freezer, so it was time to grit her teeth and get through it.

Thinking that the store would be quieter midday rather than after work, she used her lunch hour to go there. The trip there was stressful enough with lots of men she didn't recognize strolling through town. Some guy had even pulled out a grocery cart and handed it to her as she entered the store. Talk about strange.

She got through cleaning supplies, the meat counter and was halfway to the dairy case when Denise Hendrix spotted her.

"Pia!" the woman cried, abandoning her own cart and rushing over. "I heard. I'm so happy."

Pia braced herself for a warm, enveloping hug. Denise was the matriarch of the Hendrix family. An attractive woman in her early fifties, she'd lost her husband about ten years before. She was an active member of the community and the mother of six, including her daughters who were identical triplets.

They embraced, then Denise stepped back.

"Look at you, having Crystal's babies. That's such a blessing."

"Thanks. I'm still in denial, with a slight bend toward panic."

"Of course you are, but you're doing it anyway. I'm so proud of you." She smiled. "I am available anytime for advice or conversation or to talk you down from the panic. A multiple birth is completely manageable. You just need to plan."

"I've heard that." Planning was important, Pia thought. Just as soon as the idea of having three babies at once became real to her, she would start. "I appreciate the offer to talk. I'm sure I'll have a lot of questions. I just don't know what they are right now."

"Don't worry. I'm not going anywhere. Let me know when you're ready." Denise raised her eyebrows. "I also heard that more congratulations are in order." Her gaze dropped to Pia's bare left hand. "Have you set a date?"

"Not yet." She tucked her hand behind her back. She was still slightly stunned to find herself engaged.

"I imagine you'll want a small, quiet wedding. You're not going to have the energy to plan anything large. Unless you want to wait until after the babies are born. Then you could go all out."

Marriage was one thing, Pia thought, feeling slightly uneasy. But a wedding? She hadn't put those pieces together. "I, um. We haven't decided which way we're going," she admitted. "Everything happened so fast."

"I knew you'd find someone wonderful," Denise told her. "You've always been such a lovely girl. After all you've been through with your parents." She cleared her throat. "There's no need to talk about that. Anyway, you've found your happy ending. From all I've heard, Raoul is very special. And handsome. He's giving Josh a run for his money."

Pia laughed. "I don't think there's a competition."

"Then you haven't had your hair done at Julia's place lately. There was a very heated discussion about the two of them just last week."

Pia thought about the talk at the city council meeting—the argument about who had the better butt. "We need more to think about in this town."

"There are those men coming to town," Denise said. "There's a subject. Have you noticed they're everywhere? Just yesterday two men whistled at me." She sounded both outraged and faintly pleased.

"I have no idea what we're going to do with them."

"I thought there were already several events planned."

"A few, but what are they going to do the rest of the time? Troll the streets, looking for easy conquests?"

Denise laughed. "I'm old enough to be your mother, so it's not right that I'm the one to point out that no one says 'easy conquests' anymore."

"Okay, you're right, but still."

Denise still looked amused. "I'm sorry you're not excited about the influx of men, but that's because you've already found someone wonderful. I wonder if any of the men will be older."

Pia had been caught up in the fact that everyone assumed she and Raoul had fallen madly in love and wondering if they should say anything. But she found herself distracted by Denise's last comment.

"You're interested in a man?" Pia asked.

"Interested is too strong a word," Denise said with a shrug. "I'm...curious. Ralph has been gone a long time. My kids are old enough to deal with me dating. I like my life, but sometimes I think it would be nice to have someone else around."

"Way to go," Pia told her. "I think that's great. I have no idea about the ages of the men arriving, but I can let you know if I see any good ones." She grinned. "What about someone younger?"

Denise sniffed. "I'm not a cougar."

"You could be."

Denise was pretty, with her short dark hair and bright eyes. She had a body that someone fifteen years younger would envy.

"I'd prefer someone around my age," the other woman said. "Then there's less I have to explain. Do you really think anyone who wasn't there could understand the thrill of hearing 'Rhinestone Cowboy' on the radio?"

"Probably not," Pia admitted. "Point taken. We'll find you a nice man who remembers the seventies."

Denise looked worried. "You're not taking me on as a project, are you?"

"No. And I won't mention anything to your daughters. I'll let you tell them you're on the prowl."

Denise laughed and held up her hands. "No prowl. I'm thinking. There's a difference. Enough about me. Remember, I'm here if you have any questions. Also, when you get ready to register for your shower gifts, we should talk. Some things you really will need three of, but others you won't."

"Okay."

Shower gifts? As in baby shower? Pia wasn't prepared for that. Of course, as she'd already figured out, there was moving and getting married to contend with, as well. Compared with that, a baby shower should be easy.

"All right, my dear," Denise said, hugging her again. "I'm delighted. You deserve every happiness."

"Thanks."

Denise waved and pushed her cart toward the front of the store. Pia completed her own shopping, then took everything home and put it away. When she left her apartment again, she headed for Raoul's office, rather than her own.

Ten minutes later, she found him alone in the big, empty space.

"You really need to get some more furniture," she told him as she walked to his desk, her heels clicking on the cement floor. "Maybe a few employees."

"I have Dakota. She's at lunch." He rose and smiled at her. "This is a nice surprise."

"We need to talk."

He settled on the corner of his desk. "Should I be worried?"

"No. Nothing's wrong." She drew in a breath. "You do realize that word is spreading. Everyone in town is going to know we're getting married."

"I figured that out. Josh violated the guy code."

"Did you tell him not to mention the engagement?"

"Yes, but it didn't do any good."

"This isn't like Dallas or Seattle. Everybody knows everyone else's business."

He stood and pulled her close. "Is that a problem?"

"It's not something that can be changed."

"I meant are you upset people know we're getting married?"

Standing there, feeling the heat of his body against hers, wrapped in his strong arms, it was tough to be upset about anything.

"I'm not upset, I just thought we'd have more time to get used to it ourselves."

He touched her cheek with his fingers. "Meaning people are coming up to you and saying stuff."

She nodded.

"Want to change your mind?" he asked.

"No."

"Good. Me, either." He lowered his head and brushed his mouth against hers. "I meant what I said, Pia. I'm all in."

Until he said those words again, she hadn't realized there was a knot in her chest. It loosened and suddenly it was easier to breathe.

"Thanks," she whispered. "Me, too."

"Good."

He kissed her again, lingering this time, making her body heat up from the inside.

"Want to come over for dinner?" he asked. "I'll cook."

"You know how?"

He shrugged. "I'll barbecue. Fire good."

She laughed. "It's cold outside."

"It's in the forties at night. I'll survive the time it takes me to grill a couple of steaks." He pressed his mouth against her ear. "There's this new thing called a jacket. I have one."

"You're so cutting-edge."

"Tell me about it." He straightened. "Was that a yes?"

"I'll be there."

"Great. I'm heading up to the school now, but when I'm done there, I'll go get steaks and some salads. Does six work?"

"Sure."

He kissed her one more time before she left and headed back to her own office. As she walked, she felt a faint tingle on her lips—the lingering effect of his mouth on hers. The man could sure get to her.

She liked him. Considering they were getting married, that was a good thing. But Liz was right—she had to be careful. Liking him too much would leave her vulnerable. She'd already been hurt enough in her life. She didn't need to go looking for trouble. Most of the time, it seemed to find her without any help.

RAOUL ARRIVED AT THE CAMP just as the kids were let out for afternoon recess. It was cool but clear, with blue skies visible between the breaks in the trees. He found himself in the middle of a rush of children wanting to make the most of their twenty minutes of playtime.

"Hey, Raoul," Peter called as he ran past. "Come play."

He'd seen the boy a few times since they'd had lunch together. Peter was smart, friendly and interested in sports. There hadn't been a hint of any kind of abuse. Maybe Raoul had imagined Peter flinching that first day during the fire. Or maybe the fire itself had made the boy nervous.

He followed the kids onto the playground. The noise level grew as the play began. There were shrieks and calls, along with plenty of laughter.

Looking around, he was pleased at what the camp had become. This was right, he thought as several girls tried to coax him into turning one end of a jump rope. Finally he agreed.

They lined up to be the next one to jump.

"Faster," a little girl with curly hair demanded. "I jump really good."

He and the teacher holding the other end obliged, spinning the rope more quickly. The girl kept up easily, laughing as she jumped.

Out of the corner of his eye, he saw several boys on the jungle gym. A flash of red caught his attention. He turned and saw Peter climb to the top. In a moment that was like something out of the movies, Raoul saw what was going to happen, even as he knew he was too far away to stop it.

Peter started to lower himself down. His hand slipped. Raoul took off running, the boy grabbed for the bar, slipped again, screamed and tumbled to the ground. Despite all the noise around him, Raoul would have sworn he heard the thunk of the fall. Peter landed on his arm, and Raoul knew before he reached him that it was going to be bad.

"Stay still," he instructed as he reached the kid's side.

Peter looked more stunned than hurt. He started to get up, then his face went pale and he gasped. Raoul saw the awkward angle of Peter's forearm.

The boy's face screwed up. "It hurts," he said and began to cry.

"I know. It's your arm. Do you hurt anywhere else?"

Peter shook his head. Tears spilled down his cheeks.

He helped the boy shift his arm against his chest.

Peter screamed once, then continued crying. Raoul gathered him up in his arms and stood.

A bunch of students had gathered around. Teachers came running.

"He's broken his arm," Raoul said as he walked. "I don't know if he's hurt anywhere else. I'm taking him to the hospital. It'll be faster than waiting for an ambulance. Call the hospital and let them know we're coming. Call the police and see if they can meet me at the bottom of the mountain to escort us to the hospital, then find his foster parents."

Peter weighed practically nothing, Raoul thought, hurrying out to the parking lot. One of the teachers had come with them and fished his keys out of his jacket pocket. She opened the door. He crouched down and carefully slid the boy onto the seat.

Mrs. Miller appeared on his left. "I'm coming, too. I'll drive my own car and follow you down." She bent down and smoothed her hand over Peter's face. "You're going to be fine. We'll take care of you."

The boy continued to cry.

Raoul fastened the boy's seat belt. Mrs. Miller stepped back and he closed the door.

"You know where the hospital is?" she asked as Raoul hurried to the driver's side.

"Yes."

"I'll meet you there."

NEARLY TWO HOURS LATER, Raoul sat in the emergency waiting room. Peter had been seen almost at once. X-rays showed a clean break that should heal quickly. He was off getting a cast on, while Mrs. Miller waited to talk to the social worker who had been called. So far Peter's foster parents hadn't shown up.

"Mr. Moreno?"

He looked up and a saw a tall, blonde nurse with a chart. "Yes," he said as he rose.

"Hi. I'm Heidi. Peter's going to be just fine. They're finishing up now. I wondered if I could talk to you for a minute."

"Sure."

He followed her into an empty examination room.

"How do you know Peter?" she asked.

"Through the school. He goes to the one that burned down, so all the kids are up at my camp. I've played ball with him and his friends a few times. Why?"

She pressed her lips together. "He's very thin for his age. We have some concerns about the food he's getting. His bones aren't as dense as we would like. From what Mrs. Miller told us about the playground, he shouldn't have broken a bone in that fall. Do you know if he gets enough to eat?"

He shook his head, ignoring the rage that bubbled inside of him. He had no patience for people who didn't take care of the kids entrusted to them. He'd been through plenty of that himself as he'd been growing up.

"Are you going to do any tests?" he asked.

"We need to talk to his parents about that."

"Foster parents," he corrected. "He lost his parents a while ago."

"I don't like the sound of that," Heidi said. "Now I know why Mrs. Miller wanted us to call social services. I'll talk to the caseworker when she gets here and ask her to follow up."

Raoul looked at her. "Are there any signs of physical abuse?"

"We didn't see any. Do you suspect that something's going on?"

"I was there during the fire. Peter was one of the last kids to leave. When I went to help him out of the room, he pulled away. It could have just been one of those things, but…"

"Maybe." Heidi didn't sound convinced. "I'll mention that, as well. It doesn't hurt to be cautious." She made some notes. "Thanks for the information."

He and Heidi walked out of the room. He saw Mrs. Miller hurrying toward him.

"Can you come to Peter's room," the teacher asked as she approached. "He's not doing well."

"What's wrong?" Heidi asked. "He was fine a few minutes ago."

"The cast is on and they've given him something for the pain," the older woman said. "It's not his arm." She lowered her voice. "Apparently the last time he was in the hospital was after that horrible car accident that killed his parents. He keeps talking about them and asking for you." She looked at Raoul. "I think seeing you would make him feel better."

"Sure."

"You go ahead," Heidi told them. "I'm going to check on the caseworker and see when we can expect her."

As Peter was due to be released in an hour or so, he hadn't been given a room on one of the regular hospital floors. Raoul followed Mrs. Miller through the maze of hallways that made up the E.R. Peter sat up on a bed, looking small and pale. The cast went from his wrist to his elbow and was Dallas Cowboy blue. But the kid looked anything but okay as he covered his face with his free hand and tears ran down his cheeks.

"Hey, buddy," Raoul said as he walked into the room. "What's going on?"

"I want to go h-home," the boy cried.

"We're getting ahold of your foster parents," Raoul told him.

"N-not them. I want my mom and dad."

Raoul swore silently. This was a problem that couldn't be fixed. He looked at Mrs. Miller, who was obviously fighting tears of her own, then back at the boy.

Raoul moved to the bed and pulled the boy into his arms. Then he carried him to the chair in the corner and sat down, holding Peter close.

The kid clung to him, wrapping his uninjured arm around Raoul's neck and crying into his shoulder.

He was so damn skinny, Raoul thought. All bones and angles, too light for a kid his age. He held Peter, rubbing his back, not saying anything. After a few minutes, the crying softened and the kid seemed to go to sleep.

"I feel so bad for him," Mrs. Miller whispered. "I've called all the numbers his foster parents left and there's no answer. Mr. Folio's employer said the man was out of town for a few days. But if that's true, who's looking after Peter?"

Raoul didn't have any answers. He knew the situation with the boy wasn't all that unusual. That being underage and alone in the world was never a good thing. There were excellent foster parents out there, but plenty of them were only in it for the money.

An older woman entered. She looked worn and tired, with her gray hair pulled back and glasses hanging from a chain around her neck.

"I'm Cathy Dawson," she said, then saw Peter and lowered her voice. "Is he all right?"

"The break was clean and, according to the doctors, he should heal quickly," Mrs. Miller said. "I can't get ahold of his foster parents, however."

The social worker frowned, then put on her glasses and read the papers in her hand. "I see there is also some concern about his physical well-being. He might not be getting enough to eat." She sighed. "All right. Give me a few minutes."

Just then Peter stirred and sat up. He blinked at Raoul, then turned.

"Hi, Mrs. Dawson," he said, then yawned.

"Hello yourself. It looks like you fell."

Peter nodded. "I broke my arm." He held up the cast, then glanced at Raoul. "It's Dallas Cowboys blue."

"I noticed that," Raoul said. "Are you going to let me sign your cast?"

"Uh-huh." The boy smiled shyly.

"Good."

Mrs. Dawson pulled up the other chair and sat across from them. "Peter, where have you been staying for the past few days?"

"With the lady next door." He gave the name.

"How long have your foster parents been gone?"

Peter shrugged. "A while."

Mrs. Dawson's expression stayed friendly. "Since the weekend?"

Peter wrinkled his nose. "Before that, I think."

"I see. Do you know when they'll be back?"

He shook his head, then cradled his arm against his chest. "Are they gonna be mad because I got hurt?"

"Of course not," she said firmly. "They'll be happy

you're all right. We all are." She paused. "You know what I think?"

"What?" Peter asked suspiciously.

"I think you probably need a little ice cream. I know they have some down in the cafeteria. If you don't mind, I'm going to get you some."

Relief showed in Peter's expression. He grinned. "I don't mind."

"That's very nice of you. But you know, it's a big hospital. Would you mind if Mr. Moreno showed me the way?"

"Okay."

Raoul wasn't sure what the social worker was up to, but he stood and put Peter back on the bed. "I might have some silver-star stickers at my office," he said. "I'll check tomorrow and if I do, we can put some on your cast."

The boy grinned.

Mrs. Miller moved toward him. "I'll wait for you here," she said.

Raoul followed Mrs. Dawson into the hallway.

"The cafeteria is that way," she said, pointing.

"So you don't need my help finding it."

"I wanted a chance to talk to you. I assume you have people in town who know you?"

"Yes," he said cautiously.

"Good. That will help us push through the paperwork. I know a sympathetic judge. If you'll give me two or three people to use as character references, we can get this done in an hour or so."

"Get what done?"

Mrs. Dawson stopped and stared at him. "Having

Peter stay with you until his foster parents return and we can figure out if it's safe for him to go back with them, of course."

PIA ARRIVED AT RAOUL'S place at seven. There'd been so much to carry, she'd had to drive. Now she grabbed two shopping bags and headed toward the front door. He had it open before she made it to the small porch.

"What's all that?" he asked.

"Dinner for many days to come. There's more in the car."

"More what?"

Poor man, she thought, handing him the bags. "Food. Word got out about you taking in Peter. People didn't know when you'd get home, so they brought it to me."

He was still standing there looking confused when she went back to her car for the second load. She collected the last three bags, shut her car door with her hip, then returned to the house.

"I don't understand," Raoul said, following her to the kitchen.

"Pia!"

She turned and saw Peter running toward her. He had a cast on his skinny forearm and had already changed into race-car pajamas.

"Hey, you," she said, putting her bags on the kitchen table. "What happened?"

"I fell." He held out his cast. "See."

"Very impressive. Does it hurt?"

"No. I have drops."

Some kind of pain medicine, she would guess. "Cool. Have you had dinner?"

Peter shook his head. "Just ice cream."

Pia raised her eyebrows.

"Don't look at me," Raoul told her. "It was Mrs. Dawson's idea."

"A likely story," Pia teased, then shrugged out of her coat and hung it on the back of a chair. "So, what are we in the mood for? There are lots of choices."

She moved to the counter and started taking casserole dishes out of the various bags. "Lasagna, always a favorite. Seven-layer tamale pie." She read each item as she set it down. "Chicken-and-noodle casserole, a vegetable bake." She wrinkled her nose at Peter. "Probably not that one, huh?"

He laughed. "I like lasagna."

"Me, too." She glanced at Raoul. "Would you set the oven to three-fifty? It's not frozen, so it won't take long to heat up."

He stood there, staring at her. "I don't understand."

She faced him. "When people heard that Peter would be staying with you for a few days, they brought food to help out. So you don't have to cook dinner every night."

"How did they hear?"

"Someone told them. Have you learned nothing about small-town living?"

She turned on the oven, then walked to the fridge. "Tell me the freezer's empty, because you have food for days."

He nodded, still looking shell-shocked.

"Why don't you go help Peter wash his hands? You know the cast can't get wet, right?"

"Yes."

"Good. I'll get things together in here. I'll leave two dinners in the refrigerator for the next couple of nights.

Oh, and there are stickers in that white bag. For your cast."

"Cool!" Peter reached into the bag and pulled out the sheet of stickers. "Can we put them on now?"

Raoul looked at her. She laughed. "Go ahead. Dinner will be ready in about thirty minutes."

They left the kitchen. A few minutes later, Raoul was back.

"I'm sorry," he told her.

"For what?"

"We were supposed to have dinner together to-night."

"We are."

"Not like this," he said. "I don't know exactly how it happened. One second the social worker was talking, the next I had a kid."

She patted her stomach. "I know the feeling."

"You're not mad?"

"Why would I be? Peter's all alone, he's hurt and no one knows where his foster parents are. You stepped up. Honestly, it makes you even nicer."

"You hate nice."

"I'm making an exception."

"Okay. Thanks."

He disappeared down the hall.

She stared after him, telling herself that just because he was a great guy didn't mean it was safe to open her heart to him.

BY THE TIME THEY FINISHED dinner and got Peter settled in Raoul's spare bedroom, it was after nine. Pia curled up on the sofa, telling herself that she had to get it together and head home. Despite not having many symptoms of her pregnancy to date, she was a little more tired than usual. Raoul sat at the other end of the couch, angled toward her.

"Thanks for everything," he said.

"I just showed up with other people's effort. There's nothing to thank me for."

"Poor kid." Raoul sipped his beer. "Talk about a hell of a situation."

"They really don't know where his foster parents are?"

"That's what Mrs. Dawson said. I hope they investigate them when they finally get back. Peter hasn't said anything bad about them, but there are a few red flags."

He'd already told her about the possibility that the kid wasn't getting enough to eat. There was no excuse for neglect, she thought. But that didn't stop it from happening.

He set down the bottle. "I had other plans for the evening," he told her.

For a second she thought he meant sex. Her body reacted with an internal happy dance, and various parts of her went on alert.

He pulled open a small drawer from the underside of the coffee table and withdrew a small, square lavender jewelry box. She recognized the color and the design on the box. Jenel's Gems was known for elegant, upscale, one-of-a-kind designs.

Her throat went dry and she had an odd and unexpected sense of shyness. The wanting faded as confusion took its place.

"I don't understand," she said.

"We're getting married," he reminded her. "I believe an engagement ring is traditional."

"Yes, but..." Theirs wasn't a traditional engagement. "I wasn't expecting anything. You don't have to do this."

"I want to."

He eased toward her and took her left hand in his. "Pia, thank you for agreeing to marry me. We're going to make this work. I'll be there for you, no matter what."

His words made her ache. They were exactly what she'd always wanted to hear...almost.

"I'll be there for you, too," she whispered.

He smiled, then opened the box.

If she hadn't been sitting, she would have fallen. The ring was incredible. Beautiful and sparkling, and large enough to make her nervous.

"The two diamond bands are wedding bands," he said. "If you don't like them, we can get something else."

"They're wonderful. Everything is stunning, but it's too much." She looked at him. "I would have been fine with a simple gold band."

"Are you saying you're not a diamond kind of girl?"

She returned her attention to the ring. "I haven't been."

"Then we need to change that."

He drew out the engagement ring, then slid it on her finger. The fit was perfect. She stared down at the diamonds glinting on her finger.

"Thank you," she told him.

"You're welcome."

He wrapped both arms around her and held her

against him. She closed her eyes and told herself everything would be fine. That she was making the right decision. Love would have been nice, but wasn't it better to sacrifice that silly dream in order to make sure Crystal's babies would be taken care of their whole lives? Isn't that what her friend would have wanted?

CHAPTER THIRTEEN

RAOUL SPENT A SLEEPLESS night. Not that Peter was a problem, but because he kept getting up to check on the kid. But the boy never stirred.

They both woke up to Raoul's alarm, then had a busy morning of getting ready. The plastic sleeve the hospital had provided protected the cast while Peter showered. The kid had managed to dress himself, except for tying his shoes, and had shown up at the kitchen table hair damp, face smiling, eyes eager.

"What's for breakfast?" he asked.

"Waffles."

Those green eyes got bigger. "You know how to make waffles?"

Raoul showed him the waffle maker he'd bought a few months ago after wandering through a big-box store and seeing a demonstration.

"That is so cool!" Peter told him.

He scrambled out of his seat and hurried around to watch as Raoul finished mixing the batter.

"Here's the cup we use," Raoul said, pointing to the plastic container with a big pour spout. "Go ahead and fill it to the line there."

"I can do it?"

"Sure."

Peter's break was in his left forearm, and he was right-handed.

The boy carefully dipped the cup into the batter and scooped up the right amount. Raoul raised the lid on the waffle maker.

"Go ahead and pour it in the center. It's already hot so it will spread out on its own."

Peter did as instructed, then watched as the batter oozed out along the grid. "It's not filling in all the way."

"I know, but this is the fun part."

Raoul closed the waffle maker, locked the two handles together, then spun it until it was upside down.

"Whoa!" Peter stared. "That's the best."

"Want to do the second one?"

"Sure."

Raoul watched him, pleased the boy seemed rested and not in any pain. He was easy to be with. Bright and curious. When he thought about the fact that his foster parents might not be taking good care of him, he wanted to find them—or at least the dad—and beat the shit out of him.

Not an option, he reminded himself. He would trust the system to work this out. But just in case, he would talk to Dakota about what steps he could take to make sure Peter was in a safe environment.

But when he got to his office, after dropping Peter off at camp, Dakota wasn't there. She'd left early the day before. He checked the machine to see if she'd called in sick, but there wasn't any message.

By ten, he was worried and wondering whom to talk to. Just when he picked up the phone to call Pia, Dakota walked in.

She looked like hell. Her face was pale, her eyes red and swollen. There was an air of grief and loss about her, as if something important to her had been taken away from her. He was on his feet the second he saw her.

"What happened?" he demanded.

She shook her head. "Nothing."

"It's not nothing. Were you in an accident? Did someone hurt you?"

If she'd had a boyfriend, he would assume he'd beaten her or slept with her best friend. But as far as he knew, Dakota wasn't dating.

"I'm fine," she said, her mouth trembling as she spoke. "You have to believe me."

"Then you need to be more convincing."

She forced a smile that was more ghoulish than happy. "How's that?"

"Frightening."

She sighed. "I'm fine. I know I look bad. I'm not hurt, I'm not sick." She swallowed. "Everything is how it's always been."

"Dakota, get real. Something happened."

"No, it didn't." Tears filled her eyes. "It didn't." The tears spilled down her cheeks.

Instinctively, he walked toward her, but she shook her head and backed away.

"I'm sorry," she whispered. "I can't do this. I can't be here today. I need a day or two. Sick days, vacation days, whatever you want."

He felt helpless and confused. "Take whatever time you need. Can I call someone? One of your sisters? Your mom?"

"No. No one. I'm fine. I have to go."

With that she grabbed her purse and practically ran

out of the office. Raoul stared after her, not sure what he was supposed to do now. Let her go? Follow her? Call a friend?

She wasn't physically hurt—he could figure out that much. So what had happened? Had she heard bad news? But if there'd been a disaster in the family, he would have heard about it. News traveled fast in Fool's Gold.

He would give her time, he decided. If she wasn't back at work in a couple of days, he would go talk to her. If she wouldn't talk to him, he would insist she talk to someone else.

PIA STUDIED THE SIGNS and did her best not to shudder. Bad enough that busloads of men were pouring into town. Worse that there was going to be a bachelor auction.

It was embarrassing. Not for her specifically, but for the town.

"I just don't like this," she said.

Montana grinned. "That's because you already have a good guy in your life."

"Even if I didn't, this would scare me. Who are these guys? What do they want?"

"If you have to ask the question, then Raoul is doing something very, very wrong."

Pia turned away from her friend and did her best not to blush. "I'm newly pregnant. We're not…you know."

"I guess it would be weird to have sex knowing that someone else's embryos are growing inside of you."

Pia winced. "Thank you for spelling that out so clearly."

"Am I wrong?"

"No, but still."

Montana grinned. "So, did you ever…you know? Before the pregnancy?"

Pia thought about that amazing night. "Once," she admitted, then waited to be struck by lightning for the lie. "Actually it was one evening, but several times."

"Impressive. A man with stamina."

"It is an appealing characteristic." Although she was sure there would come a time when it was safe for them to do the wild thing while she was pregnant, she had a feeling she was going to have to wait until after the babies were born to have a repeat performance of that one, magical night.

"He did set the standard really high," she added, "and we should talk about something else. How's your sex life?"

"Nonexistent."

"Then you should check out the new guys."

"No, thanks." Montana stapled the cardboard handles onto the auction paddles. "I'm focusing on my career right now."

"You got the job?"

Montana grinned. "I did and I love it. The dogs are so great. Well-trained and friendly. Max is the best, too. He's really patient. I'm doing lots of reading and I've started my online class. I'm going to Sacramento in a few weeks for an intense three-week training seminar. Max is even paying for that, if you can believe it."

"You like Max," Pia said, pleased to see her friend so happy.

"Of course. He's so nice and he knows everything about dogs and…" Montana wrinkled her nose. "Um, no. Don't even go there."

"Office romances are very stylish."

"It's not like that. He's in his fifties and even if he wasn't, I admire him. I don't want a romantic relationship with him. We're friends."

"If you say so."

"I do." She nudged Pia. "It's already happening. You're engaged and now you want everyone else paired up."

"I don't. I just want my friends to be happy and if—" She paused as she saw Montana's eyes practically bug out of her head. "What?"

"The ring. It's incredible."

Pia resisted the urge to tuck her hand behind her back. She loved her engagement ring, but she was having a little trouble getting used to it. And not apologizing for it. The stones were stunning and the whole thing was so bright, it was practically a light source.

"Raoul picked it out," she murmured.

"Does he have a brother?"

Something she should know, but didn't. "I can ask."

Montana grabbed her hand and stared at the ring. "I love it more than life."

"Thanks."

"Make you a little nervous?"

"Some. Nothing about the situation feels real to me. Not the engagement or even being pregnant." She lowered her voice. "I've peed on a stick and had an ultrasound. I'm really, really pregnant. So why don't I feel different?"

"You've gone through a lot in a very short period of time. You'll get there."

"I hope." Although Pia was starting to have her doubts. Maybe there was something wrong with her.

"What if I can't bond with the babies when they're born? What if I can't love them?"

"You won't have a choice. You're going to be a great mom, Pia. Stop doubting yourself."

Pia put down the signs. "I want to believe you, but I can't. Both my parents left me. So has every guy I've ever cared about. I want to think it will be different with Raoul and the babies, but I'm not sure."

"Raoul's not going anywhere. He's a good guy."

He was a guy who was marrying her to get a ready-made family. Not because he was crazy in love with her.

"Besides," Montana continued. "You never know how things are going to work out. My parents loved each other every day of their marriage. When my dad died, we were all scared Mom wasn't going to make it. But he wasn't the only love of her life."

Pia hadn't heard that. "What do you mean?"

Montana grinned. "She has a tattoo on her hip. It says Max."

"Your Max?"

"No. He's new to the area. The tattoo is old. Over the years, Dakota, Nevada and I have tried to find out who he is, and Mom isn't saying a word. My point is, love happens. You're going to do great with the babies and I'm guessing Raoul is going to fall madly in love with you. You'll see."

RAOUL PARKED IN FRONT of the large house. "I know it's old," he told Pia, "but I had Ethan go over the whole thing and it's sound. The floor plan is great. Plenty of bedrooms, a large kitchen, which needs to be gutted, but then you could have everything you wanted. There's a big yard out back, some great trees for climbing. It's the perfect family home."

He waited anxiously while Pia glanced at the three-story house with round eyes. It was in one of the older neighborhoods in town—an affluent section built in the 1920s. The second he'd seen the house, he'd known it was exactly what he'd been looking for.

"There are eight bedrooms, including three on the third story. The second story has a decent-size master, but I thought we could tear down the wall between it and the smallest bedroom to expand it. Upgrade the bathroom, make the closet bigger."

She turned to him, her expression unreadable. "Because you have a lot of shoes?"

"I know you do. It's a chick thing."

"I guess it is."

She didn't seem that excited about the house. "Are you okay?" he asked. "Don't you like the place?"

"It has potential," she said, opening the car door. "We should go inside."

He followed her, wondering what was going on with the women in his life. Dakota had returned to work the next day, but she still wasn't herself. He'd asked what was wrong several times and she kept insisting everything was fine. Too bad she was a lousy liar. And now Pia was acting strangely.

He followed her up to the front porch. It was as wide as the house and several feet deep.

"Are you mad because I went looking at houses without you?" he asked.

"No. You said you were going to. It's fine."

He thought about mentioning he'd brought Peter with

him the previous day and the kid had loved the house, but he wasn't sure it would help.

"I know I've been busy," he said as he fished the key out of his jacket pocket. "Having Peter around. His foster parents are due back in a couple of days. Mrs. Dawson has been investigating them and can't find any kind of trouble, so he'll be going back to them."

She turned to him and pressed her hand against his chest. "Raoul, I'm not mad because you're taking care of a little boy who's hurt. I think it's wonderful and amazing. In fact, I'd love to come to dinner with the two of you, before Peter has to leave. I'm not mad about the house. I'm not mad about anything."

"You swear?"

"Yes."

She raised herself on tiptoe. He bent down and kissed her.

The feel of her mouth against his, her body so close, made him want to pull her against him and take advantage of the empty house. One night with Pia hadn't been enough. But until he talked to her doctor about when it was okay to seduce Pia back into his bed, he wasn't going to do anything to put the babies in danger.

"Tonight?" he asked, knowing they were talking about dinner but wishing it were something else.

"Sure."

He opened the front door and led the way inside.

They stepped into a large two-story foyer. The formal living room was to the left, the dining room to the right. There was a study, an eat-in kitchen and a family room, all on this level.

"Let's start at the top," he said, pointing to the stairs.

"Okay."

He led the way. At the top floor, he pointed out the three bedrooms. There were several large linen closets off the hall.

"If we give up this closet," he said, pointing, "we can have a Jack-and-Jill bath. Now with three kids, it could still be a problem, so I talked to Ethan about turning this other one into a half bath. Just a toilet and sink."

"Uh-huh."

He showed her the three bedrooms. They were all about the same size, with sloped ceilings and bay windows with window seats.

"Great for reading," he said.

"Especially on rainy days. You'd need a bunch of cushions, though, and maybe some blankets."

He watched her cautiously. She was saying all the right things, but something was wrong. He felt it in his gut.

She led the way to the second floor. The master bedroom was in the back. He showed her the small bedroom that could be made part of the master suite, the hall bath that was huge and the excess of storage.

"It's nice," she said. "Lots of light and space. I really like the craftsman details."

They went to the main floor. He told her everything he wanted to do in the kitchen. Then he led the way to the study.

"This room is great," he told her. "I don't usually like paneling, but the combination of wood and windows really works. There are plenty of bookshelves."

He waited for her to walk in, but instead of looking at the room, she took a step to the side and tucked her hands behind her back.

"Pia?"

She seemed lost in thought. "You're going through a real estate agent, right? Josh doesn't own this house."

"He recommended someone. His houses are all smaller. With three kids coming, I knew we'd need something bigger."

She looked at him. "Did the agent say anything about the family who lived here before?"

"No." His gut clenched. "Did you know them?"

She nodded. "My family owned this house."

She'd lived here? Talk about being an idiot, he thought. "Why didn't you say something? Why did you let me give you a tour?"

"I wanted to know what it would be like to be back in the house. I wanted to know..." She stared at the study. "My father committed suicide in there. I'm the one who found the body."

PIA WAS PLEASED SHE could say the words without flinching. It was almost as if she were telling a story about someone else. Perhaps enough time had passed that the past didn't have any power over her, although she had her doubts.

She turned her back on the study and walked into the living room. This space was safer, she thought. Fewer memories.

"I had the whole third floor to myself," she told Raoul. "I slept in one room and had another set up with couches and a TV. My friends all came here because I had the cool parents who didn't care what we did. We could stay up all night, talk on the phone, even steal liquor from the cabinet in my dad's study. Whatever the hot thing was, I had it. Everyone envied me. They thought I was lucky."

He didn't speak, he just stood next to her, listening. She looked out the window because it was easier than seeing the pity in his eyes.

"It took me a while to figure out neither of them ever cared about me. I was just another way to show status. We only cared about how things looked, not how they were. I grew up selfish and mean. Having more clothes than I could ever wear didn't make up for having parents who never loved me. I resented the other kids who were smarter, or had a great family."

Involuntarily, she looked at him. Thankfully, there was no emotion in his expression.

"I was mean," she said flatly. "I tormented everyone who wasn't in my circle of friends. I made fun of them, spread rumors about them, told lies. And because of who my parents were, everyone believed me." She tried to smile and failed. "You would have hated me."

"I doubt that."

"You would have. And I would have deserved it." She was sure of it. "When I was sixteen, my father was charged with embezzling from his company. The news only got worse. He hadn't paid taxes or bills. I don't know where the money went. Maybe we spent it all. By the beginning of my senior year, it became clear that he was going to be charged with some serious crimes. Rather than face the felony charges, he put a gun to his head and pulled the trigger."

Raoul reached out to her, but she stepped back. He couldn't touch her—not now. If he did, she wouldn't be able to get through the story.

"I heard the noise and came running. I burst into his

study." She paused, willing herself to say the words, but not actually remembering what it had been like. "It's not the same as the movies. It's not that clean. There was blood everywhere."

She swallowed. "I called 9-1-1 and then I don't remember very much. My mom left for Florida and I went into foster care. Everything was different. I didn't have this house or half my things. And all those kids I'd tortured got their revenge. They made my life a living hell."

She turned to look out the window again. "I don't blame them. I deserved it."

"What about your mom? Did you want to go with her?"

She nodded. "She wouldn't let me. She said she needed time. There was no discussion about what I might need. She told me it was important for me to graduate with all my friends, and when I tried to tell her I didn't have friends anymore she wouldn't listen."

She folded her arms across her chest. "I don't know what happened to the house. If it was sold or repossessed or what. I finished school. My grades had never been better, probably because I didn't have any distractions. I was voted off the cheerleading team, my boyfriend dumped me. I applied for a part-time job with the city, which is how I got involved with what I do now. My mother didn't come back for my high school graduation and she made it clear I wouldn't be welcome in Florida. I haven't seen her since."

She felt him moving toward her and even though she wanted to duck away, she didn't have the energy. She was unable to move, even as his strong arms came around her and held her tight.

"I'm sorry," he murmured, his breath whispering across the side of her face. "I'm so sorry."

"I'm fine."

He turned her so they were facing each other and stared into her eyes. "You know what? You really are. You went through hell and survived."

She shrugged out of his embrace. "Don't be nice."

"Why not?"

"Because then I might believe you."

He studied her for a long time. She felt naked and vulnerable. Alone. Broken.

Then he pulled her close again and held on so tight it was hard to breathe. She should have wanted to pull away, but it felt good. Too good.

"You can believe in me," he told her. "I'm going to marry you, Pia. Nothing bad will ever happen to you again."

She closed her eyes and let herself lean into him. "You can't promise that."

"I know, but I'll do my best." He released her just enough to cup her face in his hands, then he kissed her. "No one is ever going to leave you again."

His words made her eyes burn.

He cleared his throat. "Given what happened this time, you should probably pick the next house."

Despite everything she laughed. "You think?"

He kissed her again. "Are you going to be okay?"

She nodded. From the safety of his arms, she had a feeling everything was going to be just fine.

CHAPTER FOURTEEN

THE BACHELOR AUCTION and talent show were being held in the Fool's Gold Convention Center, a grand term for a cement-and-block-wall structure that had been planned as a big-box store. Twenty years ago some local contractor—long since out of business—had subscribed to the philosophy of "if you build it, they will come." He'd built it and no one had shown up to rent the space. The city had bought the building and used it for various events.

The advantage was plenty of open space that could be broken up into nearly any size room. About ten years ago, the interior had been updated with a huge industrial kitchen and lots of bathrooms. Pia had taken over about half the building for the night. The place wasn't exactly elegant, but it was functional and free, which was important, given her meager budget.

A stage had been assembled at one end, and several city workers were setting up chairs. Off to the side the banner proclaiming Fool's Gold's Bachelor Auction had yet to be hung and she did her best to avoid looking at it. Talk about a hideous event. The talent show was only going to make things worse. No doubt all the media attending would go out of their way to make the town look like a refuge for men-starved women of a certain age.

Because her days weren't already crammed with plenty to do, Raoul had called that morning and informed her his former coach was visiting. Pia knew how much Hawk had meant to him. No doubt he was looking forward to the visit. Pia, on the other hand, was having a case of nerves brought on by meeting the emotional equivalent of the in-laws. Hawk was bringing his wife, Nicole.

She had no idea if Raoul was going to tell them the truth about the engagement, and honestly she couldn't decide which she wanted. Faking being in love in front of the two people who cared about Raoul most seemed like a challenge. But if they knew what was really happening, wouldn't they try to talk him out of it? And as freakish as the idea of marrying for reasons of practicality might be, Pia had found herself depending on the fact that Raoul was going to be there for her.

Dakota crossed the cement floor of the convention center, her arms filled with an overflowing box of auction paddles. "Do you really think we're going to need this many?"

Pia nodded. "Oh, yes. We're having quite the turnout. It's not just ladies from Fool's Gold who will be attending. We're pulling them in from the whole county."

"Lucky us."

Montana followed her sister. She had a box full of programs for the talent show. "Did you look at these?" she asked. "There's a woman who's dancing with her dog."

Pia led them to the table against the wall. "I saw her audition. It's not as scary as it sounds. They both do ballet."

The sisters stared at her.

Dakota set down her box. "On what planet isn't that scary?"

"At least they're not dancing together."

"Okay," Montana said slowly, lowering her box to the table. "Tell me it's not a poodle."

Pia pressed her lips together. "Sorry. It's a big one, if that helps."

"It doesn't."

They all laughed, although Dakota's amusement seemed a little forced. Montana must have noticed that as well, because she turned to her sister.

"Are you okay? You don't seem perky."

"I'm perky."

"Want to take a vote?" Montana asked.

Dakota shrugged. "I'm thinking about some stuff in my life. Reevaluating. I feel as if I've been drifting."

That was news to Pia. "Drifting how?"

Montana sank into a folding chair. "Oh, God. If you getting your PhD and helping children is drifting, what does that make me? An earthworm?"

"It's not about what I do," Dakota said. "Getting the work done isn't the point. You have so much passion for your life. I feel like I'm going through the motions. I'm not sure what's important to me. I'm not dating, but it doesn't really bother me. I want to wake up excited about my life." She shrugged. "I have some thinking to do."

Pia had to agree with Montana. Dakota was one of the most together women she knew. It was kind of scary to think someone she'd always thought of as borderline perfect had issues. If Dakota had trouble figuring things out, what hope did the rest of them have?

Montana crossed to her sister and hugged her. "I want you to be happy."

"I *am* happy."

Montana shook her head. "You're not."

Dakota smiled. "Okay. Then I will be. How's that?"

"Better," Montana said. "I love you."

"I love you, too."

Pia felt her throat get a little tight as she watched the sisters hug each other. She'd always wondered what it would be like to grow up with a sibling. While she would never know, Crystal's babies would have that experience.

She lightly touched her stomach. "You're always going to have each other," she whispered. "Won't that be great?"

Before the moment could spiral into a hugging, tearful vat of emotion, two other women approached. Pia recognized one as a head nurse from the hospital. The other was a lawyer in town. Both were in their fifties, with the lawyer slightly closer to sixty than her friend.

Bea, the lawyer, stopped in front of Pia. "About this auction," she began without a greeting. "Have you vetted the men? Done background checks? Will they have papers?"

Pia had worked with Bea before and was used to her abrupt style. "They're coming to a dinner-dance, not immigrating into the country. What kind of papers are you looking for?"

"How do we know they're safe?"

Pia sighed. "Buyer beware."

Bea's friend, Nina, smiled at Pia. "Will there be a

preview? Can we look them over before we bid? Is there a list of what they will or won't do?"

Crap, crap, crap. "We're sponsoring the auction, ladies. We're talking dinner and dancing, not anything else."

Bea snorted. "She thinks you're looking for sex, Nina."

Nina, a petite brunette, flushed. "Oh, no. Not that. I was wondering if I could ask the guy to clean out my gutters. There's a lot of leaves up there and I hate getting on a ladder."

Gutters? From the corner of her eye, Pia saw Dakota and Montana trying not to laugh.

"You win a night that includes dinner and dancing," Pia repeated, telling herself it was important to be patient. "The woman pays. Proceeds from the auction itself go to the city for various charity projects."

"Who needs a man for dancing?" Bea muttered. "I'm too old to care about that."

Nina tilted her head. "I don't know. A night of dancing sounds kind of nice."

"There are plenty of young women who'll be in competition with you, Nina. Bidding against you."

Nina grinned. "Yes, but being of a certain age has advantages. We have more money."

Bea didn't look amused. "Perhaps you should use some of that precious money of yours to hire someone to clean out your gutters."

"You're always so crabby," Nina complained, then turned back to Pia. "Thanks for the information. I guess I'm going to have to find another way to get the gutters cleaned."

"Pick up the phone book," Bea muttered. "I know you can spell."

The two women walked away.

"I thought the auction was going to be boring," Montana admitted when Bea and Nina were out of earshot. "But now I can't wait to be here."

"Are you going to bid?" Dakota asked.

"No, but I'm bringing popcorn. Talk about a show."

Pia sank into a chair and rubbed her temples. "I don't get paid enough to do this."

"Probably not," Dakota said cheerfully, "but at least it's never boring."

"Right now, boring sounds really, really good."

RAOUL WALKED ONTO THE playground at the mountain school only to find himself surrounded by kids.

"Come play with us."

"No, me."

"Can you help me throw harder?"

"We want to jump rope. Will you hold the rope?"

Raoul felt like the leader of a very short tribe. He raised his hands in the air. "I'm here to check on my main man. Then we'll talk about playing."

There were a few grumbles, but the kids fell back, allowing him to walk over to Peter and his friends. The boy grinned when he saw Raoul and launched himself at him. Raoul caught him easily.

"How are you doing?" he asked the boy. "All settled?"

Peter had returned to his foster home the previous afternoon. Mrs. Dawson had done a thorough investigation and while she admitted the Folios weren't her favorite family, she couldn't remove a child based on a feeling. There had to be something closer to proof.

The boy hung on to Raoul. "It's okay. They're being really nice. Don says he's going to sue the school 'cause of my fall. But I don't know who Sue is."

Raoul put down the boy and made a mental note to talk to Don about his plan. If he thought he could get some easy money out of the school district and keep it for himself, he was about to have a change in attitude.

"I've been practicing throwing," Peter continued happily.

"Just throwing, right? No catching."

The kid sighed. "I know. Not until my arm is better."

"If you want to play football, you need to be strong all over. That means letting your arm heal."

"Will I be as big as you?"

"I don't know." Raoul didn't have any details about Peter's real parents. He wondered if he could ask around and get some information. "Want to show me what you can do?"

"Uh-huh."

Peter ran over to the box of balls. Several other boys spotted what he was doing and followed. Raoul quickly organized them into groups and had them throwing back and forth to each other, like in a training camp.

"Good," he said, walking behind them, watching them throw. "Billy, straighten that arm. Your strength is in your shoulder, not your wrist. Nice, Trevor. Great follow-through."

He felt someone tug on his jacket and looked down to see a girl in glasses and pigtails staring up at him.

"Can I throw, too?" she asked.

The boy closest shook his head. "No girls. Go away."

The girl ignored him. "I want to learn."

"Girls play, too," Raoul said, leading her to the end of the line. He motioned for Jackson to throw him a ball, then get in position to catch. "Why don't you show me what you can do."

The girl took the ball, pushed up her glasses, then threw the baseball with enough power to make a pop when it hit the glove. Jackson winced.

Raoul grinned. "You've got quite an arm there, young lady."

"I want to be able to hit my big brother in the head and knock him out. He's always teasing me."

"Okay. I'm happy to help you with your throwing, but you have to promise never to aim at your brother's head. The way you throw, you could hurt him really bad."

Her eyes widened. "He says I'm a weak, whiny girl."

"Probably because you're better than him."

She beamed. "I never thought about that."

Dakota walked up. "Creating dissension between the sexes at such a young age?"

"I'm not that young."

She laughed. "You know what I meant."

"I do." He studied her, seeing that she looked rested and a lot less sad. "You're feeling better."

"I am.

"Good. Want to talk about what happened?"

"No."

The bell rang, indicating that it was time to head back into class. The kids threw the balls and gloves into the box and raced past them. Peter looked back and waved.

"You did good with him," Dakota said.

"He made it easy."

"You hold yourself back from most of the kids, but with him, you're different."

They walked toward the main building. He wasn't surprised she'd figured out the truth about him.

"Old habit," he said.

"I'm sure there are a lot of reasons," she said. "The fame, for one thing. You can't know who's interested in you for you or because they want something."

"Less of an issue now."

"Possibly. Plus I would guess there are just too many kids to help individually. You can't be in more than one place at once. So you created the camp to help as many kids as you can. It has the added benefit of allowing you to keep your distance."

"You really feel the need to use your psychology degree, don't you?"

"Sometimes. It can be very flashy at parties."

He knew she was right about all of it. He did hold himself back. He'd been burned plenty of times in college and during his first few years in the NFL. Finally he'd learned the lesson that helping from a distance was a whole lot easier.

Since things had gone bad with Caro, it was also smarter. Her betrayal had shaken him on many levels. She'd made him question his ability to read someone.

"You don't have to do anything at all," Dakota said. "It's not required."

"Sure it is. I was taught that if life gives you advantages, you give back."

"Your former coach?"

"Uh-huh. If I wasn't doing something, he'd come down here and kick my ass."

She smiled. "Cheap talk. You didn't buy this camp for him. You bought it because you wanted to."

He shrugged. "Hawk can be the voice in my head, telling me what to do."

"My mom is that for me. I think it's a good thing."

"Psychologically sound?" he asked.

She laughed. "Definitely. I think it's important to stay on the side of sanity."

"You're the professional." He held open the door to the main building.

"How's Pia doing?" she asked.

"Good. Why?"

"Aren't Hawk and his wife coming to visit for a couple of days?"

"Sure."

"Technically they don't qualify as family, but emotionally, these are the in-laws. Don't you think that's going to make her nervous?"

He hadn't thought of it that way. "There's nothing for her to worry about. They'll like her."

Dakota's expression turned pitying. "You've been married before. Do you really think that's what she's sitting around thinking?"

His face fell. "Oh. Right. I should probably go talk to her, huh?"

Dakota patted his arm. "Don't take it personally. You can't help it, just being a man and all."

PIA TOLD HERSELF THAT pacing counted as exercise and exercise was healthy. It's not as if her body knew she was wearing a path in Raoul's carpet rather than striding through the park or doing time on a treadmill. Life was about reframing, she told herself.

"Would you relax?" Raoul walked into the living room and crossed to her. After putting his hands on her shoulders, he leaned in and kissed her. "They're going to love you."

"Do you have proof? Because proof would be nice."

"They'll love you," he repeated.

"Saying something over and over again doesn't make it happen. No matter how many times I tell you I'm a giraffe, you're not going to believe me."

He eyed her. "Have you had coffee today?"

"No. This isn't me hyped on caffeine. I'm doing this all myself."

"You should try breathing."

As if that would help. "What if I don't want to meet them?" she asked. "I'm sure they're very nice people, but this all seems so unnecessary. I'll be taking up your visiting time. Why don't you meet them by yourself and tell me about it. You can take pictures. It'll be like I was there."

"I'd rather you *were* there."

"Think of the babies. All this stress can't be good for them. I think I need to throw up."

"Relax," he said softly, right before he kissed her.

It was a good kiss, too, damn him. One that lingered and made her feel all melty inside.

"That's cheating," she said when he straightened.

"I prefer to think of it as getting the job done."

"It's still cheating."

He stared into her eyes. "I'm going to marry you,

Pia. Hawk and Nicole are my family, so they'll be part of your life, as well. Why put off the inevitable?"

"Because putting it off makes me feel better." She heard the sound of a car pulling into the driveway. Her stomach twisted. "I think they're here."

He took her hand and led her to the front door, then stepped outside.

A large four-door BMW pulled up. Pia wasn't sure there was a name or number, mostly because she couldn't tell one fancy car from the other. Okay, it was green, but that was the best she could do.

As she thought seriously about throwing up, she watched a tall, good-looking man step out. Based on what she knew about Hawk, he had to be in his late forties, but he looked a lot younger. Then his wife got out of the car. She was a beautiful, elegant blonde. Despite the jeans and button-down shirt, she looked sophisticated—like the kind of woman who always knew what to say.

Pia held in a whimper.

"You made it," Raoul said as he stepped off the porch. He walked to Hawk and the two men hugged. Nicole joined them. Raoul kissed her cheek. She held on to him for several seconds before letting go and stepping back.

"Small-town life agrees with you," she said. "You look good."

"Always," Raoul said with a laugh. "Come meet Pia."

She'd agonized about what to wear, wanting to make a good impression without trying too hard. There was also the pregnancy to consider. Despite having puffy and bloated moments, she wasn't really showing. In the end, she'd settled on a tunic-length forest green top over black jeans. As a tour of the town was on the agenda, she'd put on flats.

"Hello," she said, holding out her hand first to Hawk. "Nice to meet you."

"Didn't you warn her?" Hawk asked as he ignored the outstretched hand. Instead he grabbed her around her waist and pulled her into a bear hug. "Welcome to the family, Pia." He swung her around a full 360 degrees before setting her on the ground.

"Thanks," she managed while doing her best to regain her footing.

"You'll scare the poor girl," Nicole said, stepping close and hugging Pia more gently. "He's just a big lug of a man. You'll have to forgive him."

"Of course," Pia said, feeling a little disoriented. She'd been worried about Raoul's family judging her and being standoffish. Apparently that wasn't going to be a problem.

Nicole linked arms with her and they walked inside. "I understand you and Raoul are looking for a house. That's so fun. Hawk and I have been in our place forever now. And as much as I love my children, I am, I confess, delighted to be away from them for a few days."

"Raoul said you drove down from Seattle."

"Yes, we're going to Los Angeles."

"Road trip," Hawk said, coming in with Raoul. "One of my former students is playing for USC. We're going to catch a game, then drive home."

"I said let's fly," Nicole told Pia, her tone weary but her eyes bright with amusement. "We could have stopped in Sacramento and rented a car to come here. But no…"

She released Pia's arm. Hawk came up behind Nicole

and slipped his arms around her waist. "Are you saying you haven't enjoyed being in a hotel room with me for the past two nights?"

"Hawk! The children."

Pia wanted to point out that she was twenty-eight and that Raoul was a few years older than her, but she didn't. In a way it was kind of nice to have someone a little older than her worrying about her. It had been a lot of years since that had happened.

Hawk kissed his wife. "Nicole, I hate to break it to you, but they've already had sex. They know what it is."

Pia hoped she wasn't blushing.

Raoul caught her eye and grinned. "See what I have to deal with?"

Everyone laughed.

They settled on the sofa and chairs in the living room and talked. Nicole brought Raoul up to date on what her kids were doing. Hawk and Raoul talked football. Pia mostly listened. After about half an hour, Raoul stood.

"Let's do a tour of town. Then we can have lunch."

"Want us to drive?" Hawk asked.

Raoul shook his head. "We'll walk. There's not that much to see."

As they walked down the sidewalk, Pia noticed that Nicole kept pace with her while Hawk and Raoul seemed to be getting ahead of them. She recognized the separation of the sexes for what it was.

"Why don't you two meet us at the restaurant in an hour," Nicole called. "Go talk about sports. I get enough of that at home." The older woman smiled. "We can entertain ourselves until then."

Pia forced a smile and told herself that Nicole seemed really nice. Everything was going to be fine.

They strolled down by the park, toward the lake. Pia pointed out Morgan's Books, the store with the fabulous fudge and the entrance to her office. She noticed there were a lot more men out and about than usual, but she didn't want to bring that up. Telling Nicole about Fool's Gold's sudden influx of men would probably scare her.

They chatted about the weather, reality TV and how it would be a good thing if cropped pants never came back in style.

Nicole pointed to the Starbucks. "Come on. I'd kill for a latte."

When they had their drinks—a mocha for Nicole and an herbal tea for Pia—they settled at a table by the window. Pia did her best not to acknowledge the men watching them.

"Raoul mentioned you're in charge of the festivals in town," Nicole said. "Thanks for taking time off work to meet us."

"I wanted to," Pia said, telling herself that now that she'd met Nicole, it wasn't exactly a lie. "You're his family."

"He's been important to us for a long time." She glanced out the window and sighed. "I love it here. What a great place to grow up."

"We do have less rain than Seattle."

"I think the Amazon jungle has less rain than Seattle," Nicole joked. "I was worried about Raoul after his divorce. He couldn't figure out what to do with himself. I thought he'd come back home, but this is better. He needs to make his own way. Hawk was lucky. When he left the NFL, he knew he wanted to coach high school football. Not everyone is so clear."

"You know about the camp Raoul bought?" Pia asked.

"Uh-huh. It sounds great. And now there's a school up there?"

Pia explained about the fire. "It's probably going to take a couple of years for the regular school to be repaired. They're hoping to get the money quickly and get started, but who knows. Without the camp, the kids would have been shoved into already crowded schools."

"Raoul is hero material," Nicole said with a smile. "He gets that from Hawk."

From what she'd heard, the couple had been together for a long time, yet they were still obviously in love. Pia felt a twinge of envy. Loving someone that long, being loved…it had to feel very safe and yet exciting at the same time. For a second she allowed herself to imagine what it would be like to experience that herself. To have love grow stronger every year.

Longing filled her, a physical ache that made it difficult to breathe. She wasn't going to get that with Raoul. Theirs was a practical arrangement. Perhaps, with time, they would grow to love each other, but it wouldn't be the same, she thought sadly. The history of a courtship would never be there. The "falling in love" that made everything seem right in the world.

Nicole leaned over and touched Pia's left hand. "Beautiful ring."

"Thank you." She pressed her lips together, telling herself *not* to say she hadn't been expecting a ring at all—let alone one this amazing.

"We're happy Raoul's found someone."

The statement made Pia nervous. She couldn't tell if Nicole knew why they were getting married. Though she was willing to stay quiet on the whys of the engagement, she wasn't willing to lie about the pregnancy.

"Did Raoul tell you I was pregnant?" Pia asked.

Nicole raised her eyebrows, then laughed. "No, he didn't. How wonderful. Raoul's finally having a child. Excellent."

She felt as if she'd just stepped into something sticky. "Maybe I shouldn't have said anything."

Nicole laughed. "Much like pregnancy itself, there's no do-over. Sorry. Besides, I'm really happy. For what it's worth, I was pregnant when Hawk and I got married."

"Yes, but it was probably his baby."

To give her credit, Nicole barely blinked. She picked up her mocha, took a sip and said, "Why don't you start from the beginning?"

CHAPTER FIFTEEN

PIA EXPLAINED ABOUT Crystal and Keith and the embryos. "I'm still not sure why she left them to me, but she did and they're implanted and I'm pregnant."

"Triplets," Nicole said. "I'm a twin and I had twins, so I know what that's like. You're going to have three. That's a lot of diapers."

"I try not to think about it," Pia admitted. Or feedings, or getting them all to sleep at the same time. In fact, she was pretty much in denial.

"What did Raoul say when you told him what you wanted to do?" Nicole asked.

She was assuming they'd been dating, Pia thought. That the embryos had added an extra dimension to an already ongoing relationship.

"He offered to be my pregnancy buddy," she said, determined to stick to the truth as much as possible.

"That sounds like him." Nicole studied her. "You could have walked away from them."

"No," Pia said firmly. "I would never abandon them." She knew what that felt like.

"What about giving them to someone else?"

Pia shook her head. "Crystal left them to me. I may never know why, but I'll do the best I can with her children. She was my friend."

Nicole reached out and squeezed her hand. "You're nothing like Caro, are you?"

"I don't know much about her. What was she like?"

Nicole released her hand and leaned back in her chair. "Beautiful. Smart. She's a news anchor."

Pia already hated her. "Great."

Nicole laughed. "Please don't tell Raoul, but that was my reaction when I met her. She says all the right things, but I always had the feeling she would rather have been anywhere but with us. I want to say I'm sorry about their divorce, but honestly I was relieved. I'm so glad he found you."

"Me, too," Pia said. Maybe theirs wasn't the fantasy love every little girl dreamed of, but it was stable and solid and for her, that was going to be enough.

RAOUL AND HAWK made their way to Jo's Bar.

"Brace yourself," Raoul said as he pulled open the door. "It's not what you think."

Hawk stepped inside, then came to a stop as he stared at the big-screen TVs. Three were on the network soaps and the fourth was on a home shopping channel.

"What the hell?"

"Don't ask," Raoul told him, then glanced toward the bar. "Jo, could you send over two beers?"

"Sure. Going into your man cave?"

"As fast as we can." He pointed to the doorway off to the side. "Through there. You'll feel better."

The smaller room had a couple of pool tables, a couple of TVs tuned to sports and was a masculine dark blue color. A relief from the pink and lime green Jo had recently painted the main room. For once it was relatively crowded with men, most of whom Raoul didn't recognize.

Jo delivered the beers and left them with a bowl of pretzels.

"Interesting place," Hawk said, then took a sip of his beer. "You like it here."

Raoul nodded.

"Are you happy?" his former coach asked.

"Not a real masculine question," Raoul joked.

"I've been married nearly all my adult life," Hawk told him. "I can barely hang on to any masculinity. Just don't tell anyone I talk about my feelings."

"I won't say a word." Raoul rested his forearms on the table and looked at his mentor. "I'm happy. I didn't know what to expect when I moved here, but it's turning out even better than I thought."

"You have the camp."

Raoul explained how it was being used as a school. "It'll be a while until they're able to move back into their old building. We'll still have camp in the summer, when the local kids are out of school, but we've had to put our winter plans on hold."

"You okay with that?"

"I would have liked to get started with the math and science programs sooner rather than later, but they needed a place to have school. I'm not going to put three hundred kids out on the street because I have an ego problem."

Hawk slapped him on the shoulder. "I like hearing that. It means I did a good job raising you."

"It couldn't be my sterling character?"

"Not likely."

They laughed and clinked bottles.

"Pia seems nice," Hawk said.

"She is. She was born and raised here. I told you she runs all the festivals in town. It's a lot of coordinating, working with different people. When the school needed an emergency fundraiser and supply drive, she got it done in a couple of days." He glanced at his friend. "She's pregnant."

Hawk raised his eyebrows. "You okay with that?"

"Yeah. I'm happy." He hesitated. "The babies aren't mine."

Hawk picked up his beer bottle but didn't drink. "Okay," he said slowly. "Tell me about it."

Raoul explained about Crystal and the embryos.

"That's a lot to take on," Hawk said when he'd finished. "Responsibility, time, money. They're not going to be yours."

Raoul didn't fall for it. "They'll be mine. I'll be there when they're born and see them through their whole lives. How could they not be mine?"

Hawk didn't look convinced. "You doing this because of Caro? Are you secretly figuring it won't be as big a problem because they're not your biological children? You're wrong—they'll be yours in every sense of the word. You won't be able to hold back with them."

"I don't want to hold back."

"You sure about that?"

It was a question Raoul had wrestled with since finding out about Pia's plans for the embryos. He'd meant it when he'd promised to be there for her, to be a real father to those children.

"I want to be their father. I want to be involved with them, the way you were there for me. You might have come into my life when I was in high school, but that doesn't mean you didn't shape everything about me. I can do this. I want to do this."

Hawk took a long drink of his beer. "Kids aren't easy under the best of circumstances. Triplets. That's a load and a half."

Raoul grinned. "It's probably three loads."

"Smart-ass." Hawk shook his head. "You sure about this? Once you commit, there's no turning back."

"I'm sure." It was what he wanted.

"Make sure you get married for the right reasons."

Raoul could do the translation. Hawk wanted him to be sure he was marrying Pia because he loved her and couldn't live without her. Not because it was the right thing to do.

It was the only secret he would keep from his friend. The truth was, not loving Pia was part of the appeal. He'd been in love once, had married Caro and had paid the price. Never again, he'd promised himself, and he meant it.

"Pia's the one," he said, sidestepping the issue.

"Then I'm happy for you."

Raoul couldn't tell if Hawk believed him or was simply going along with things. In the end, he supposed it didn't matter. Whatever the outcome, Hawk would be there for him, just like he would be there for the babies Pia carried.

PIA LOOKED UP FROM HER desk to find Charity Jones-Golden standing in the doorway.

"You're busy," her friend said.

"I have the auction tonight, followed by the dinner-dance in a week. Busy doesn't cover it. Hysterical is closer. In fact, I think hysterical is pretty accurate."

"So you probably don't have time to go shopping."

Pia perked up. "I certainly do. In fact a little retail therapy is exactly what I need. On the way back, I'll grab a sandwich to eat at my desk and call it lunch."

Charity smiled. "Really? You'd do that for me?"

"Mostly I'm doing it for myself, but you can pretend it's about you if it makes you feel better." Pia saved her computer program, then closed it, grabbed her purse and stood. "What are we shopping for? Jewelry? Furniture? A vacation in the south of France?"

"Maternity clothes."

Pia plopped down on her seat, her gaze settling on her friend's growing tummy. "Tell me you're kidding."

"I need to buy some things, and you're way better at the stylish thing than I am. I want to look good as I approach my whale days. Or as good as I can. 'Help me, Obi Wan. You're my only hope.'"

"Oh, please. Don't try *Star Wars* on me. I'm too young to remember anything but the remastered versions, and so are you."

Charity continued to stare at her, all wide-eyed and pleading.

"Fine," Pia grumbled, standing again. "I'll help you buy your stupid maternity clothes."

"The point of bringing you along is so they're not stupid. Besides, you might want to get a few things for yourself. It took me a while to pop out of my regular clothes, but I'm not carrying triplets."

"Thanks for mentioning that."

"Anytime."

Pia followed her into the hallway, then locked the door. As they made their way down the stairs, she had to admit that Charity was right...sort of. Lately it had

seemed her pants were getting snug, and she would
swear her breasts had gone up a full cup size. She was
starting to spill out of her bras. In the few weeks between now and looking like a woman who had swallowed a beach ball, she could probably make some great
money posing for breast-enhancement ads.

"How are you feeling?" Charity asked. "Any morning
sickness?"

"I'm fine as long as I stick to crackers for the first
hour. Then I can pretty much eat what I want. Of course,
based on the list of things I should be eating, all those
fruits and vegetables, the protein and dairy, there's not
much room left for empty calories." She sighed. "I miss
empty calories."

"Me, too. And coffee. I would kill for a glass of
wine." She glanced at Pia. "Do you think it's wrong to
bring a saucy little Merlot into the recovery room?"

"I think they'd frown on it. Plus, won't you be
breastfeeding?"

They reached the street and turned left. There was
an exclusive maternity boutique right next to Jenel's
Gems.

"Breastfeeding is in the plan," Charity admitted. "Are
you?"

"I haven't gotten that far," Pia admitted. "I'm one
breast short, to begin with, so I'm not sure how it would
work. I'm not really doing a lot of reading yet. I have
time."

"Of course you do. It's nice that you're not totally
obsessed with your pregnancy. The first two months,
I couldn't stop reading about it, or talking about it. I
became one of those horrible, self-absorbed friends who
only cared about herself."

"I remember," Pia said, her voice teasing.

Charity gave her a mock glare. "A true friend wouldn't mention my slip in judgment."

"A true friend would have given you a good slap if it had continued much longer."

Charity laughed.

Pia joined in but was pleased when the conversation changed topic. In truth, the reason she hadn't started doing a lot of reading about her pregnancy had nothing to do with being calm and everything to do with the fact that she still didn't feel connected to the babies growing inside of her. They were an intellectual exercise, not an emotional bond. She knew she was pregnant, but those were just words.

In time things would get better, she told herself. From finding out about the embryos to implantation had only been a matter of a few weeks. It made sense that she would need time to catch up emotionally. At least that was the plan.

"Josh keeps saying we have to register." Charity grimaced. "I've gone online where they have those lists of what is 'essential,' and it's enough to freak me out. They talk about things I've never heard of. And some other stuff that's really weird. Do you know there's a device that keeps baby wipes warm? You drop in a container of wipes and it keeps them toasty. The reviews say not to get it because then the kids scream when you're away from home and have to use a cold baby wipe."

Pia felt the first hint of fear. "I have to make a decision about baby wipes? Can't I just buy what's on sale?"

"Sure, but then do you heat them? It's incredible. I swear, if you took along everything that they said, you wouldn't need a baby bag so much as a camel. And you'll have three times that amount."

Pia felt a little light-headed. "We should talk about something else," she murmured.

"And the diapers. Do you know how many diapers babies go through in an average week?"

"No," she whispered.

"Eighty to a hundred."

Charity kept talking, but Pia was too busy doing the math. With triplets, she could be looking at two hundred and forty to three hundred diapers in a week. If she used disposable ones, wouldn't she be personally responsible for any overflow in the Fool's Gold landfill?

Three hundred diapers? How many were in a box? Could she fit that many in her car? Was Raoul going to have to buy a semi to bring in supplies?

"That's pretty." Charity had stopped in front of the window of the maternity store. A pregnant mannequin wore a sophisticated burgundy pantsuit, with a fly-away-style jacket. The fabric was a high-quality knit that skimmed the body and held its shape but would probably wash like a dream.

"The color would be great for you," Pia said. "With your light hair."

"I wonder if the set comes with a skirt. Or I could get a black skirt and a patterned top. That would give me a lot of work outfits." She glanced at Pia. "Or am I being too matchy-matchy?"

"You're doing just fine. Let's go in and see what they have."

The store was larger than it looked from the outside. There was plenty of light, lots of mirrors and racks of clothes set up by type. In the back, an archway led into a massive separate store that sold everything baby. Pia caught sight of a stroller and crib before carefully averting her eyes. She was here to shop for her friend, not freak herself out. Later, when she could sit down, she would think about all the equipment babies apparently required and try not to hyperventilate. And maybe she would take Denise Hendrix up on her offer to explain what exactly the mother of a triplet needed three of and what she could avoid buying in bulk.

"Hi, ladies," a salesclerk called. "How are you doing?"

"Great," Charity said. "I'm browsing first."

"Let me know if I can help."

Pia wandered toward the dress racks. Maybe dresses would be easier, as they would give her more breathing room—so to speak. But as it got colder, she preferred pants or nice jeans. Plus, did she really want to deal with maternity tights or nylons?

She crossed over to the jeans and grimaced when she saw a very unattractive elastic kind of band thing stuck in front. Was that what she had to look forward to?

"Look at this," Charity said, pointing to a mannequin. "It's a tummy sleeve." She leaned in and read the sign. "Oh, this is great. It helps with transition. When you're too big for your regular pants but maternity ones are too big for you. It covers the open zipper." She grinned. "I wish I'd thought of that. You should get one."

What Pia should get is out of the store. She wasn't ready for any of this. Not yet. She was barely pregnant and she still hadn't accepted she was having one baby, let alone three.

She watched Charity collect several items of clothing, then waited while her friend tried them on.

"You look adorable in everything," Pia told her.

It was the truth. Charity genuinely glowed. She was pleasantly rounded, blissfully happy and excited about being a mother. Pia felt like a crabby fraud.

"You don't want to pick out anything?" Charity asked as she paid for her clothing.

Pia shook her head. "I'm not ready."

"I would guess with triplets, you're going to have to get ready soon. Is this where I ask you to come with me next door to look at furniture and you refuse?"

"I'll look."

Maybe poking around in a baby store would help. If nothing else, she could look for a book on multiple births. The books she had at home only had a chapter or two on multiples.

They walked through to the baby store. There were cribs and changing tables, mobiles and teddy bear lamps.

"Come see," Charity told her, pointing to the left. "There's a bedroom set I really love. But it's pretty girly and if we have a boy, I'm not sure it's appropriate."

Pia followed her friend to a display done in pale wood. The small nightstand, crib, dresser and changing table were all carved with fairies and angels, the edges scalloped. Pink-and-gold drawer pulls sparkled with a touch of glitter.

"Too girly doesn't describe it," Pia said with a grin. "I think it's great, but you need to make sure you're having a girl before you get this."

"It's too over the top for a boy?"

"It will give Josh a heart attack, and that's the last thing you want."

"I know." Charity sighed. "I had planned not to know

the sex of the baby until the birth. I thought that would be fun. I've always been such a planner. This seemed like the ultimate in letting go."

"Then you're going to have to let go on the furniture selection," Pia told her. "This is a whole new dimension of girly."

"You're right," Charity said, sounding reluctant. "What are you going to do?"

Pia turned to her. "About what?"

"Knowing the gender of the babies."

"I haven't really thought about it."

"From what I know about IVF, you're going to have fraternal rather than identical triplets," Charity said. "Three embryos mean they fertilized three different eggs. That could make things interesting. Does Raoul want to know?"

They hadn't talked about it, Pia realized. In fact they hadn't talked much about the babies at all. She didn't know anything about his thoughts on children, except he wanted them. What were his hopes and dreams for these babies? Did he spank or prefer time-outs? Would he want to know if they were having boys or girls?

She put her hand on the dresser to steady herself. There was more. They hadn't talked about financials or their goals for their lives. She didn't know what religion he was, if he opened his presents Christmas Eve or Christmas morning. They hadn't even discussed which way to load a dishwasher.

How could she have agreed to marry someone she didn't know at all? Shouldn't they have a plan to get to know each other? Of course, she was the same person who had blithely had her friend's babies implanted into her body without considering the future.

She was going to be the mother of three children. She was going to have to raise them for the next eighteen years. Longer if housing prices kept going up. She could barely take care of herself. There was the whole humiliating relationship failure with Jake, the cat.

"I can't do this," she said.

"What's wrong?" Crystal asked, sounding concerned.

Pia had to get out of there. She couldn't breathe, couldn't think.

She glanced at her watch. "I have to go. I have..." Her mind went blank, then rebooted and provided her with the perfect excuse. "I have a city council meeting tomorrow. I need to get back to work and prepare."

"Me, too," Crystal told her. "We're talking about the budget, which is a serious drag. Neither of us can have caffeine. How are we supposed to stay awake?"

Pia was amazed. She must still look and sound normal, when on the inside, she was seconds from a meltdown.

Somehow she made it back to her office. But instead of preparing for the meeting, she stood in her tiny bathroom, her arms braced against the sink.

The obvious question was what had she been thinking. But she knew the answer to that. She hadn't been. She'd been reacting to the loss of a dear friend. And now that she was pregnant, was she doing her very best to be informed? Had she made even one change in her life to support the babies?

Okay, sure she'd given up alcohol and caffeine and she was taking the vitamins and eating lots of fruits and vegetables. But was that enough? She hadn't known how many diapers a baby needed a day. She didn't want to look at furniture or maternity clothes. If Crystal really knew what she was like, she would be horrified to know her future children would be in Pia's custody. Because for the first time ever, the babies were finally real to her and she was terrified.

THE ENTIRE TOWN TURNED OUT for the auction. Pia stared at the huge crowd and found that being the object of so much male attention was kind of good for her emotionally fragile state.

Since arriving at the convention center, she'd been ogled, had her butt pinched twice and asked out more times than she could count.

There had to be at least three hundred guys milling around the open space and twice that many women. The concession stands were doing a brisk business, which meant plenty of income for the city. All good.

"Hey, pretty lady."

Pia glanced up from her clipboard and saw a tall, slightly grizzled older man smiling at her. He was missing a couple of teeth and needed a shave.

"You gonna bid on me tonight?" he asked, wiggling his eyebrows.

"Would that I could," she said with a heavy sigh. "But I'm pregnant."

His gaze dropped to her belly and he took a couple of steps back. "I'm not interested in no kids."

"I hear that a lot."

The man turned and nearly ran in the opposite direction. Montana hurried up to her.

"This is great. I can't wait for the talent show. Some guy just felt me up. I should probably be mad, but it's so strange, it's almost funny."

"Give it an hour," Pia told her. "It'll get annoying. I'm telling every guy who talks to me that I'm pregnant. It's very effective."

Dakota joined them. She had a soda in one hand and popcorn in the other. "The lady with the dancing dog is first up in the talent show. I can't wait."

Pia laughed. "This is a serious event, you two. Act accordingly."

"It's a woman dancing with her poodle," Dakota said with a laugh. "I do love this town."

Pia glanced around at the crowd filling the convention center. Despite the craziness, she loved it, too.

THE NEXT AFTERNOON, PIA managed to sit through the city council meeting without dozing off. Given her wild night at the auction, that was a serious accomplishment.

The performances had gone off on time, the bachelor auction had been nearly orderly. The more attractive men who claimed to have jobs had gone for the most money, and nothing really embarrassing had happened, which meant the media coverage should be relatively benign.

One crisis endured, forty-seven others waiting in the wings, she thought. At least the activities of last night had kept her from dwelling on her inadequacies as a potential mother.

She was trying and that should count, she told herself. As she got more pregnant, she would bond more with the babies. She promised herself she would read more and figure out what she was supposed to do next.

"We're hoping revenue from the influx of tourists helps," the city treasurer was saying.

"By tourists she means men," Mayor Marsha said with a heavy sigh. "Pia, the auction went very smoothly last night. Thank you for that."

"You're welcome. I don't have the money totals yet, but we made a lot. We're taking costs out of the auction proceeds, and then all the profits go directly to the city."

"I suppose if we have to be in the middle of this circus, we might as well benefit in some way," Marsha said. "What's next?"

Talk turned to budgeting. At one point, Charity tried to stifle a yawn, then caught Pia's gaze and grinned.

Pia nodded in agreement. Not exactly a topic to keep one up in anticipation. She shifted in her seat, feeling a faint cramping in her stomach. At first she didn't think anything about it. She listened to the latest information on the cause of the fire at the school and the projections for repair costs.

The cramps increased. She frowned as she tried to remember if her period was due. Usually she noted that on her calendar so she could be prepared with...

Dread swept through her. She wasn't going to get her period. She was pregnant. She shouldn't be cramping. Not like this.

"Oh, God," she breathed, terrified to move, not sure what to do.

Everyone turned to look at her. Another cramp hit her. This one was horrifyingly worse.

Then she felt it. A rush of something liquid. Involuntarily she stood and looked down. Blood pooled in the seat.

Pia began to scream.

CHAPTER SIXTEEN

PIA GULPED FOR AIR. Even as she gasped, she choked on a sob. Despite the nurse's insistence that she had to calm down, she couldn't stop crying.

The nurse held on to Pia's hand. "Honey, is there someone I can call? Do you want me to get your mom?"

The irony of the question only made Pia cry harder. Marsha would have phoned Raoul already, and he would get here as quickly as he could. There was no one else.

"I'm fine," Pia managed.

"You've got to quiet down. This isn't good for you or the babies."

Babies. Because there were two left. At least that's what the ultrasound had shown. Only one had been lost.

Pia did her best to slow her breathing. Getting upset only made things worse. She knew that, but she couldn't seem to control herself. Not when she knew she was to blame.

"Where is she?" a male voice asked from the hallway. "Pia O'Brian. She's my fiancée."

"Raoul!"

The nurse left her side and hurried to the open door. "In here."

Raoul rushed in and raced to her side. "Pia." He bent over her and took her hand in his, then kissed her forehead. "Are you all right?"

The worry and concern had her crying again. But instead of backing away, he leaned close and wrapped his arms around her.

She cried and cried until she felt empty inside. Until there was no way to find relief.

"I lost one of the babies," she said, the words hoarse in her swollen throat.

"I know." He smoothed her hair. "It's okay."

"It's not. It's not okay. I'm the reason. It's my fault." She felt her eyes fill again. Grabbing his hand with both of hers, she stared into his eyes. "It's my fault. I did this. They were never real to me. I didn't want to tell you, but they weren't. I knew in my head I was pregnant, but I didn't feel it. I wasn't maternal. The baby knew. It knew and now it's gone."

"Pia, no. That's not what happens."

"It is. I did it. I was out with Charity yesterday. She wanted to look at maternity clothes and I didn't. I didn't want to think about how big I'm going to get, or what's going to happen to my body. Then I freaked out about the furniture. I didn't even know how many diapers a baby uses in a week."

The tears flowed again, trickling down her cheeks. "Crystal trusted me. She trusted me and one of her babies is gone and I can't fix it. I can't make it better. I loved her and she believed in me and look what I've done."

Raoul shook his head. He looked uncomfortable and helpless. "Sometimes babies don't make it."

She raised her bed a little, so she could see him more

easily. "There's more. I'm the reason." She swallowed, knowing she had to tell him the truth, even if it meant he would walk away from her forever.

Maybe that would be for the best, she thought, feeling sick to her stomach. Then when the babies were born, he could have child protective services take them from her so she wouldn't damage them further.

"I got pregnant when I was in college."

RAOUL DIDN'T WANT TO HEAR anything more. He knew where the story was going, what she was going to say. Anger grew. He pulled his hand back.

Pia was talking. He forced himself to listen, to pretend he wasn't judging.

"I knew he wouldn't marry me, and I started…" She gasped for breath. "I started wishing the baby would go away. That's what I thought in my head. How everything would be better if it just went away."

She closed her eyes. The tears continued to flow, but they no longer touched him.

"Then it did," she whispered.

"It didn't go away," he said harshly. "You did something."

She nodded. "I know. The baby knew or sensed and then it was gone. Dr. Galloway said I can't take responsibility. That not every baby starts out right and when they don't, nature takes care of things. That's the medical explanation. The baby wasn't right. But it wasn't the baby, it was me."

He stared at her, confused by what she was saying. "You didn't have an abortion?"

"What?" Her eyes opened. "No. Of course not. I was figuring I'd give the baby up for adoption. I even had a few brochures. But it was gone, just like today. That's what I kept thinking. That I was being punished for not wanting that first baby. So I don't get to have these."

His anger and sense of betrayal faded as if they'd never been. Shame replaced them—for thinking the worst of Pia. She was nothing like Caro. He already knew that.

He returned to the bed, grateful she hadn't noticed his retreat, and pulled her close again.

"I'm sorry," he said, apologizing for his mistake.

"You didn't do anything."

He would tell her later, he thought. When she was better.

"Neither did you," he told her. "You're not being punished."

"You can't know that."

He looked into her eyes. "Yes, I can."

"I lost one of Crystal's babies."

"No," he said quietly, for the first time understanding exactly what had happened. "We lost one of ours."

Twins, he thought sadly. Twins, not triplets.

Her eyes widened. More tears came. "You're right," she said on a sob. "Oh, God. Make it come back."

A prayer that would never be answered, he thought sadly as he held her.

They hung on to each other for a long time. When she seemed to have calmed down a little, he sat next to her on the bed and stroked her face.

"I look terrible," she said. "Puffy and swollen and miserable."

"You're beautiful."

"You're either a liar or you need your eyes checked."

He gave her a smile, then let it fade. After kissing her mouth, he said, "Don't for one minute think it's your fault. It's not. It can't be. Blame comes with a deliberate action."

He paused, then decided it was time. "You know that I was married before. Caro was a former beauty queen turned local news anchor. We met at a charity function in Dallas."

Pia leaned back against her pillows. "Is it okay to hate her?"

"Sure."

"Good. Because I do."

At one time he had hated her more. But time had healed him. He would never understand, but he'd ceased wanting her punished.

"We were the perfect couple," he continued. "Shortly after we got engaged, she was offered a job with a national affiliate in Los Angeles. Her career was important to her, so we moved to L.A. and during the season, I commuted."

"That sounds very civilized."

"It was. We talked about starting a family. We both wanted kids. One day I got a call that Caro was in the hospital. I came as fast as I could. I didn't understand what was wrong and she didn't want them to tell me."

He could remember everything about that moment. Standing in the hallway, staring at a doctor who wouldn't tell him what was wrong with his wife.

"I don't understand," Pia said. "The doctor wouldn't tell you?"

"Not without her permission. I went into her room. She was pale. There were a couple of IVs and blood. I remember seeing the blood dripping into her."

That had scared him the most. The thought that she might die.

He looked at Pia. "She'd had an abortion that afternoon and something had gone wrong. She'd been bleeding internally. She had surgery and was fine. That's what she said. 'I'm fine.'"

He shook his head. "I didn't even know she was pregnant. She hadn't told me. She said she wanted kids one day but not right then. Not when her career was going so well." He turned away. "If she hadn't ended up in the hospital, I never would have known. She made the decision without me. While I believe a woman has a right to choose, this was different. We were married. We were trying to have a kid—actively trying to get pregnant right then so I could be with her when it was born during the off-season. But it was all a lie."

Pia's breath caught. She couldn't believe what she was hearing. That Raoul's wife had betrayed him, betrayed *them* that way. It was one thing to put off having kids, or to discuss an unexpected pregnancy, but to pretend to be trying for a baby, then abort it when it happened was inexcusable.

"I'm sorry," she whispered. "I know that's a stupid thing to say, but I'm sorry."

He turned back to her. She saw the hurt in his eyes and the loss.

"I'm sorry, too."

They stared at each other, sharing their pain. Despite their practical arrangement, she'd never felt closer to him. More connected.

There was a short knock on the door. They both turned and saw Dr. Galloway walk in.

"Pia, my dear," she said. "I'm so sorry."

"Me, too."

The doctor shook hands with Raoul, then moved to her side. "From what we can tell, the other two babies are hanging on just fine. They're growing and look healthy."

"You're saying don't give up hope."

The older woman patted her shoulder. "I'm saying don't beat yourself up about this. I want you to try to relax. You'll stay here tonight and we'll do another ultrasound in the morning. I expect everything will be fine and you'll go home. There's no reason for us to believe you'll have any other problems, but we'll take precautions, just to be sure."

Pia nodded.

"I'm going to have the kitchen send up some dinner. I want you to eat. Do you promise?"

"Yes."

"I'm staying," Raoul said firmly. "I'll make sure she eats."

"I suspect you will," the doctor said cheerfully. "All right, Pia. Get some rest. I'll see you in the morning."

"Thank you."

"You're welcome." Dr. Galloway's mouth straightened. "No blaming yourself for this, hear me?"

"I'll try."

When the doctor left, Raoul moved to her side again.

"We'll get through this," he promised.

"I know."

Having him here helped, she thought, relaxing back against the pillows. He was someone she could depend on, and right now that seemed like the best thing of all.

PIA STRETCHED OUT ON the sofa and tried to get comfortable. It wasn't that she was hurting, she just felt weird inside. Unsettled. Afraid. Unworthy. Not exactly emotions designed to make her day restful.

She'd come home from the hospital that morning. It had taken a while to convince Raoul that it was perfectly safe to leave her for a few hours. Actually, it hadn't been her words that had done the trick—instead it had been the steady stream of visitors, showing up with flowers, cards, food and baby gifts for the remaining twins. When he'd figured out she was unlikely to be alone for more than a few minutes at a time, he'd agreed to head out to check in at his office.

Now she breathed a sigh of relief at the silence and hoped it would be hours until she next heard a knock on the door. It was a whole lot easier to feel sorry for herself and guilty when she was alone.

The second ultrasound had shown the two remaining babies were doing very well. They seemed unaffected by what had happened to their sibling. One of her visitors— Nina, the nurse from the hospital—had brought over a chicken casserole and had explained about vanishing twins. That it wasn't uncommon to lose one baby during gestation.

Pia appreciated the attempts to make her feel better, but right now she felt mired in guilt and depression. It was possible that in time she would feel better, but she couldn't imagine that ever happening.

There was a knock on her front door.

"Come in," she called, hoping she sounded at least slightly enthusiastic.

Denise Hendrix pushed open the door and walked into Pia's living room.

"Hi," she said, smiling gently. "How are you feeling?"

Pia shrugged. "Okay, I guess. Sad."

"Sure you are. You're going to be for a while." Denise held up the grocery bag she had. "Ice cream. Nearly every Ben & Jerry's flavor. Think of it as your dairy. I'll go put it in the freezer."

She returned in a few minutes. Instead of sitting in the chair opposite the sofa where Pia lay, Denise sat on the coffee table and leaned close.

"You look miserable," she said flatly. "Like you lost your best friend."

"Or killed her baby," Pia murmured, then shook her head. "Sorry. I didn't mean to say it out loud."

"You didn't kill Crystal's baby."

"It feels like it. They weren't real to me, Denise. I was going through the motions."

"So? Why isn't that enough? You're growing children inside of you, not providing a spiritual education. Right now your only job is to take care of yourself and them to the best of your ability." She sighed. "I raised six kids. Do you think I was fully present every second of every day? Do you think I liked it when the boys were fighting and the girls had colic? That I didn't wish myself away to some tropical island with nothing more than a quiet room to sleep in and a good book to read?"

Pia blinked at her. "But you're a great mom."

"Thank you. I loved my kids and tried my best, but I wasn't perfect. No one is. And if the babies you had implanted aren't real to you, so what? You'll get there. It's not as if you've violated the universal pregnancy time line. This is a huge change in your life, Pia. You've given up so many things to honor your friend's request.

I liked Crystal a lot, but I have to tell you, there's a part of me that thinks she had no right to do this to you."

Pia felt her eyes widen. "What are you talking about?"

"You don't just leave someone embryos without talking to them first. It's wrong. She should have talked to you, made sure this was what you wanted, too. She was asking a hell of a lot, and she didn't give you the chance to say no."

Pia hadn't thought about it that way. "I could have walked away."

"Walking away was a possibility, yes, but not for you. That's not who you are. We all see it in how you are with this town. You get the details right, you do the work. And anyone who knows you personally, knows that you've been hurt by the people who were supposed to protect you. And that you would never do that to anyone else. You don't need to worry about connecting with the babies you're carrying. It will happen. The reason you're sad is you've lost one of your children, as well. If this was just about Crystal, you'd only feel guilty."

Pia turned the other woman's words over in her mind. "You're right," she said slowly. "If I didn't care, I guess I'd secretly be relieved. Two babies is going to be a lot easier than three. But I can't get away from the sense of loss. And letting Crystal down."

"This isn't about your emotions. An embryo could have been lost at any point in the process. It's a miracle all three of them got this far. Do you know how unlikely it was for you to get pregnant at all? You've done great."

"Thanks."

Somehow Denise had cut to the heart of the problem. In a way, exposing the issue to the light made Pia feel better.

"I worry that I won't do a good job," she admitted. "I'm not ready to buy maternity clothes or look at baby furniture."

"Most women get married, then plan having a baby. This was thrust upon you without warning. You need time to catch up. As for maternity clothes, trust me, it won't be long until you don't have a choice." She smiled. "The baby-furniture issue will take care of itself. Pretty soon you'll have freakish hormones coursing through your body. You'll be biologically compelled to nest. But until that happens, don't sweat it. You're being too hard on yourself."

"I'll try to do better."

"I hope so. You're going to be a great mother. You already are. If you need anything, you know we'll all be there for you. This whole town loves you."

The two women hugged. As Denise straightened, Pia heard footsteps on the stairs. Seconds later, Raoul entered the apartment.

He'd brought a small duffel with him. More clothes, she thought.

"Denise," he said. "Thanks for stopping by."

"I had to see our girl. She's doing better."

Raoul glanced at her anxiously. "I hope so." He hesitated, then said, "I'm trying to convince her to move in with me, at least temporarily. My house is all one level."

Pia rolled her eyes. "I'm fine."

"You can't take the stairs."

There was a difference between can't and don't want

to, Pia thought. Although she was supposed to take it easy for the next few days, after that, there weren't any restrictions. Which might be medically sound, but emotionally, the thought of taking stairs made her beyond nervous.

Denise glanced between them. "Pia, it might be a good idea. You'd be more relaxed if you didn't have to worry about stairs. It's only for a week or so, then you can move back." She raised her eyebrows. "Although I'm not sure how long you're going to want to climb those three flights as your pregnancy progresses."

Raoul looked both pleading and smug. "See."

It might be the practical solution, but Pia didn't like it. Moving in with Raoul said something about their relationship. Or maybe it simply made things more real. Not that she'd been able to ignore the very large engagement ring on her left hand.

"I'll think about it," she promised. It was the best she could do.

Denise hugged her again. As she was bent over, she whispered, "He's very handsome and doting. There are worse traits in a man."

"I know. Thanks for coming by and talking to me."

Denise kissed her forehead. "Anytime." She straightened. "Take care of her. She's precious to all of us."

"I will," Raoul told her, then walked her to the door.

They spoke for a few seconds. Pia couldn't hear what they were saying, which was probably the point. She leaned back against the sofa and closed her eyes. Despite being exhausted, she couldn't seem to fall asleep. Every time she tried, she flashed back to the sight of the blood on the chair and felt the same terror flooding her. Not exactly a sequence designed to get her to nod off.

Instead she thought about what Denise had told her. Denise's observation that it was amazing that the babies had gotten this far was the most help. Maybe it was okay that she hadn't totally absorbed the idea of being pregnant. Maybe all that would change with time.

She opened her eyes and saw Raoul close the door. He glanced back at her.

"Why don't you try to rest," he suggested.

She nodded because it was easier than admitting she couldn't sleep. She closed her eyes and tried to think about nothing at all. That seemed safest.

But she found herself remembering his story about his first wife. How Caro had betrayed him. There was no excuse for what she'd done. Pia couldn't imagine lying to the one person you were supposed to love more than anyone. Not like that. If she hadn't wanted to have children, she should have told him and gone on the Pill or something.

But the most difficult part of what he'd told her had been the realization that he'd loved Caro. The truth had been in the way he'd spoken about her, in the emotion in his eyes. He'd met her, dated her, fallen in love with her and proposed. Just like it was supposed to be.

She wasn't going to get that. She wasn't going to have the kind of love Hawk and Nicole shared, or that Denise had had with her late husband. There might be respect and a growing affection, there might be a shared goal of raising the twins and perhaps having more children, but there wasn't a heart-pounding, hair-raising, oh-my-God kind of falling in love.

The knowledge hurt more than she would have

expected. It made her want to curl up and give in to tears. Some for what she'd lost, but also for the realization of how much she'd wanted that in her life. She'd wanted her happy ending.

With Raoul.

She sat up straight and opened her eyes. After checking to make sure he wasn't in the room, she turned the thought over in her mind. With Raoul? As in… What? She was falling for him?

A dangerous place to go, she told herself. It was insane to fall for a guy who'd made it clear he didn't want his heart to get involved.

She reminded herself she'd always been practical. This was completely the wrong time to be thinking with her heart.

"My hands still smell funny," Peter said with a laugh, holding one up for her to inspect. "And I washed 'em like five times."

"Garlic's tricky that way," Pia told him, enjoying having the boy to talk to. It was difficult to stay depressed in the presence of a happy ten-year-old.

"Raoul said a bad word when he dropped the spaghetti in the boiling water," Peter said in a whisper. "It was funny."

"I'm sure it was."

Despite her misgivings about moving in with Raoul, practicality and her fear of stairs had won. He'd packed up her stuff and carried her down two flights of stairs—a testament to his workout commitment. Now she was settled in his guest room.

He'd called Peter's foster parents and asked if the boy could join them for dinner. Pia appreciated having someone else there that first night. It made her feel less weird about being in Raoul's house.

He appeared in the doorway, a dish towel over his shoulder. "I drain the meat before putting in the sauce, right?"

"Yes. But don't put the grease down the drain."

"Cooking is complicated."

She laughed. "I told you not to start with making spaghetti. You could have heated up one of the casseroles. That would have been easier."

"But I love a good challenge."

"Typical man."

He chuckled and left.

Peter sat down next to her on the sofa. "Raoul said you were sick and you have to be careful." He held out his arm which now sported a green cast. "Is it like my arm?"

"A little like that. You still have to be careful about not getting it wet, right?"

"Uh-huh."

"But it will get better."

"Like you?" Peter asked, leaning against her.

She put her arm around him. "Like me," she said, and hoped she was telling the truth.

CHAPTER SEVENTEEN

LIZ STRETCHED OUT ON THE other sofa in Raoul's living room. "Seriously," she said. "You have to be bored."

"I'm getting there," Pia admitted. This was day four and her last day of resting. "I keep thinking about everything that has to be done and how behind I'm going to be."

Liz winced. "Yes, well, about that. Montana organized a work party."

Pia straightened. "Do not tell me she let people into my office."

"Okay, I won't."

"Are you kidding? They were touching my files?"

Liz laughed. "It's not like they were feeling up your underwear drawer. It's just files."

Pia groaned. "They're my files. I have a system. What if they messed it up?"

"What if they were just trying to help because they care about you?"

"Helping is nice," Pia said. "But not if it makes more work for me."

"Someone needs her attitude adjusted. You should be grateful we all care about you. This town takes care of its own."

Pia narrowed her gaze. "You weren't so happy with all the meddling when you first moved back to town.

If I remember correctly, you wanted to leave and never come back."

"That was different."

"Why?"

"It was happening to me."

Pia relaxed back on the sofa and laughed. "Typical. We're all so self-absorbed."

"Speak for yourself." Liz's humor faded. "How are you doing?"

"No. I'm tired of talking about myself. How are you doing? How is life with three kids and a fiancé?"

"You forgot the puppy," Liz said. "Ethan's bright idea, although I get the blame. I allowed a vote. Of course everyone wanted the puppy but me and now in addition to everything else, I'm potty training a very energetic Labradoodle named—wait for it—Newman."

Pia giggled. "Newman?"

"Can you believe it?"

At the beginning of summer, Liz had discovered she had two nieces she hadn't known about. The oldest, a fourteen-year-old, had contacted her through Liz's Web site, admitting their father was in prison and their stepmother had taken off, leaving them on their own. Liz had packed up her son and her computer and driven to Fool's Gold to rescue the girls.

The difficult situation had been complicated by the fact that Ethan, the oldest of the Hendrix children, had been the father of Liz's ten-year-old son. Through a series of miscommunications, Liz thought he knew about Tyler, but he hadn't been told. After a very rocky few months, they'd realized they were still madly in love. Now Ethan was building them a house, they were engaged and Liz had custody of her two nieces. And Newman.

"Don't you have to go on a book tour soon?" Pia asked.

Liz was a bestselling mystery author.

"Next week," Liz said with a sigh. "Denise is moving in for the duration. I've warned her it's not going to be the big party she's expecting. The good news is Newman is about ninety percent on knowing where to pee."

"Meaning not in the house?"

"Exactly. I finally have a chore list for the kids that seems workable, and everyone is doing their own laundry. It means that Tyler sometimes has pink socks, but he's learning to deal with that." Liz shook her head. "I'm normally gone about three weeks, but under the circumstances my publisher very graciously agreed that ten days was better. Honestly, I'm looking forward to being alone in a hotel room. No loud music or TV, no fighting over the Wii control, no yells asking what time is dinner."

"No Ethan."

"That's the downside, but I'll survive. Actually, he's a big help with the kids. The girls adore him. He's helping Abby with her pitching. There's a softball team in middle school and she wants to get on it."

"You've settled in to living here. For a while I didn't think that was going to happen."

"Me, either," Liz admitted. "It was tough at first, because of my past, but eventually the town and I made peace with each other."

Pia studied her friend. She considered it a sign of her good character that she didn't mind that Liz was beautiful, with shiny red hair and a perfect body.

"You look happy," Pia said.

"I am. I know you don't want to talk about it, but how are you doing?"

"Better. I'm sleeping. I'm desperately bored, which is probably a good sign. Now that I know people are mucking around in my office, I'm even more anxious to get back." She lightly touched her stomach. "It's hard not to be scared about the two little ones still in there."

"Not surprising. When's your next doctor's visit?"

"In a couple of days. I want her to tell me everything is going to be all right, and I know she can't make that promise."

"She can get close," Liz told her.

"I hope so. Right now I feel as if everything I do puts the babies at risk. Once they're born, I'll be able to relax."

Liz raised her eyebrows. "Sorry to disillusion you, but no. In some ways it will be better, but in others, it will be worse. Every stage brings new joys and new traumas. It's amazing that any of us ever have kids, given all that can go wrong."

"The need to procreate burns hot and bright."

"Apparently. In the end, it's worth it though. You'll love those babies in a way you've never loved before. It's magical and you'll be so grateful to have them."

"I look forward to that," Pia admitted. "Losing one has brought me closer to the others. I'm thinking of them as tiny, little people inside of me. I want to see what they're going to look like and hold them and keep them safe."

"Look at you. A few weeks ago, you didn't know why Crystal had left the embryos to you. Are you still asking yourself that question?"

"Less than I was."

"So we're both happy," Liz said. "Which is the way it's supposed to be. Have you and Raoul set a date for the wedding?"

"No." Despite his proposal and the very impressive ring she wore, she couldn't imagine getting married. Visualizing the ceremony was beyond her. "One crisis at a time."

"Ethan and I are thinking of doing something quiet over the Christmas holidays. Just friends and family. I told him the pressure is on, because I'm not marrying him until the house is finished. There's no way I'm starting my married life in the house where I grew up."

Pia understood. Liz had never known her father, and her mother had been distant and an alcoholic. Men had come and gone with a frequency that had led many people to believe that Liz's mother was in it more for the money than the relationship. Liz had been emotionally and physically neglected, and sometimes there had been unexplained bruises.

"So Ethan is a motivated guy," Pia teased. "That's very smart of you."

"It's more desperation than intelligence. I keep telling myself that the house is great. It's all fixed up and there aren't any ghosts, but I'm looking forward to moving out."

Pia leaned back against the sofa. "When did you realize you'd fallen back in love with him?"

"It was more finding out I'd never stopped loving him. That was a shock," Liz admitted. "Time and distance had done nothing to kill my feelings. I guess it's sometimes like that. People can love for a lifetime. Why?"

"Just curious." She held up a hand. "Don't read more than that into the conversation."

"You're not falling for Raoul?" Liz asked cautiously.

"I don't think so." Pia told herself it wasn't a lie—she hadn't decided yet.

"If you are, maybe it's not a bad thing."

"Why do you say that?"

"Because you're you and he'd be a fool not to love you back."

Pia sighed. "If only," she whispered.

DR. GALLOWAY HELPED PIA into a sitting position, then settled on her stool.

"You're fine," the doctor told her. "Everything looks just as it's supposed to. Both babies are growing very well. Developmentally, they are on target. Your blood work is good, you're healthy."

Pia allowed herself to relax a little. "So they're going to be fine?"

"Sometimes babies don't make it, Pia, and we can't know why. Nature has her own way of solving problems. Although they check the embryos before implantation, science is not perfect. But there is no reason to think you'll have a difficult time from here on. Have you resumed your regular life?"

"Except for stairs. They scare me."

"They are exercise and exercise is good. I'm not saying this is the time to take up a new sport, but do what you did before. Walk, talk, laugh, take the stairs."

Pia drew in a deep breath. "All right. I will."

"Good. Keep stress to a minimum, as much as you can. Get plenty of rest and enjoy that handsome man of yours." Dr. Galloway's expression turned stern. "Are you having sex with him?"

"What?" Pia felt herself blush. "No. Of course not."

"Probably best for the first few days, but now, it's fine."

Pia couldn't imagine ever doing that again. "Even with the babies in there?"

"It's not like they know what's happening. Nor can they see what you're doing. For them, it's a gentle ride and when Mom has an orgasm, then it's even more fun."

Babies and sex didn't go together in Pia's mind. Besides, she was confused about her feelings for Raoul. Making love at this point would only complicate an already difficult situation.

"I'll think about it," she said.

"I want more than thinking," the doctor told her with a grin. "I want doing." She rose. "Be happy, Pia. All is well."

"Thank you."

She waited until Dr. Galloway left before standing and reaching for her clothes.

The babies were okay. That was the main thing. Knowing that, she would try to relax. To, as Dr. Galloway had said, live her life.

One month down and only eight to go, she thought, wishing there was a way to hurry along the pregnancy. Or maybe not, she told herself, remembering the eighty-to-a-hundred-diapers-a-week statistic. Maybe it was better to let things happen in their own time.

"It's my job," Pia said, wondering if she hit Raoul with something really, really hard, she could make him understand. Or knock him unconscious, which would allow her to do her job. At this point, either worked for her.

"You can't spend the day on your feet."

"I won't. I have chairs set up all over the park, and several people who are going to make sure I sit." Despite Dr. Galloway's all clear, she wasn't willing to take any risks. "I'll be fine."

He moved close and wrapped his arms around her waist. "I worry about you."

"I worry about me, too, but I have a job that I love and I need to get to it."

He held her a second longer, his dark eyes gazing into hers.

In truth, she didn't want to move just yet. She loved being in his arms, feeling his body against hers. There was something so right about them being together. But there was a time and place for the mushy stuff, and this wasn't it.

She stepped back. "I have to get going."

"I'll see you tonight."

"Yes, you will."

She grabbed her purse and left. On the way to the park, she found herself thinking about Raoul instead of the impending event. Not a good thing. Thinking about him was dangerous to her heart. Work was safe.

She walked the few blocks to the park and found the setup had been completed in the early hours of the morning. Booths lined the walkway and vendors were already putting out their goods. The smell of barbecue mingled with the sweet scent of melting caramel.

The Fall Festival was one of her favorites. Sure the days were getting shorter and the first snow was right around the corner, but she loved the changing colors, the promised quiet of winter, the scent of a wood fire.

Each festival had its own personality. This one was going to be a little different because of all the men in town. She'd added extra games to keep them happy and a second beer vendor. To counteract the latter, there were also extra police on patrol.

A heavyset man in a Fool's Gold safety vest walked up to her. "Pia, we're five portable toilets short. The guy's lost."

"Not for long," Pia said. "Have someone get his cell number, then call him and talk him in. We need the extra bathrooms."

An electrician needed to be dispatched to fix a faulty outlet, the shift in the wind meant smoke from the meat smoker was choking the jewelry vendors and someone had forgotten to put up the no-parking cones to reserve spots for the fire truck.

Pia handled each crisis quickly and easily, as she had for years. She turned to take a quick tour, only to find Denise Hendrix walking toward her, a folding chair under one arm.

"I have the first shift," Denise said cheerfully. "It is now eight-thirty. You are to sit until nine."

"But I have to go check on the setup."

"No, you don't. And you're not going to." Denise batted her eyelashes. "Don't make me use my bad-mom voice, because you won't like it."

"Yes, ma'am," Pia said meekly and sank onto the chair.

Denise saw Montana and waved her over.

"Hi, Mom," Montana said, then grinned at Pia. "I

have the eleven-thirty-to-twelve shift and then I'm on again this afternoon. Bossing you around is fun."

"Gee, thanks." She was being forced to sit for thirty minutes of every hour. "Can you go talk to the vendors and make sure they have everything they need? Also, there's water for them in the back of Jo's pickup. Find her and make sure it's put somewhere the vendors can find. And if you see a guy driving around with portable toilets on the back of a truck, let me know."

Montana stared at her. "You expect me to do all that?"

Pia flashed her clipboard. "That's not even all of page one."

"Jeez, I wouldn't want your job," Montana grumbled. "Mom, if you see Nevada, tell her to come help me."

"Of course, dear."

Montana left.

"Impressive," Denise told Pia. "You're resting *and* getting your work done."

"I'm an expert multitasker."

Denise stared after her daughter. "Montana seems excited about her new job."

"She does. I admire her—she gives her all to whatever she does."

"I know she's worried about finding the right kind of work. Not that she won't but that it's taking too long. I keep telling her that everyone finds his or her own path in his or her own time, but she won't listen. One of the thrills of being a mother." Denise smiled. "Wait until your little ones are teenagers."

"At this point I simply want them to be bigger than a rice grain."

"That will happen, too."

The sound of a large truck caused them both to turn. Denise shaded her eyes with her hand, then turned to Pia.

"That's interesting. Were you expecting elephants?"

RAOUL WALKED WITH PETER through the crowded park. Fool's Gold was holding yet another of its many festivals. Knowing Pia was going to be working, he'd arranged to take Peter for the afternoon. The Folios didn't seem to mind him spending time with the kid, which was good. While the couple seemed pleasant enough, Raoul was still concerned about their caretaking abilities.

He and Peter had already checked on Pia, who was being confined to a lawn chair until the top of the hour. She swore she wasn't the least bit tired and that she'd never had so many assistants or done so little work at any festival.

"Want to get ice cream?" he asked, pointing to a stand.

"Sure!"

Peter led the way. They both got two scoops, then went over to a bench.

"This is so cool," Peter said between licks. "I like how there are different festivals at different times of the year. It's really fun. My parents used to bring me all the time."

"You grew up in Fool's Gold?"

"Sort of. My dad worked at one of the wineries and we lived out of town. But I went to school here." His smile faded. "After they died, I was in a group home for a while. I didn't like that. It was really hard because the other kids made fun of me when I cried."

Raoul felt his pain. "It's okay to feel stuff and be sad."

"Boys don't cry."

"Plenty of boys cry." Raoul hesitated, knowing there was a fine line between saying what was healthy and the reality of being tortured by peers. "Losing your parents is a big deal."

"I know." Peter licked his cone. "I still miss them."

"That's good. You loved them. You're supposed to miss people you love."

"Mrs. Dawson says they're watching me from heaven, but I don't know if that's true."

"Every time you remember them, you know how much they loved you. That's what's important."

Peter took a few more licks, then held up his cast. "I get this off in a couple of weeks. The doctor says I'm healing really fast."

The advantage of youth, Raoul thought, remembering feeling like roadkill the morning after his last few games. There was nothing like being trampled by a few three-hundred-pound guys to make a man feel humble.

"Wait until you see your arm," Raoul told him. "It's going to look weird from being in the cast."

"Cool! I wish I could see it now." He raised his arm and turned it back and forth, as if trying to see inside the cast. Then he turned to Raoul. "You know there's a school carnival next week, right? We're gonna have games and stuff. It won't be as big as this, but it will still be fun."

While the boy went on about the different events at the school, Raoul was aware of three women standing on the path a few feet away. He'd never seen them before, so he guessed they were tourists, in town for the festival, or possibly the influx of men. They were in their mid-thirties, talking to each other and pointing at him. The tall brunette raised her camera and took a picture.

When they realized he'd noticed them, the smaller blonde waved and walked over.

"You're Raoul Moreno, aren't you?" she said, her voice high and excited. "I recognized you right away. Oh my God! I can't believe it. You are just as good-looking in person. This is really exciting. We came here when we heard about all the men. There was an auction and everything. Too bad you weren't in it. You would have gotten a lot of money."

Her friends joined her.

Raoul tossed his ice cream and rose. Normally this sort of thing didn't bother him, but it had been months since anyone had approached him as a fan. Living in Fool's Gold where everyone treated him normally had spoiled him for the real world. Right now he wanted to spend the day with Peter—not deal with three women who probably weren't going to be satisfied with a picture.

"Is that your son?" the taller blonde asked.

"He doesn't have children," the brunette said scornfully. "Are you in one of those charity programs? Is he disadvantaged? Look at his poor broken arm."

Raoul stepped between the women and Peter. "That's enough. Take your pictures and then move on."

The petite blonde stepped closer. "This is a free country. We don't have to do anything. We can spend the whole day just following you around."

"I don't think so."

The firm words came from behind him. He turned

and saw Bella Gionni walking up. With her were Denise Hendrix and a few women he didn't recognize. They looked serious.

"Morning, ladies," Denise said pleasantly. "How can we help you?"

"You can't," the brunette said. "This is a private conversation."

"You can say anything in front of us." Bella moved between him and Peter. She put her hand on the boy's shoulder, then slipped her arm around his. "We're close."

Her friends took up places around him and Peter.

The younger women looked at each other and frowned.

"What's going on?" the taller blonde asked.

"You're welcome to say hello to Raoul and even take his picture, but that's as far as it goes. You don't follow him or disturb him in any way. Nor do you get to talk to Peter." She smiled at the boy. "Girls," she said in a mock whisper.

He was wide-eyed, more interested than scared. "I know," he whispered back.

Raoul was as startled by the rescue as by the potential stalkers. While he appreciated the concern, his pride didn't welcome the idea of being protected by a half dozen women in their forties and fifties.

Not that he was willing to take them on either. Ego be damned—for now he was keeping his mouth shut.

The three women turned their attention to him. "Are you serious? You're going to let them tell us what to do?"

He gave them his best grin. The one he wore in all his publicity pictures. "Absolutely."

"This town is stupid," the petite blonde said. "We should leave. I don't know why we thought we could have a good time here."

"Us, either," Bella told her. "Drive safe, ladies."

The brunette flipped her off.

Bella only smiled. "Looks like you need a manicure, missy. Chipped polish is so cheap. Just like you."

The three stomped off.

Raoul watched them go, then looked at his posse. "Thank you."

"You're welcome," Bella told him. "I'm sure you could have dealt with them yourself, but why waste time on trash?"

"If I was ten years older," he began.

Bella patted his shoulder. "Sorry, but no. If you were ten years older, I'd wear you out and then you'd die of a heart attack. So let's not go there."

Denise moved up to him and kissed his cheek. "Admit it. You're secretly humiliated."

"Some."

"Then our work here is complete." She glanced at Peter. "Do you mind if I borrow this handsome young man? There are bumper cars set up across the park and I do love a good bumper car. My kids are all too old. I'll return him right after that."

"Sure. If it's okay with you, Peter."

"Sure."

Peter took Denise's outstretched hand and went off, still licking his ice cream. Raoul thanked the other women, then waited until they'd left before making his way to where Pia held court from her lawn chair.

"Talk to the peanut guy," she was saying. "He always packs up early. Like he's going to beat the traffic. Tell him if he does that this time, he's not coming back. Remind him I can get fifty peanut vendors to replace him with just a phone call."

She smiled at Raoul. "Hi. Where's Peter?"

"Riding bumper cars with Denise." He sank down on the grass next to her chair. "I was just rescued by middle-aged women."

"What are you talking about?"

He told her about the women who had stopped by and how Bella, Denise and their friends had taken care of the situation.

"That's sweet," she said, amusement dancing in her eyes. "The big bad football player rescued by older women."

He winced. "This isn't good. I'm capable of taking care of myself. But I just stood there and let them do all the talking."

"Did you think they would allow it to happen any other way? You're one of us now. We take care of our own. It's just like the food everyone brought over after I lost the baby."

"It's nothing like that."

"Don't freak. It's adorable."

He wasn't amused. "You can't tell my friends."

"What will you give me if I don't?"

"Anything."

She laughed.

He enjoyed the sound, and looking at her. She was lovely, with her large eyes and laughing mouth. Her tumbling curls bright in the sun. She was the perfect combination of attitude and kindness.

It wasn't just her, he thought, glancing around at the crowd enjoying the Fall Festival. It was the town. He'd lived in a lot of different places and while he'd always enjoyed the cities, he'd never felt connected to the community. Not like here. A few people recognized him, but the most they wanted was an autograph.

While he wasn't happy that he'd been rescued by a bunch of women, he knew the significance went beyond their gender and age. It was that they'd seen the problem and acted. They'd stepped in—as if he were their responsibility. He'd moved to Fool's Gold to find a place to settle, and what he'd found instead was home.

CHAPTER EIGHTEEN

NORMALLY, AFTER A DAYLONG EVENT, like the Fall Festival, Pia would be exhausted. But as she'd spent exactly half her day just sitting, she felt rested and ready to party at the town's dinner-dance. Well, in a very quiet, protect-the-babies kind of way.

She finished applying mascara and leaned back to check her makeup in the mirror. She'd taken Dr. Galloway's advice about stairs and taken the two flights to come back to her place to get ready. All her clothes were here, along with her serious makeup. Raoul was going to pick her up and take her to the dance, then back to his place.

She fluffed her hair, then tightened her robe around her waist. The big question was what to wear.

Sometime in the last day or so, she'd gotten a case of serious bloat. Her pants were tight and no matter how much lemon water she drank, she couldn't get her belly to go down. There were a couple of dresses she knew wouldn't fit. But she had one that had an empire waist. The style was forgiving and—

She stopped in the doorway to her bedroom. Her mind replayed her last thoughts, then she started to laugh. She wasn't bloated, she realized. She was pregnant. Talk about an idiot.

She touched her stomach. "I'm hoping you two

weren't thinking your mom would be a rocket scientist, because that's simply not going to happen. Pregnant. You'd think I would have grasped that by now."

She crossed to the full-length mirror on the back of her closet door, then opened her robe. When she turned sideways, she saw the rounding she'd thought was too much water.

"How are you two doing?" she asked, lightly touching her stomach. "Everything okay? I'm fine. Still sad, but recovering. It's going to be okay. I want you to know that. I'm going to take really good care of you both. I promise."

There wasn't an answer, which was probably good. Voices from inside her body would scare the crap out of her. But she felt a sense of peace—a knowing. The rightness of what she'd done settled on her. She was having Crystal's babies. More important, these were also *her* babies. They might not have her DNA, but they were growing inside of her. She was nurturing them with every beat of her heart. When they were born, she would be their mother in every sense of the word.

"It's going to be great," she whispered.

She went into her closet and pulled out the black dress. The bodice was lightweight velvet, with a deep vee. The skirt began just under her breasts. That fabric was lighter, more flowy, ending just above her knee.

She'd already rubbed a shimmering body lotion on her bare legs. Now she hung the robe on a hook and reached for the dress. After slipping it on, she secured the side zipper. She stepped in front of the mirror to see if it worked.

"Oh my."

While she'd had breasts since she was about thirteen,

they'd never looked like this, she thought, staring at the cleavage filling the vee of the dress.

"At least now I know what I'd look like if I got implants."

Fortunately the dress had a short jacket. She pulled that on and saw it hid virtually nothing. Raoul was simply going to have to endure.

She'd chosen a medium-heel black sandal. She'd barely slipped them on when she heard a knock at the front door.

"Come in," she called as she walked to the living room.

The door opened and Raoul stepped inside.

She'd never seen him in a suit before. The dark, tailored fabric fit him perfectly, skimming over impossibly broad shoulders. He was elegant and handsome and hers.

The latter admission was as difficult to believe as the pregnancy had been. Were they really going to get married?

His gaze swept over her, starting at her shoes and working his way up. When he reached her chest, she saw him tense. He crossed the room in two strides, cupped her face in his hands and kissed her with a passion that had her trembling in her heels.

His mouth moved against her, claiming, enticing, promising. Heat poured through her.

Without thinking, she grabbed his hands and lowered them to her chest. He pushed aside her jacket and cupped her eagerly, finding her already tight nipples and rubbing them.

Fire shot through her. She was wet and ready in seconds. She shrugged out of her jacket and fumbled with her zipper. He undid it for her, then pushed down her dress to her waist. Then her bra was gone and his mouth was on her breasts.

The feel of his lips and tongue, the stroking and sucking, nearly brought her to the brink. Her breath came in sharp pants. Need threatened to drown her. She hung on to him to keep standing.

He moved one hand between her legs, slipping under her panties and finding her center with one sure stroke. He rubbed that place hard, as if aware how close she already was. Around and around, his mouth still on her breasts, her hands on his shoulders, her legs shaking so hard she wasn't sure she could stay standing.

She came without warning. One second she was riding the wave, the next she was shivering and convulsing, rubbing herself against his fingers, gasping out his name. The contractions faded and the world righted itself.

She straightened, as did he. They stared at each other. Then his mouth curved in a very satisfied male smile.

"You look good," he said. "Did I get a chance to mention that?"

She was still dealing with aftershock. Where had that orgasm come from? Fifteen minutes ago—five minutes ago—she would have sworn she wouldn't have a single sexual thought ever again. Or at least not until after the babies were born.

She paused to take stock of her body. Except for the lingering sense of well-being, she felt fine.

She smiled at him. "You didn't."

His gaze lowered to her bare breasts. "Those are new."

"You like?"

"The other ones are great, but these will be fun, too."

She stepped out of her shoes. "Your turn."

He hesitated. "We probably shouldn't."

She could see his erection straining against the fabric of his pants. "Dr. Galloway said it was fine. That the babies can't see anything."

She reached for his belt. "How about we get you almost all the way there and you finish inside me? Everybody wins."

Wanting and concern battled. "I don't want to put you or them in danger."

"Me, either."

She unzipped his pants and withdrew him. He was hard and thick and when she ran her hand down the length of him, his breath hissed between clenched teeth.

He moved closer and kissed her. She gripped him in her hand, moving up and down in a steady rhythm. As they kissed deeply, she moved faster. He touched her breasts, using his fingers to lightly toy with her nipples. Arousal began again inside of her. She felt the need building.

"Raoul," she breathed.

He must have heard the desperation in her voice because he dropped one hand to her thigh, then moved it between her legs and found her center.

The sure touch pushed her closer. She felt him tense.

She quickly pushed down her panties. He pulled them the rest of the way off and drew her to the sofa.

"Now," she said and guided him inside of her.

He thrust in slowly, carefully. She felt the restraint

in his hard muscles. She grabbed his hips to pull him in. He withdrew and she whimpered. Another thrust. He slipped a hand between them and found that magical spot again. It only took a second for her to feel the shuddering beginning again, deep inside.

She breathed his name and lost herself in her release. He pushed in again and shuddered.

They clung to each other, breathing hard.

When she could speak, she asked, "Was that okay?"

He kissed her lightly. "It was great. There's something to be said for going slow. How do you feel?"

She knew he wasn't asking about her afterglow. "Good. Really good." There was no way to explain it to him, but she had a sense of certainty. A knowledge that everything was going to be all right from now on.

She glanced at the kitchen clock and gasped. "We're going to be late. We have to hurry."

"Yes, ma'am."

He stepped back and was dressed in a matter of seconds. It took Pia a little longer, but they were out the door in less than five minutes.

At the bottom of the stairs, he pulled her close and kissed her again. She let herself feel the warmth of his embrace, the safety she found in his arms and knew that somewhere along the way, she'd gone and fallen in love with him.

THE DINNER-DANCE WAS HELD at the convention center. Tables had been set up in the center, with the dance floor up by the stage. A local DJ would provide the music during dinner before the live band arrived at eight. Dancing went on until midnight. There was a cash bar, plenty of tacky decorations and balloons floating on the ceiling.

"Impressive," Raoul said as they walked in.

She laughed. "You're mocking our efforts."

"I would never do that. It's charming."

"Small-town America at its best."

They wove their way through the crowd, stopping to talk to people they knew. Pia was aware of all the unfamiliar men in the crowd. It was odd to have so many male strangers around. During festivals, most of their visitors were families.

Dakota greeted them.

"You look beautiful," she told Pia. "Positively glowing."

Pia did her best not to blush. She had a feeling that any glow came from making love with Raoul rather than the pregnancy, but there was no need for anyone to know.

Raoul must have been thinking the same thing because his hand tightened on hers.

"Thanks," Pia said. "You look great, too."

Dakota turned, showing off her blue dress. "I'm dateless, so I'm only here for the dinner. Then I'm heading home to my small, spinster life."

Raoul looked around the room. "There are plenty of single guys. Go find one."

She wrinkled her nose. "Not this week. I'm not in the mood. Nevada and Montana are coming over and we're having a chick-flick marathon. They're both staying the night." She raised her eyebrows. "Besides, compared with you, they're just not that interesting."

"Oh, please." Raoul didn't look the least bit impressed.

Pia laughed. "If I see anyone special, I'll send him your way."

"Please don't."

They parted and continued to their table. Pia spotted a tall, thin man talking to Mayor Marsha. He was gesturing wildly, talking quickly, although it was impossible to catch any part of the conversation over the other talking in the room.

"Let's go see what that's about," she said, pointing.

They walked between tables and reached Marsha just as the man moved off. The mayor gave Pia and Raoul hugs, then sighed.

"I'm getting too old for this job," she said. "Do you recognize that man?" She pointed at the guy she'd been talking to.

"No," Pia said.

Raoul shook his head.

"I didn't recognize him, either," Marsha said. "Which insulted him deeply. Apparently he's some Hollywood-producer type."

"As in movies?" Pia asked.

"As in reality television. According to him, we're hot right now."

"Lucky us," Pia muttered.

"That's what I said. He wants to do a show about the bachelors coming to Fool's Gold. He's going to get me the details in the next day or so."

A reality show? "Is that something we want in town?" Pia asked.

"No, but I'm not sure how to keep him out. If he's not blocking traffic or otherwise getting in the way of everyday life, there's not much I can do. California has very supportive laws when it comes to filming."

"Want me to beat him up for you?" Raoul offered.

Marsha smiled. "Aren't you sweet? Let me think about it. At this point I'm more inclined to have a glass of wine and not deal with any of this until tomorrow." She smiled at them. "You two have a good time."

"We will," Raoul said.

"A reality show," Pia said as they found their table and sat down. "That's kind of icky."

"It should bring in revenue."

"And weird people." She leaned against him. "Like Marsha said, a worry for tomorrow."

He wrapped his arms around her. "Did I tell you how beautiful you look?"

"About three times, but it never gets old."

"You're stunning."

"Thank you. You're pretty hunky yourself."

AFTER DINNER, THE DANCING began. Pia excused herself to use the restroom. Along with her puffy tummy came the need to pee forty-seven times a day. Charity joined her along the way.

"How's it going?" her friend asked.

"Good. I feel much better."

"Nice to hear."

Pia turned to her. "I wasn't ready before, but I think I am now. Want to try the shopping thing again?"

Charity smiled. "I'd love to. I still have to make that all-important baby-wipe-heater decision. We can have an intense conversation about it over hot chocolate and cookies to gain our strength, then face the maternity clothes and baby store, ready to conquer."

"It's a date."

They reached the restroom, only to find the usual line.

"I knew we needed more women's restrooms when we remodeled," Pia grumbled. "But did Ethan listen?"

"Complain to Liz," Charity told her. "She'll punish him."

An older woman walked out of the restroom, then stopped by Pia. "How are you feeling, dear?"

"Fine."

"I was so sorry to hear about your loss. I miscarried two before having my Betsy. She was a blessing. I know it's sad but you have to trust that happier days are ahead."

"Thank you," Pia said.

The woman in front of them turned around. "I lost a baby, too. At four months. It was horrible, but you go on. It's hard, but moving forward helps with the healing."

A white-haired lady using a cane to walk stopped by Pia and patted her arm. "Just make sure you're taking care of that stud of yours in the bedroom. If God hadn't meant for us to have sex while we're pregnant, he wouldn't have made it so much fun. My George, God rest his soul, and I went at it until two weeks before I gave birth. All six times. As soon as the doctor gave us the all clear, we were at it again." She winked. "One time a little sooner than we should have."

Pia felt her mouth drop open. She consciously closed it, then swallowed.

"Yes, ma'am. Thank you for the information."

"You're a good girl, Pia. Have lots of sex. It helps."

The woman teetered off, leaning heavily on her cane.

Beside Pia, Charity burst out laughing. "I can't decide which is worse. Her calling Raoul a stud or the intimate details of her marriage."

"I know which is worse," Pia muttered. "I'm just trying not to think about it."

After using the restroom, she returned to the table. Raoul stood.

"What's wrong?" he asked, sounding worried.

"Nothing."

"You look…" He frowned. "Shocked."

"Old ladies are telling me how important it is to have regular sex with you."

He grinned. "Did I ever tell you how much I love this town?"

THEY ARRIVED BACK at Raoul's place a little after ten. The long day had caught up with Pia and she felt exhausted. Raoul guided her into the house, then put his arms around her and leaned his forehead against hers.

"I want us to share a bed tonight," he said, then smiled. "I'm not going to try to have my way with you. I just want to know you're okay."

He'd never asked her that before, she thought, both tempted and frightened by the invitation. In theory, they would be married soon, and after that, they would share a bedroom like every other couple. It wasn't that big a deal. There was no reason the idea should make her uneasy.

"Sure," she said, ignoring the warning voice in her head. "That would be nice. You're not a blanket hog, are you?"

"You can have all the blanket you want."

A lovely invitation, but in truth she was interested in a whole lot more than a blanket. She wanted him. All of him. Not just a practical invitation to a marriage that made logical sense. She wanted his heart and soul. She wanted to be the most important part of his life and the best part of his day. She wanted him to love her.

Afraid he would sense what she was thinking, she stepped back. "I'm going to go get ready for bed."

By the time she'd taken off her makeup and changed into a nightgown, she'd nearly convinced herself that everything was going to be fine. That she was over-reacting. Sleeping with Raoul shouldn't be that big a deal. It was probably better that they get used to each other one night at a time. She could think of this as a practice run.

But when she walked out of the bathroom and found him already in bed, her heart seemed to stumble a little. Although they'd shared a bed the first night they'd made love, somehow this was more intimate.

She shrugged out of her robe, then got into bed.

"Tired?" he asked.

"Exhausted."

"Back sleeper or side sleeper?"

"Side."

"Go ahead and get comfortable," he said, then turned off the bedside light.

She felt self-conscious as she turned on her side, away from him. He moved up behind her, putting his arm around her. His thighs nestled the backs of her legs, his chest pressed against her spine. He wrapped his arm around her waist, holding on as if he would never let go.

"Good night," he murmured.

"Night."

Pia found herself getting more awake by the second. She wasn't used to sleeping with anyone, and everything about being so close to him felt strange. And scary.

She knew in her heart she could get to like this. That it wouldn't take much for her to want him nearby all the time. And then what? Did she spend the rest of her life loving a man who wouldn't love her back? Did she get lost in her kids' lives so as not to notice that her marriage was only a shell of what she wanted?

His steady breathing told her that he'd fallen asleep. She wasn't sure how long she lay there, fighting tears and a crushing sadness that told her the engagement was a mistake.

RAOUL READ THE GRANT proposal he'd received. A grad student had come up with an idea to link high school math and science programs to specific industries. The industries as a whole would underwrite the cost of the special math or science classes with the idea that most of the students would want to study that field and after college would come back to work for the sponsoring companies. The student wanted to study feasibility and approach different industries. The grant amount was modest enough.

Raoul made some notes in the margin of the proposal. He would call a couple of friends in aerospace, one of the suggested fields, and get their thoughts on the idea.

The door to the large office opened and Pia walked in.

He rose and smiled at her, pleased she'd stopped by. The last few days had been better than he could have anticipated. He liked having Pia around. They got along well. She made him laugh and always had an interesting world view.

Now, however, she looked serious and concerned.

He walked toward her. "Is everything all right?" he asked. "The babies?"

"We're fine." She drew in a breath. "I know why Crystal left me her embryos."

While he hadn't questioned the reason, he knew she'd had several concerns. "Tell me."

"She believed in me. She knew she could trust me to care for her children, to raise them as my own. The only person who had doubts was me. I couldn't believe in myself. I didn't think I was capable. So I took the easy way out."

She squared her shoulders. "I've moved out, Raoul. I did that this morning, after you left. Liz helped me. I'm back in my apartment."

"I don't understand. Why would you do that?"

Leaving him? She couldn't. He wanted her there— maybe even needed her in his life.

Her gaze flickered, then grew steady again. She pulled the engagement ring off her left hand and held it out to him. "I'm not going to marry you."

He stared at the ring, watching how it twinkled in the overhead lights.

She couldn't mean it, he told himself. She needed him. They needed each other.

"We're going to be a family. I'm helping you with the babies. What's changed?" They'd made plans. They were going to raise the children together. Have a kid of their own. He thought it was what they both wanted.

"I appreciate the offer," she told him. "You're a really great guy." She paused for a second. "But it's not enough. I don't want a practical solution to a difficult problem. I want what Hawk and Nicole have. I want to be in love and be loved in return. I want a passionate, loving, messy marriage, practical or not. I want it all."

What Hawk and Nicole had came around once every thousand years, he thought bitterly. He'd tried to find it with Caro and had been shot down. She wanted it all. Meaning she wanted him baring it all for her, handing over his heart. And then what? There weren't any promises, no guarantees.

She wanted more than he was willing to give.

Her mouth curved into a sad smile. "I can see by your face that you're not exactly excited about my news. I'm not surprised. I was hopeful, of course."

"We don't need that," he told her. "We can make it work the other way. We don't have to be in love to be happy."

"Too late," she said lightly. "I already am in love with you. And I won't be with someone who doesn't feel the same way about me."

She loved him? Impossible. Was she trying to trap him?

Even as he thought the words, he wondered if they were true. After all, he'd been the one to propose, not Pia. He'd been the one pushing for them to be a family. He wanted to be a part of the babies' lives. She'd never come to him.

But no matter how logical it all sounded, he couldn't believe it. Or maybe he wouldn't. Either way, he wasn't taking the next step. He'd already done it once. He refused to be betrayed a second time.

"What happens now?" he asked stiffly, feeling as if he'd been sucker punched but not wanting that to show.

"We go on like we did before. People knew about the

engagement, so you'll have to answer a few questions. Don't worry. I'm going to make it clear this was my decision. You won't get run out of town."

She held out the ring again, but he didn't take it. She walked around him and set it in the center of the desk.

"You're playing it safe," she said quietly.

He turned to face her. She stared down at the ring, then returned her attention to him.

"You're looking for an easy solution to a difficult problem," she repeated. "You can't play at being a family, Raoul. Life isn't that tidy. If you want to be happy, you're going to have to give it all—risk it all. Life demands that from us. You think if you're logical enough you can make sure no one ever hurts you again. But the only thing that makes life worthwhile is loving other people and being loved by them."

She sighed. "For what it's worth, I didn't mean to fall for you. It just happened. If you change your mind, if you want to take a chance, I'd love to be that girl."

Then she turned and walked away, leaving him alone in an empty office. Everything he'd wanted was gone, and all he had to show for it was the engagement ring he'd bought for the woman he'd just lost.

CHAPTER NINETEEN

PIA TOLD HERSELF THERE WAS no reason to believe she was going to throw up. That the churning in her stomach would eventually go away. At least she wasn't crying. It was one thing to walk through Fool's Gold nauseous—at least no one could tell. But sobbing hysterically might get a question or two.

She reached city hall and went inside. She automatically greeted everyone she passed, smiling and waving, as if everything was fine. Only a few more feet, she told herself as she rounded the corner and saw Charity's office. The door stood open, so she knew her friend was at least in the building.

Luck was on her side. Charity sat behind her desk, staring intently at her computer. She looked up as Pia entered.

"Thank goodness. I'm going crazy with—" Charity stood, her pregnancy obvious in her brightly colored knit shirt. "What's wrong?"

Pia sucked in a breath and twisted her hands together. "I told Raoul I couldn't marry him. That while I appreciated the offer, I can't be in a practical marriage with someone I've fallen in love with."

She paused, waiting for Charity to burst out laughing. After all, what did Pia expect? That he would fall at her feet and beg her to let him love her back?

Instead Charity walked around the desk and hugged Pia. "Good for you."

Pia held herself stiffly. "What? Good for me? I've just walked away from a guy worth millions who wanted to marry me and take care of me for the rest of my life."

"You love him."

"So?"

"You're convinced he doesn't love you. Therefore you made the right decision."

Pia sank into the chair and covered her face with her hands. Reality crashed all around her, leaving her breathless and shaking. "What was I thinking? I can't do this on my own—be the single mother of twins. How will I pay for it? When will I sleep? I don't know anything about infants or children."

Charity pulled up another chair and sat across from her. "You'll be fine. You can do this. You were planning to do it before Raoul proposed."

"I was an idiot."

"No, you were exactly the same person you are now. Capable and loving. Pia, if you can organize the four thousand festivals we have every year and get a fundraiser up and running in three days, you can certainly handle having a couple of kids."

Pia lowered her hands to her lap. "You think?"

"I know. You'll be amazing. Besides, you might technically be a single mother, but you're not going to be alone. You have your friends and you have this town. We all love you and we'll be there for you."

"But Raoul would have given me everything."

"Not his heart."

Pia felt her chest tighten. "No. Not his heart."

"So this is better."

"How can you be sure?" Pia desperately wanted to know she hadn't made the wrong decision.

"You convinced me," Charity said kindly. "When you said no."

PIA HAD SPENT THE REST of the day buried in work. Maybe it wasn't the most mature way to handle heart-break, but it sure cleared out her in-box. Now tired and ready to have some serious pity-party time, she walked home. As she entered her building, she heard a lot of people talking. The higher she climbed, the louder the noise got. She stepped out onto the landing to find most of her friends waiting for her.

Their arms were filled with packages and grocery bags. Liz spotted her first.

"Here she is."

Everyone turned.

"Pia!" Montana hurried over. "Are you okay?"

From the various looks of concern, Pia realized that word had spread. Not just about the broken engage-ment, but about their practical but ultimately unworkable relationship.

All three triplets were there, along with Charity and Liz. Marsha held a basket filled with what looked like baby stuff. Denise Hendrix, several women from city hall, along with Bella and Julia Gionni, the feuding hairdressers.

Everyone crowded into her small apartment, pulling in chairs from the kitchen or settling on the floor.

"Jo wanted to be here," Nevada told her, "but she has to work. She sends her love."

Pia quickly realized no one expected her to provide anything for the impromptu party. There were plastic cups and paper plates, all kinds of food, from Chinese dumplings to taquitos. Wine was opened, along with sparkling water for Pia. She was settled in the center of the sofa, handed food and drink and surrounded with love.

"How are you doing?" Charity asked anxiously.

"Better now," Pia admitted. "It's been a tough day, but I know I did the right thing."

"I don't know. Marrying a guy worth millions seems like a smart decision, too," Bella muttered.

Everyone laughed. Julia rolled her eyes at her sister and stayed on her side of the room.

"You did the right thing," Montana assured her. "You have to marry for love. You deserve that. The proposal, the begging."

"You need the begging," Denise assured her. "Trust me. Courtship is the best time in a relationship for a woman. Marriage is the best time in a relationship for a man. Who gets their best time longer? So you need to make it last. Besides, you deserve someone who adores you, Pia."

There were several nods of agreement.

"Do you want us to call him names?" Dakota asked helpfully. "Or have him beat up?" She frowned. "That might take two guys, but we can arrange it."

Pia felt her eyes burning. She blinked away tears. "He hasn't done anything wrong. Don't forget, he wanted to take care of me. That's a good thing. I'm not mad. I'm the one who changed the rules, not him."

Julia shook her head. "It's been a long time since I've seen a man beat up. I was hoping to watch."

"There's something wrong with you," Bella snapped.

Denise raised one hand. "Ladies, it's a testament to

your love for Pia that you're both here. Let's not forget our purpose."

The sisters grumbled at each other.

Charity, who sat next to Pia, leaned close. "I never did hear why they aren't speaking. What's the story?"

"No one knows. It's a big secret."

Charity grinned. "I thought Fool's Gold didn't have any."

"There are a few."

"We have many gifts," Montana said, taking charge of the piles. "Most of this you can open later, but you should see this one now."

She handed Pia a large white envelope. Pia set her plate of food on the coffee table and opened it. Inside were dozens of pieces of paper. Each one was from someone different. Most offered hours of babysitting or company after the babies were born. There were consultations for baby room decorating, the promise of a weekly massage from now until birth, coupons for free diaper service for the first three months and a sheet where the women in town had signed up to deliver dinners for the first six weeks she was home with the babies. Three flyers showed houses for rent.

This time she was unable to stop the tears. They spilled down her cheeks before she could brush them away.

"I don't know what to say," she admitted. "This is wonderful."

"We all love you," Denise told her. "And we want you to know that we'll be there for you. No matter what."

It might not be the romantic proposal she'd dreamed about, but it was damned close. These women and this town were going to take care of her. Pia allowed herself to accept the love offered and let it heal her shattered heart. Then she touched her belly and silently told her growing children that no matter what, they were going to be just fine.

RAOUL SAT AT THE BAR, ignoring the reality show playing on the big TVs around him. Jo's Bar was quiet tonight, for which he was grateful. He'd tried staying home but he'd been unable to stand the solitude. While he wanted to be out, a crowd would have been too much. There were times when a man needed a little space to get drunk, and this was one of those nights.

He'd started on his second beer when Josh slipped onto the seat next to him.

"Hey," he said. "Jo called and said you looked like you needed a friend."

Raoul glanced at the bartender, who gave him a level look as if daring him to challenge her.

"She's wrong," he said flatly.

"Doesn't matter to me," Josh told him. "Charity's out. There's some girl thing going on at Pia's. They're making her feel better, which I guess makes you the ass who broke her heart."

Raoul sipped his beer and kept his gaze on the TV screen. A dozen or so people were bent over sewing machines. What the hell? A show about sewing?

Josh turned toward him. "Did you hear me?"

"I didn't break her heart. I asked her to marry me. I offered to spend my life with her, to take care of her and the kids. I'm not the bad guy."

Josh took the beer Jo offered and drank some. "So why are you here and why is she back at her place drowning in Ben & Jerry's ice cream?"

"She wouldn't be practical."

"An impractical woman. There's a stunner."

He turned to Josh and saw the raised eyebrow. "You don't understand. We had a deal. I didn't change it. I didn't change anything. I care about her."

"But?"

"It wasn't enough." Raoul drained his glass and pushed it toward the front of the bar. Jo turned her back on him. Typical, he thought grimly. "I wanted to take care of her."

"Did it ever occur to you that Pia can get all that without you? Right now my wife and several of her friends are reminding her that she's not alone. Except for the sex, which I doubt was very good, she's covered."

Raoul continued to stare at the TV screen. "You know I could take you."

"In your dreams."

He thought about taking Josh on, of showing the other man how unprepared he was. But there wasn't any point. Beating up Josh wouldn't make the hole inside of him go away.

The bottom line was he missed Pia. She wanted the impossible and he couldn't give it to her, but he still wanted her in his life. They could have been good together.

"The problem you have," Josh said conversationally, "is that she was never alone. It took her a while to remember that, but once she did, you became a lot less interesting."

Raoul turned and glared at him. "Do you think that's why she left? She loves me, you hothead."

Josh's expression turned satisfied. "I'd wondered if you'd caught that. You're right. She loves you. Like most women, she's not willing to settle. She wants it all. That's what women specialize in—demanding every scrap of humanity we have. Our hearts, our souls and our balls. You can fight it, my friend, but I've learned it's a whole lot smarter to hand it all over quietly. They're going to win in the end and if you resist, you only end up having to beg more." He took another drink. "Unless you don't love her."

I don't.

Raoul started to say the words but couldn't. He knew that was the real problem. If he could convince himself that he'd only been doing a good thing, something noble and important, the rejection was easier. That's how this whole problem had started. It should have been easy to forget her.

But it wasn't and that bothered him. Because it meant there was a possibility that Pia was more than a project, more than a way to get what he wanted without having to risk anything.

Without saying goodbye, he tossed a twenty on the bar and left. Once outside, he sucked in the cold night air, then started walking. But instead of heading to his rental, he crossed the street and went by Pia's apartment building.

Most of the units were dark, except for one on the top floor. A window was partially open and he heard the sound of voices and laughter drifting down to him.

She wasn't alone. While the information wasn't news, the proof of it made him feel better. He didn't want her to be by herself. He didn't want her to suffer. He'd really been trying to take care of her. Maybe he'd gone about it in an unconventional way, but he wasn't the bad guy in this.

And neither was she.

He stood there for a long time before turning around and heading to his own place. The echo of the laughter stayed with him, making him feel more alone than he ever had before. He missed her. Even if he couldn't be with her, surely he could talk to her. Explain.

Explain what? That his way was better? The truth was Pia deserved more, and that's what ate him up inside. She'd been right to walk away from him, to demand more. He respected her, admired her, wanted her...

But for the rest of it—she needed more than he had left to give.

THE SCHOOL CARNIVAL WAS LOUD, a crowded funfest with plenty of kids and parents in attendance. Raoul had gone to support all the kids he'd made friends with and found himself dodging dads who wanted autographs or to talk sports.

"Ah, the price of fame," Dakota said, coming up behind him as he explained that no, he hadn't had his head up his ass during that third-quarter play at his last Super Bowl.

He glanced at her gratefully. "Excuse me," he told the group of men and grabbed her arm. "I need to talk to Dakota about some business."

"Using me as a getaway?" she asked.

"Whatever works." He led her out of the crowd, toward the main building. "The mothers are either snubbing me or telling me I'm a jerk, and the fathers all want to talk about specific plays during games I barely remember. There's no elaborate planning in the middle of a football game. You have to react to what's happening. If you aren't prepared to trust your gut and go with what you feel is right, you'll never win."

He paused as she stared at him with rapt attention.

"Oh, please," she breathed. "Tell me more. Don't leave out any details."

"Funny," he muttered, then drew his eyebrows together. "Hey, you're speaking to me. Aren't you supposed to ignore me?"

"I work for you."

"I thought you'd be pissed about Pia." Everyone else was.

As she'd promised, Pia had spread the word that she'd been the one to break up with him. The problem was not enough people believed her. Or they assumed he'd done something so awful she'd been forced to end things with him.

"You didn't change the rules," Dakota said easily. "She did."

He stared at her, waiting for the "but."

"Not that you weren't an idiot," she continued. "If you're not willing to risk your heart for someone like her, you're completely cowardly and stupid. If you can't see you're already in love with her, then you're just dumb."

So much for having someone on his side. "Tell me what you really think," he said.

She patted his arm. "You'll figure it out. I have faith."

He liked her theory, but she didn't have all the information. She didn't understand the past he was fighting.

"Did that guy really want to know if you had your head up your ass?" she asked.

"Those were his exact words."

She laughed. "I want to say it must be refreshing to have people talk to you like you're a regular guy and not a sports celebrity, but I'm thinking right now you'd enjoy a little reverence."

"It wouldn't hurt. Want to stick around and be my wingman?"

"Not really. You'll be fine. Chin up and all that. They're people, too."

"Are you paid by the cliché?" he asked drily.

She smiled and walked off.

Alone in blissful quiet for a few seconds, he thought about what she'd said. About him being stupid for not risking his heart for someone like Pia.

As much as he wanted to give Pia all that she wanted, it wasn't as if there was a switch inside that he could simply turn on and off. He wasn't willing to take the chance again. Period. There was nothing anyone could say or do to change his mind. If that meant losing Pia permanently, then so be it.

He turned to return to the carnival, only to see Peter heading toward him. A short, beefy man trailed behind.

"Hi!" Peter waved his left arm. "Look. My cast is off. And you're right—my arm looks really weird. All scaly and skinny. The doctor says I'm doing really good, though."

"I'm glad to hear it," Raoul said, then held out his fist to start their elaborate greeting. The one Peter and Pia had come up with.

The downside of small-town living, he realized. There wasn't going to be anywhere to escape.

"My foster dad wants to meet you," Peter said in a low voice when they'd finished. "I hope that's okay."

"Sure."

Raoul walked over and shook hands with the other man. Don Folio eyed him from under thick, dark eyebrows.

"You've been spending a lot of time with Peter," he said.

"He's a great kid. Very special."

There was something about the man Raoul didn't like.

"We appreciate your taking care of him when we were out of town."

"It wasn't a problem." Raoul smiled at Peter, who grinned back.

Don dug a dollar out of his pocket and handed it to Peter. "Raoul and I need to talk, kid. Go play a game or something."

Peter hesitated, then nodded and hurried toward the arcade. Don faced Raoul.

"I can see you have a soft spot for the boy."

"Sure. I like spending time with him."

Don raised his eyebrows. "How much do you like spending time with him?" he asked.

Raoul felt a flicker of alarm over the oily nature of the question, but he wanted to see where Don was going with this. "If I could have more personal time with Peter, that would be ideal," he said slowly.

Don nodded energetically. "I'm a man of the world and I get these kind of things. But the foster care system, they have some rules."

Raoul ignored the burst of fury that flared up inside

of him. He kept his expression neutral, his body language open.

"The way I see it," Don continued, "there are options. You want the kid and I don't care if you have him. Only it's going to cost you."

Out of the corner of his eye, Raoul saw Mrs. Miller approaching. Casually, he stepped to the right to block her path.

"You're saying I can have Peter for a price?" he said just loud enough for the other woman to hear.

She froze, her face going white. He risked a single glance. She nodded, as if to say she was going to stay back and keep listening.

"Sure. And I don't care what you do with him. To each his own."

"You have a price in mind?"

"Fifty thousand. In cash." Don held up his hand. "I'm not interested in bargaining on the price. This is a one-time offer. If you don't want him, I can find someone else who does."

Raoul pretended to consider the offer. "You have a way of clearing this through social services?"

"Sure. I go to Mrs. Dawson and say Peter would be happier with you. You had him before and he never said what happened. The kid knows how to keep a secret, I guess. Boys aren't my thing, but I'm an understanding kind of guy."

Raoul wanted nothing more than to put his fist in the man's face. It would give him pleasure to grind Don Folio into the dirt.

He didn't know how this man had gotten ahold of Peter in the first place, but it was going to stop now. Today.

Don handed over a business card. "My cell's on the back. You have twenty-four hours."

Raoul nodded, and the other man walked off. When he was gone, Mrs. Miller hurried up to him.

"It's disgusting."

Raoul closed his hands into fists. "He has to be stopped."

She pulled out her cell phone and scrolled through the contacts. "I'm calling Mrs. Dawson right now."

The social worker arrived in less than thirty minutes. Less than ten minutes after that, Police Chief Barns was threatening a very nervous-looking Don Folio. Raoul didn't think they could charge the guy with much—money hadn't actually changed hands—but he wasn't likely to ever take in a foster kid again. At least that was something.

Peter came running toward him.

"I heard," the boy said, grinning and slightly out of breath. "I'm not going to be with them anymore. You're going to take me."

Raoul stared at the kid, then held up both his hands. "Peter, I think you misunderstood. You'll be safely away from the Folios and another family will be found for you."

Peter's expression froze. The happiness faded from his eyes and tears appeared. He went pale and his mouth trembled. "But I want to go with you. I stayed with you before. You're my friend."

Raoul ignored the sense of being kicked in the gut. "We *are* friends. We'll still be friends and I'll see you at school. But I'm not a foster parent."

"You were before," he insisted, the last word coming out on a sob. "You took care of me."

Mrs. Dawson hurried toward them. "Peter, we need to go."

Peter lunged for Raoul. For a second, he thought the kid was going to hit him, but instead Peter wrapped his arms around Raoul and hung on as if he would never let go.

"You have to take care of me," he cried. "You have to."

Mrs. Dawson shook her head apologetically. "Come on, Peter. I have to get you to the group home. It's only for a few weeks until we find something else."

Raoul stood there, not moving. Although the boy wasn't doing anything, he still felt his heart being ripped out all the same. People were stopping to stare.

Just when he thought he was going to have to forcibly push the kid away, Peter let go. Mrs. Dawson led him away, and neither of them bothered to look back.

MONDAY MORNING, RAOUL arrived at work at his usual time. Seconds later, Dakota walked in, slammed her purse down on his desk and put her hands on her hips.

"I can't decide if I should quit or back my car over you," she announced.

He stared at her. "What are you pissed about now?"

"What you did to Peter."

Raoul didn't want to talk about that. He hadn't slept all night and he still felt as if he'd been hit in the gut. "He's safe now," Raoul said flatly. "I talked to Mrs. Dawson this morning and from what the psychologists can tell, he wasn't abused by anyone. Folio's threats about giving the kid to someone else were designed to make me hurry. He's not part of a big child-stealing ring. He's just an asshole."

She glared at him. "And that's all you see?"

"What else is there?" He knew he sounded defensive, but it was all he had.

"Peter's crushed," she snapped. "You swept in and saved him. Do you think he doesn't know what you did? You've been there for him all this time. You took him home when he broke his arm. You've been his friend."

She spoke as if he'd been burning the kid with a cigarette.

"All that stuff is great," he yelled. "So what's your problem?"

She jabbed him in the chest with her index finger. "You led that poor kid on, you jerk. You let him believe that you cared about him and when they took his foster dad away, he thought he'd be going home with you."

"You think I don't know that? It was a mistake. All of it." Getting involved in the first place. He knew better. He did his best work from a distance.

"It wasn't a mistake." She spoke more calmly now. "Don't you remember what that was like? Packing everything you owned into a trash bag because you didn't have a suitcase and moving on? Do you remember how scary it was to find yourself in a new place, to not know the rules? Now it's happening again. And you've made that reality worse. You let him believe in you, trust you, and it all turned out to be a lie."

Raoul wanted to protest that he'd never promised the boy anything. That he'd been there in a crisis, but that was all it was. Nothing more.

Only Peter wouldn't have seen it that way, he thought

grimly. He would have expected Raoul to rescue him again.

She shook her head. "I didn't blame you for the Pia thing, but I'm starting to see a pattern here. You play at making a difference, at being the good guy, but none of it is real. You're too afraid to give what really matters. You're all flash and no substance."

She turned away, then spun back to him. "Do us all a favor. Stay away from 'causes.' You've already done enough damage here."

CHAPTER TWENTY

RAOUL'S DAY OF HELL ONLY went downhill from there. Dakota left him alone with his guilt. He wanted to do something, hit something—mostly himself. Nearly as bad, he honestly didn't know if she'd stalked off because she was mad or if she'd quit.

He paced back and forth in the large empty space he'd rented, trying to find an answer. But it all came back to the same thing. He'd let Peter believe in him, and then he'd let him down.

About an hour later, when he was still trying to come up with a plan, Mayor Marsha Tilson walked into his office. Normally, she was someone he enjoyed talking to. But there was something about the way she moved so purposefully that made him aware he might not like what she was going to say.

"I've heard what happened with Peter," she said, getting right to the point. "I must say, I wish things had turned out differently, Mr. Moreno."

Looking at her, seeing the disappointment in her eyes, was nearly the toughest thing he'd ever done, but he would be damned if he'd allow anyone to make him flinch.

"I do, too."

"Do you?" she asked. "When you first arri were all impressed by your financial genero continued, her blue eyes dark with disillusionment. "Your reputation elsewhere was that of a man who cared about others. One who gave back to the community. So when you indicated you wanted to move here, we welcomed you as one of our own."

She pressed her lips together. "I don't know all the details about what happened with Pia, but I do know that she is a loving, giving young woman. To see her unhappy pains me. It pains us all."

His body tensed. He squared his shoulders. "I didn't hurt Pia. We had a deal. She changed her mind."

"If she's not hurt, then why was she crying over you?"

Pia crying? She'd been so sure when she'd left. How could she be wounded?

The mayor drew in a breath. "I'm sure you have some measure of guilt for all this, but fear not. It will pass. Peter will be taken care of, and Pia, too, because that's what we do here. We protect our own." She put her hand on his arm. "I want to believe you're a good man trying to be a better one. But from what I can see, you're getting in your own way when things get personal." She stared into his eyes. "For your own sake, and for Pia and Peter, maybe it's time to risk more than your money."

With that, she turned and left. Raoul watched her go, feeling the slice of every honest word. He had never been what Hawk had raised him to be. It *was* all on the surface.

He crossed to the window and stared out at the town.

He'd wanted to settle here, to make a difference. He'd thought he would grow old here. But that wasn't going ɔ happen. He didn't belong. No one would say it to his face, but it was true. He deserved to be run out with pitchforks and torches.

He swore, not knowing which was worse—that he'd lost Pia, or that he'd broken the heart of a little boy who'd been foolish enough to believe in him.

He continued to stand by the window, waiting for the day to pass. He needed it to be dark so he could slink home without being seen and figure out what he was supposed to do next.

"APPARENTLY MARSHA GAVE him one of her famous talks," Charity said, as she and Pia sat at the Fox and Hound having lunch. "She wouldn't give me details, but I'm sure she got inside his head and messed with him."

Pia felt awful. Not only was she still hurting from missing Raoul, she felt terrible about Peter's situation. While she agreed that Raoul had given the boy the impression he would be there for him, she knew the man she loved would never deliberately hurt anyone. It seemed there were no winners in this situation.

"Did she say how he looked?"

"No." Charity studied her. "You really do love him, don't you?"

"You sound surprised."

"I thought this would disillusion you."

"No. He has a good heart and he's a good guy. None of this is easy for him."

She thought about his past, how Caro had betrayed him. How he was afraid to trust.

"Everyone needs to give him a break," she said firmly.

Charity hesitated. "Marsha thinks he might be leaving town."

Pia's breath caught. "Leaving? Why? He's settled here. He has the camp, which is what brought him here. There are plans for special classes and intensive learning. He would never give that up." The camp represented his future.

She looked at her friend. "There's no way he would make the decision on his own. What happened? Did Marsha run him out of town?"

"No, but she made it clear she was disappointed. How will he handle that?"

"I don't know," Pia admitted. Would he leave? If he didn't feel comfortable in town, he might. She hated the thought of Fool's Gold without him.

"I'm sorry," Charity told her.

"Me, too," Pia said. "I want him here. I want him to stay. While I'm at it, I want him to love me back."

"You don't get to decide any of that," her friend reminded her.

If only things could be different, Pia thought sadly. But they weren't.

RAOUL'S PLAN TO WAIT until dark lasted about an hour. He paced in his office, tried working, then had to fight the need to throw the damn computer across the room.

He was furious and ashamed and disappointed—all with himself.

He'd come here with big ideas for finding the right place, the right way to give back. Being like Hawk, changing lives, had driven him. Everything about Fool's Gold had appealed to him. The friendly small town had made him feel welcome. Then what had he done? Blown it.

Years ago, in college, he'd screwed up big-time. Hawk had been the one to get him back on track. Since then, Raoul had managed to find his way on his own. Until now.

He couldn't figure out where it had all gone wrong. With Pia, he supposed it had been when he'd offered to marry her so he could have everything he wanted without putting any part of himself on the line. He'd taken the easy, safe way out, and it had all gone to hell.

He should have known he couldn't have it all for free. That was like making a deal with the devil. If it looked too good to be true, it was.

As for Peter, he'd simply stepped in it with the kid. His motivations had all been aboveboard, but somewhere along the way, he'd forgotten he was dealing with a ten-year-old boy's heart. He'd befriended Peter, wanting only to save the kid. Instead he'd hurt him again.

Unable to stand the confines of his office, he stalked to the door and opened it. He half expected an angry mob with pitchforks waiting for him, but the town looked as it always had. The turning leaves fluttered in a light breeze. The sky was blue, the sun a little lower in the horizon than it had been a month ago. Winter was coming.

He'd wanted to see the town in snow, to experience the changing seasons. He'd wanted to ski at the resort, to lie with Pia by a fire, to watch her grow heavy with their two babies. It didn't take much effort to add Peter to the mix. He could see the boy playing by the fire, or laughing as he and Raoul played video games.

As he stepped out into the afternoon, he realized the

solution was obvious and simple. He could have them both, if he was willing to hand over all he was. What had Josh said? Heart, soul and balls. Without Pia, he had no use for them anyway. As for Peter, the kid probably deserved better, but Raoul hoped he was willing to accept what was offered.

He half expected the heavens to open and angels to sing. He got it. He really got it. After all this time and running to avoid the only thing he wanted, he understood the point.

It wasn't about giving money or loaning a camp to a school. It was about giving all he had, all he was. It was about risking his heart.

Pia, he thought frantically. He had to get to Pia.

He turned toward her office, only to nearly run into a half dozen middle-aged women. They were staring at him purposefully, which wasn't a good thing.

"Hi," the one in front said. "I'm Denise Hendrix. Dakota's mother? We met at the Fall Festival."

He held in a groan. "Yes. Nice to see you again." He nodded at the other women. "Ladies."

The other women stared at him without responding. He noticed Bella in the crowd, but she didn't look as happy as she had the day she'd also helped rescue him from the overaggressive tourists.

"We need to talk to you," Denise told him.

"This isn't a good time for me."

"Do we look like we're getting any younger?" the oldest in the group snapped. "You'll listen, young man, and you'll listen good. We have ways of making your life a living hell. Do you really want to test us on that?"

Like any good sportsman, he knew when he'd met a superior opponent. "No, ma'am."

"I didn't think so." She sniffed. "Go on, Denise."

"We've been talking," Dakota's mother told him. "We looked you up on the Internet. I don't know what went wrong with your first wife, but she wasn't anyone we would trust."

The other women nodded in agreement.

"You've been single a few years now, so you're obviously over her. You came here to settle down, which shows you're intelligent. You seem like a nice enough man."

Obviously these women hadn't been talking to Mayor Marsha, he thought grimly.

"But you're stuck."

Bella pushed through the other women and moved in front of him. "Pia loves you, so we want her to have you."

Denise patted her friend's arm. "Bella, I think we need to be more delicate. Raoul might not know he's in love with Pia. We might have to explain things."

"He gets it," another woman said. "How could he not? She's wonderful. If he doesn't love her, he doesn't deserve her."

"I agree," someone else said. "But I've said it before. If we wait for the man we deserve, we'll never get married."

"At least he's handsome."

"And rich."

"He has nice, thick hair," Bella told them.

"And a great butt."

The last comment was Raoul's tipping point. "Ladies," he said loudly. "I appreciate the intervention. I know Pia will be grateful when she hears of your very vocal support." Humiliated, he thought while smiling for the first time in hours, but grateful.

"However, this is between me and Pia. Now if you'll excuse me, I need to go talk to her."

Denise grabbed his arm in a surprisingly strong grip. "Not so fast. What are you going to say?"

He stared at them all. While he could easily tell them it wasn't their business, he hadn't changed his mind about settling here. Fool's Gold was going to be his home for a very long time, and these women were his neighbors.

"The truth," he said simply. "That I'm desperately in love with her and I'm begging her to give me a second chance."

Several of the women sighed.

Denise gave him a shove. "Don't just stand there," she said. "Go find her."

He took off at a jog, trying to figure out where to go first. It was midafternoon. He would start with her office and spread out from there.

He took the stairs two at a time and burst onto the landing. Her door stood partially open. He hurried toward it, aware of voices down by the first-floor entrance. Ignoring them, he pushed open Pia's door and found her alone in her small office.

She looked much as she had the first time he'd seen her. Pretty with curly brown hair and bright, hazel eyes that showed every emotion. The difference was now he knew that she was kind and loving, funny and smart. That she was rational and compassionate, even when panicked, that she gave with her whole heart and that he could search the world and never find anyone even close to her.

She looked up, startled. "Raoul. Are you okay? I heard about Marsha's visit and I want to tell you I had nothing to do with that."

"I know."

"She's upset, but no one wants you to leave town."

"Good, because I'm not going."

"Really? Well, that's great. I mean of course you can live where you want. This is a free country. Sometimes small towns have an inflated sense of themselves."

He moved around the desk and drew her to her feet. Her gaze flickered, as if she was afraid to stare directly at him.

"Pia?"

"Yes."

"Look at me."

She sighed, then did as he requested.

He knew her face. He'd seen it hundreds of times. But he would never get tired of seeing her and touching her. Only her, he thought. He would take the chance with her, because he didn't have a choice. Without her, he was only half-alive.

"I offered you a marriage of convenience," he began. "Because I wasn't willing to get involved again. My first marriage ended badly. I'd made a mistake and I didn't know where I'd gone wrong. Rather than figure that out, I decided to never take the chance again."

Her fingers were warm against his. He felt her faint trembling. While he wanted to reassure her, he knew he had to tell her the truth, first.

"What Caro did was wrong, but I don't believe she meant to betray me. Her career mattered more than anything else. I'd known that, but I didn't think through what that meant. I wanted a wife and a family. She said the right words, and I took them at face value because it gave me what was important to me. I think she knew I wouldn't like hearing that she wanted to wait to start a family."

He brought one of Pia's hands to his mouth and kissed her palm.

"I moved here, thinking it would be easy," he continued.

"Foolish man."

"Tell me about it. It wasn't easy, but it was where I belonged. This is home. But it's an empty, cold place without you." He stared into her eyes. "I love you, Pia O'Brian. I was too stubborn and scared to admit it until now, but I love you. Please marry me. Not because it's convenient, but because we can't imagine life without each other."

Hope brightened her face. Her lips curved into a smile.

Everything inside of him relaxed. She still cared. They could be together. Except...

"But it won't just be us," he told her. "You, me and the twins. There's also Peter. I can't leave him in the group home. I want to talk to Mrs. Dawson about adopting him."

She bit her lower lip. "And if I say no to that?"

He tensed again, feeling the fist hit his gut. "We're a package deal."

Everything he'd ever wanted and needed hung on what she would say next. He wanted to tell her that he would take care of her forever. That he would always love her and their children. But he couldn't bribe her into accepting. They both had to follow their hearts.

"Right answer," she whispered. "And yes."

Happiness exploded inside of him. He hauled her against him and kissed her with all the love and passion he had. Behind them he heard something that sounded like both cheering and sniffing. After a few seconds, he raised his head and glanced over his shoulder.

The women he'd met on the street all stood there, joined by the mayor and Mrs. Dawson.

"I'm so happy," the social worker said, dabbing at her eyes. "You were cleared as an emergency foster parent when Peter went to stay with you the first time. You can go get him now."

The other women nodded. Marsha smiled. "I knew you had it in you."

"You didn't say that earlier."

"It wouldn't have helped."

Note to self, he thought, kissing Pia again. Do *not* get on the mayor's bad side.

Pia wrapped her arms around Raoul's neck and leaned against him. She'd hoped, prayed and done her best to believe it would all work out, but she'd also been scared. Scared that she would spend the rest of her life loving a man who wouldn't love her back. It was nice to be wrong.

He kissed her again. Her insides started that melty thing, which was also very nice.

"We've got a lot to do," he said, his forehead resting against hers. "Approve the house plans, get married, start birthing classes."

She laughed. "Don't worry. I'm really good at details. Right now there's only one thing that matters."

He nodded. "Peter."

"Yes. He should be home from school by now. Let's go tell him the good news."

Raoul hesitated. "You're sure about this? We'll have three kids."

"I'm sure."

There were other considerations. Like the fact that being a mom to newborn twins and Peter probably meant she was going to need an assistant to help her with all the festivals. And that until their new house was built, things were going to be a little crowded in the rental. And that they should get married right away so she could move in with Raoul and Peter. But those were for later. Now they were off to make a little boy's dreams come true.

PETER SAT ON THE NARROW bed he'd been assigned. This was the same group home he'd been in before, but the kids were different. Not so mean. No one teased him about crying himself to sleep every night.

He tried really hard not to be scared all the time. He told himself he was bigger now. He didn't need anyone. He was strong. Except when he thought like that, his chest hurt and his throat got tight and then he started crying.

He knew what would happen next. He would be sent to a foster home where he wouldn't know the rules and the other kids would stare at him. He would try to do everything right, but he wouldn't and then he'd get yelled at and maybe hit. And he would be alone.

From downstairs, he heard voices. Adults talking. For the first couple of days he'd waited for Raoul to come. To say he'd made a mistake, that he'd changed his mind. That he wanted Peter with him forever.

He'd thought…he'd hoped…

He shook his head. He'd been wrong. No one was coming for him. Not ever.

"Peter?"

He heard Mrs. Goodwin call his name.

"Peter, would you please come downstairs?"

Peter stood and wiped his face so no one would know he'd been crying. He moved to the landing, his head down, his shoulders hunched.

He took one step, then another. When he glanced up, he saw Raoul and Pia standing in the living room, watching him.

Without meaning to, he came to a stop and stared at them. They both looked kind of funny. Not mad, exactly but… Scared, he thought at last. Only adults didn't get scared, did they?

Raoul walked to the bottom of the stairs and looked up at him.

"I'm sorry," Raoul said. "For making you come here. I messed up."

Peter shrugged. "Whatever." He knew people were supposed to apologize, but he didn't know why. Saying you were sorry didn't change anything.

"No. Not whatever," Raoul said, his gaze intent. "All I could think about was getting you away from the Folios. But there was a next step. You didn't just need to be away from them, you needed to find your way to a real home."

He cleared his throat. "Pia and I are getting married. We wanted to know if you'd like to come live with us." Raoul paused. "No, that's not right. We want to adopt you, Peter. If you'll have us as your family."

Peter's whole body felt hot and cold at the same time. The words were like magic, making everything okay again. Okay for the first time in forever. Tears filled his eyes, then he was coming down the stairs so fast, he was practically flying. He launched himself at Raoul.

Raoul caught him and held him so tight it was hard to breathe, but that was okay. Peter was crying, then Pia was there, hugging them both. She was saying something about babies and puppies and his own room.

Peter didn't understand it all and he knew it didn't matter. All he cared about was that he'd finally found a place to belong. A family with people who loved him. Raoul's strong arms held him. Pia kissed his cheek and smoothed away his tears.

For the first time since the car accident, he looked up at the ceiling and knew his parents really were watching him from heaven.

"You can stop being sad now," he whispered. "I'm going to be okay."

* * * * *

Don't miss these deliciously sexy tales
in the *Buchanan* series from
New York Times and *USA TODAY* bestselling author

SUSAN MALLERY

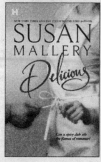
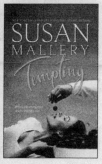

Available now wherever books are sold!

HQN™

We *are* romance™

www.HQNBooks.com

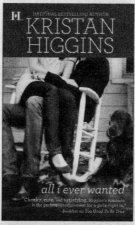

REQUEST YOUR FREE BOOKS!

2 FREE NOVELS
FROM THE ROMANCE COLLECTION
PLUS 2 FREE GIFTS!

YES! Please send me 2 FREE novels from the Romance Collection and my 2 FREE gifts (gifts are worth about $10). After receiving them, if I don't wish to receive any more books, I can return the shipping statement marked "cancel." If I don't cancel, I will receive 4 brand-new novels every month and be billed just $5.74 per book in the U.S. or $6.24 per book in Canada. That's a saving of at least 28% off the cover price. It's quite a bargain! Shipping and handling is just 50¢ per book.* I understand that accepting the 2 free books and gifts places me under no obligation to buy anything. I can always return a shipment and cancel at any time. Even if I never buy another book, the two free books and gifts are mine to keep forever.

194/394 MDN E7NZ

Name _____ (PLEASE PRINT) _____

Address _____ Apt. # _____

City _____ State/Prov. _____ Zip/Postal Code _____

Signature (if under 18, a parent or guardian must sign)

Mail to **The Reader Service:**
IN U.S.A.: P.O. Box 1867, Buffalo, NY 14240-1867
IN CANADA: P.O. Box 609, Fort Erie, Ontario L2A 5X3

Not valid for current subscribers to the Romance Collection
or the Romance/Suspense Collection.

Want to try two free books from another line?
Call 1-800-873-8635 or visit www.morefreebooks.com.

* Terms and prices subject to change without notice. Prices do not include applicable taxes. N.Y. residents add applicable sales tax. Canadian residents will be charged applicable provincial taxes and GST. Offer not valid in Quebec. This offer is limited to one order per household. All orders subject to approval. Credit or debit balances in a customer's account(s) may be offset by any other outstanding balance owed by or to the customer. Please allow 4 to 6 weeks for delivery. Offer available while quantities last.

Your Privacy: Harlequin Books is committed to protecting your privacy. Our Privacy Policy is available online at www.eHarlequin.com or upon request from the Reader Service. From time to time we make our lists of customers available to reputable third parties who may have a product or service of interest to you. If you would prefer we not share your name and address, please check here. ☐

Help us get it right—We strive for accurate, respectful and relevant communications. To clarify or modify your communication preferences, visit us at www.ReaderService.com/consumerschoice.

MROM10R

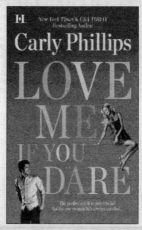